W9-BGB-532

Pets

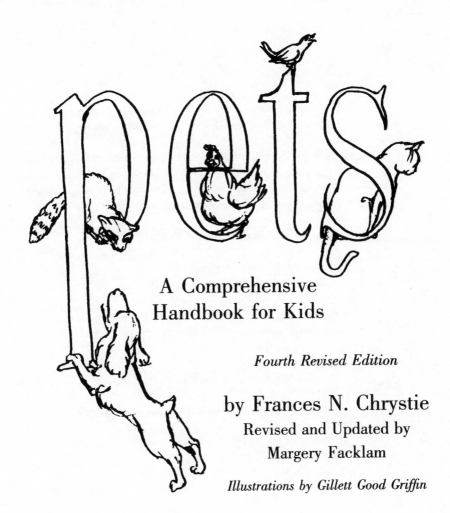

pets

A Comprehensive Handbook for Kids

Fourth Revised Edition

by Frances N. Chrystie
Revised and Updated by
Margery Facklam

Illustrations by Gillett Good Griffin

Little, Brown and Company
Boston   New York   Toronto   London

Fourth Revised Edition

Library of Congress Cataloging-in-Publication Data
Chrystie, Frances N. (Frances Nicholson).
    Pets : a comprehensive handbook for kids / by Frances N.
Chrystie ; revised and updated by Margery Facklam ; illustrations
by Gillett Good Griffin. — 4th rev. ed.
        p.   cm.
    Includes bibliographical references and index.
    ISBN 0-316-14281-6
    1. Pets — Juvenile literature.   2. Animals — Juvenile
literature.
    [1. Pets.   2. Animals.]   I. Facklam, Margery.   II. Griffin,
Gillett G. (Gillett Good).   ill.   III. Title.
    SF416.2.C495   1995
    636.088'7 — dc20   94-41229

                    10 9 8 7 6 5 4 3 2 1

                              MV-NY

Published simultaneously in Canada by Little, Brown & Company
(Canada) Limited and in Great Britain by Little, Brown and Company
(UK) Limited

Printed in the United States of America

To T. W. C.
especially Chapter 2

Foreword
to the Third Edition

A NATURAL enthusiasm for animals has prompted me to own a number of pets and to always notice those of other people. To write this book, I have supplemented what knowledge and understanding of animals I already had with research of various kinds. I have attempted to gather only the essential basic facts about each animal mentioned so that readers may get off to the right start with their new pets. Then they can have the pleasure of making a special study of their own and of becoming an expert in their particular sort of animal.

In the course of my research, I have asked endless questions of many persons experienced in special fields. To all the people involved I am most grateful. There are many in the country whose profession it is to teach animal care to children and also to adults. Each of those whom I approached was extremely kind in taking time to encourage me in my project and in making valuable suggestions and corrections.

Specifically I wish to acknowledge my thanks to Miss

Elizabeth Jacob and Mr. Herbert J. Knobloch of the New York Zoological Society; to Miss Mary Priscilla Keyes of the American Society for the Prevention of Cruelty to Animals; to Miss Shirley Miller, Mrs. Mildred Finney, and Mr. Andrew Bihun of the National Audubon Society; to Miss Marie E. Gaudette of the Girl Scouts of the United States of America; to Miss Ruth Teichmann of Camp Fire Girls, Inc.; to Marguerite B. Gulick, V.M.D., of Great Barrington, Massachusetts; and to Dr. Clive M. McCay of Cornell University. For his suggestions and for verifying Chapter 9 of the Third Revised Edition, my thanks go to Mr. S. A. Asdell of the New York State College of Agriculture at Cornell.

I am fortunate that for this edition Vernon R. Thornton, D.M.V., made extensive revisions, bringing up to date all sections on diet and health.

F. N. C.

Acknowledgments
for the Fourth Edition

I AM grateful to Michael Daley, Jessie Haas, Mary Jane Luce, Robert McAllister, David Metz, Peggy Thomas, Barbara VanSlambrouck, and David Whitelaw for reviewing sections of this book and advising me about raising goats and sheep, cockateels and parakeets, pigeons, turtles (especially box turtles), horses, and cattle. Thanks as well to Dr. Linda A. Ross, associate professor of medicine and associate dean for clinical programs at Tufts University School of Veterinary Medicine and director of Tufts New England Veterinary Medical Center, and Dr. Gretchen Kaufman, clinical instructor in medicine at Tufts University School of Veterinary Medicine and staff veterinarian at Tufts New England Veterinary Medical Center, for their expert advice. I also appreciate the bulletins and information from 4-H agents at the Cornell Cooperative Extension office in Niagara County, New York, and from the New York State Department of Environmental Conservation, Division of Fish and Wildlife.

M. F.

Contents

Introduction

Hᴀʀᴅʟʏ anything is more fun than a pet. It
is better than a bicycle, a dollhouse, or anything else
I can think of. But it is also a great deal of trouble. Even if
you just naturally like animals and don't like to hear any
of them called "a trouble," don't fool yourself. No matter
how much you usually enjoy being with your pet and caring
for it, there will be times when you would rather do something else. You can play with a toy all week and then forget it
for a day, but you can't do this with an animal. Both its
feelings and its health will be hurt if you neglect it a single
time.

An animal must have confidence in you before you can pet
it, play with it, or watch its natural games. And you can't even
begin the simplest kind of training until your pet is feeling
happy and safe and knows you are its friend.

Part of the fun of any pet is knowing that it is your own
and that it feels especially happy with you. But this owner-
ship is never complete, either, in the same way as owning a

toy. The animal has feelings and rights of its own. And since you are housing and feeding it for your own amusement — preventing it from caring for itself in its natural way — you are under a big obligation to take the best care of it that you can.

If you are wise and lucky, you will do most things for your pet yourself, but you will need some help, too. To a degree a live animal becomes a member of the family, and therefore the others in your house ought to have a say in the matter. You are probably too old to do anything so unfair and mean as to tease a pet, but you may have a younger brother or sister who will have to be taught kindness. And certainly your parents will share in the trouble as well as the fun of your pet, so choose a kind of animal they, too, will enjoy. There is no use in your promising to do every single thing yourself, because what about the hours you are in school? Or the time you have the measles? Or go camping with a friend in the summer? Besides, it costs money, space, and time to have an animal. It costs to buy it and to feed it, and when it gets sick, it costs to have the veterinarian's advice and to buy medicine.

I am writing all this discouraging part to urge you to select the sort of pet that is right for your family and not, by any means, to discourage you from having an animal of some sort. If you are a true animal lover, you will greatly enjoy any kind of animal, and it is exciting to widen your acquaintance among them. If you live in a small apartment with a large family and have parents who have not yet found out what pleasure an animal can be, don't set your heart stubbornly on a big Saint Bernard just because you have read of their faithfulness and bravery. Give other pets a chance. Maybe you will be surprised to find how much you like goldfish or tropical fish, when the shadow of your feeding hand above the water makes them rush expectantly to the surface, especially if you wiggle your fingers.

To Parents

Besides the great pleasure a child derives from owning and caring for a pet, there is of course the permanent value of learning to accept and carry out the responsibilities of training and daily care, which are so necessary for success with an animal. No one has the figures on the number of animals that have been brought enthusiastically into the house and have soon died or become unmanageable because no one has known how to care for them, but the number of such mishaps is undoubtedly staggeringly large. Careless treatment is obviously hard on the animals, but it is also extremely bad for the children involved. Either they feel a deep disappointment and heartbreak over the death of the animal or, worse still, in order to protect themselves, they harden their heart and close their imagination and sensitivity to the feelings of others. A child who learns to understand and treat an animal fairly and to be self-controlled and patient with it is getting invaluable training in dealing with people in the same way.

It is for this reason that more and more is being done in the schools and by humane societies to teach proper animal care, and to relate it to natural history, conservation, and human enterprise. Natural history museums throughout the country have prepared interesting pamphlets and movies on the subject. The many humane societies, such as those for the prevention of cruelty to animals, work unceasingly to teach animal care, and so do the 4-H clubs, the educational departments of zoos, the Audubon Society, the Defenders of Furbearers, the Scouts, and the Campfire Girls. The thought behind all this intelligent planning is not at all a sentimental love of animals but a recognition that cruelty to animals — and ignorant treatment that amounts to cruelty — has as bad an effect on the child as on the animal.

All this sounds solemn, but it is intended as a plea to you not to allow your child lightheartedly to bring any sort of pet into the home unless you have time to support the enterprise and see that your child learns how to take care of the animal and treat it kindly. You wouldn't buy a bicycle and let your child leave it out in the rain. It is only common sense to have him or her learn about whatever he or she tries to do.

A large part of the fun and interest of a pet for a child is in considering it his or her own and being the one to feed and care for it. But no child knows how to do this instinctively, and no child can be depended on to follow out a daily routine without supervision and training. So you will need to be alert in the background to take up the slack, as you do in other matters. I hope that if you are not experienced with all kinds of pets, you and your child will get help from this book and that your child will want to go on and learn more than is included here.

It would be a practical plan to find out what animal-care

organizations there are in your neighborhood and to interest your child in joining one. He or she will get detailed help from experts and will learn to be observing and thoughtful and to take his or her responsibilities in a more adult way. It's also a good opportunity to do things in a group and become part of the community. Even if a child does not live near enough a city to take advantage of the lectures and tours that are a part of the educational programs of many humane organizations, he or she can learn a lot through pamphlets and news brought in the mail. The Department of Agriculture in Washington will supply bulletins. There are radio and TV programs that give sound information on animal care. Many commercial bulletins are useful. Throughout the country there are zoos, natural history museums, and societies for the prevention of cruelty to animals that are equipped to give information either by mail or on personal visits. Find out how your local one can help your child with his or her animal.

The Boys' Clubs of America, in their camps and through such activities as pet shows and obedience training classes, teach the proper care of animals. The Audubon study programs, which deal with other aspects of natural history as well as with birds, are most worthwhile, whether a child joins the groups or belongs only by mail, and their pamphlets are authoritative, inexpensive, and interesting. The 4-H clubs, which spring from the Department of Agriculture in Washington and are administered through state colleges and thence county agents, have something very valuable to offer your child.

Since you will need to prepare for the animal, make sure that you are getting the kind your child really wants and that you can help care for it. If possible, make the project a family one in the first place, and together look at different animals in the pet shops or wherever the pet is to come from. This is fun for both you and the child. If you can manage to let your child see the animal he or she is to have while it is very little and pick out, say, his or her own puppy or kitten from a litter, it will add to the pleasure to think about it ahead of time. Naturally the child will want to bring the animal home before it is ready, but it does no harm to wait for pleasures. It's a good start in training to let a child realize that a pet is not a toy but a creature with feelings, and to learn that its own mother's care is necessary.

If for any reason the pet you have chosen is not a success or you move away and cannot take it to new quarters, I cannot urge you too strongly to provide for your animal in a reasonable and humane way and never to abandon it. To leave it, under any circumstance, is cruel to the animal and dangerous for your neighborhood. Perhaps you have a friend who would like your pet, and if you are sure the animal will be well taken care of, you can give it away. Otherwise all you need to do is telephone your local humane society, and without charge to you — although you might like to give a donation to support its valuable work — it will call at your home and take the animal away, where it will be kindly treated and put up for adoption. If a good home cannot be found, your pet will be painlessly put to death. It is far better to destroy an animal than to abandon it. If your pet is old and you think it cannot adjust happily to new surroundings, the most sensible thing you can do is either pay a veterinarian to put it to sleep or ask a humane society to do so.

Pets

1.   Dogs

THERE's an old saying that "a dog is a man's best friend." Dogs were also humankind's *first* friends, the first animal to be domesticated, more than twenty thousand years ago. And they are still particularly fine pets because it is the nature of dogs to love their human families and to wish to please them.

CHOOSING A DOG

There are many different breeds of dogs to choose from. The American Kennel Club registers only about 130 breeds that are called purebreds, although there are more than 300 other breeds registered in other kennel clubs around the world. Some breeds aren't registered because there are still too few of them to form classes in dog shows. A purebred is a dog whose parents and ancestors are the same breed as far back as anyone knows.

There is pride and pleasure in owning a purebred dog,

one that you can register and possibly show. But a good dog of any breed is a delight, and because certain traits are inherited, you can make a guess at the type of disposition you are going to find in the breed you choose. Do you want the whirlwind companionship of an Irish terrier or the sedate, strong-minded habits of a Scottie? An intelligent poodle will probably entertain you with the tricks it learns so easily, and the dignified collie will be a devoted, loyal companion, happiest when given the responsibility of a job. Each breed has its virtues. Many breeds, do, however, also have some hereditary disorders such as hip dysplasia. Check with a veterinarian before you make a final choice.

Although generalizations can be made about the characteristics of breeds, there is nothing set about them. Puppies from the same litter vary as much as sisters and brothers raised in the same family. Some are timid, and some are bold, some are intelligent, and some are not. Even stronger than these natural differences will be the effect you have on your own dog. A dog will sense your moods. It wants to please you. It will be happy if you are, and sorrowful when you are sad. If you are nervous and excitable, your dog will be jittery. If you are calm and self-controlled, your dog will learn to be so, too. A dog's natural intelligence will not develop unless you talk to your pet and give it a chance to learn. People who don't like dogs or who haven't been around them often will think that this is sentimental nonsense, but it is not. Guide dogs for blind people, dogs trained to help people in wheelchairs, police dogs, and shepherd dogs, all prove how close the understanding can become between humans and dogs.

In spite of the many shapes and sizes and kinds of purebred dogs there are to choose from, most of the 52 million or more pet dogs in the United States are mixed breeds. Some people call them mutts or mongrels, but no matter what they're called, one of these all-purpose dogs of mixed parentage can be as lovable a companion as any champion. And they don't cost as much! When you choose a mixed breed puppy, you will have to take a chance on its final size and appearance. Some people claim that these dogs are brighter than purebreds, but it all depends on the individual dog and on the amount of training it has had. Many show champions and many hunting or working champions are devoted house pets. Some people believe that female dogs (called bitches) are more affectionate and intelligent than males, but there are so many exceptions to this idea that it can't be counted on. It is all a matter of personal preference. Select your dog, and if you do your part, it will be the best dog for you.

The most sensible way to choose a dog is to decide which type of dog you think you'd like and then compare that dog's characteristics to the way you live. You may have to change your mind. You may happen to like the idea of a big sporting dog, such as a foxhound, but if you live in a city or suburb with many neighbors and a small yard, how are you going to keep a dog that size exercised? You would do better to consider a smaller dog with the same general characteristics, such as a beagle. Some breeds cost more than others, and big dogs are more expensive to feed than small ones. Beware of making up your mind until you have read about all sorts of dogs. Go to see them whenever and wherever you can — at local dogs shows, in kennels, or at an animal shelter.

If you are determined to buy a purebred and if your

family agrees with you, it's best to buy it from a breeder whose kennel specializes in the kind of dog you want. Do not buy it from a pet store that displays a dozen different breeds in small cages, unless they can tell you where the dogs came from, so that you can go and see the mother dog if you want to. Too many of these pet-shop dogs come from "puppy mills," which are badly run kennels that usually force the mother dogs to have too many litters each year, often under unsanitary and cruel conditions. Some of the puppies may be healthy, but too many are not. Humane societies and dog breeders' organizations are trying to close down puppy mills, but as long as people keep buying puppies that come from disreputable kennels, these greedy breeders will stay in business. It's all right to buy from someone who advertises puppies for sale from their home, where you can see the mother dog and choose your puppy from the litter.

You may also find a perfect companion at an animal shelter. In most cities, the SPCA and similar organizations have all kinds of dogs, both purebreds and mixed breeds, eagerly waiting to be adopted. Each adopted dog gets a checkup from a veterinarian and is given all the proper shots before you take it home.

A big decision is whether you want a puppy to train or an older, more settled dog. Puppies are fun, but they take a lot of care, so if you are going to have one, make sure that you can spare a good deal of time. If you have little experience with dogs or if your time is limited, consider getting an older, housebroken dog. If you are short on patience as well as time, you had better not have a dog at all. Select a pet that will not need so much of your attention. Patience, common sense, and a realization that a dog has strong feelings, individuality, and rights of its own are the three things you must be sure you can supply if you have a dog. Common sense includes finding out as much as you can about its needs before you own the dog.

PUPPY CARE AND TRAINING

A puppy should be at least two months old before you take it home. Somewhere between two and six months is ideal. The puppy will be so charming that you will want to pick it right up and hug it, and here is your first lesson in controlling yourself. When you pick up a puppy, or any other animal, don't let it dangle in the air, or you will both frighten and injure it. Put one hand under the dog, and support it firmly and gently with the other hand. Talk to it softly, saying anything you like, because it is the tone of your voice that will be reassuring. Instead of squeezing it, be careful of its young bones as you would of a baby's, and stroke it from head to tail, the way the hair grows. (An older dog, which knows you, may enjoy a little ruffling, but not a new puppy. Remember never to touch any unfamiliar dog before introducing yourself. First squat down to the dog's level and speak to it, then hold out your hand, palm up, for it to sniff.)

Before you take a puppy home, make sure you have picked out a warm place for its bed or crate and a place for its training papers if needed. When it first comes to your house, imagine how new and strange it will seem to the puppy to be away from its mother and its brothers and sisters. You probably look very big and scary. Don't try to teach the puppy anything at first except that it is safe and that you can be trusted. Give the puppy time to wander around a little, sniffing and exploring. Don't be surprised if your puppy puddles on the floor, but since you have prepared a place, maybe in the bathroom or kitchen, and have spread the floor with newspapers, it won't matter. After the puppy has explored a bit, lapped up some warm milk, and had a nap on its own bed, you can gradually introduce it to the rest of the house.

One of your first duties is to take your new dog to a veterinarian as soon as possible. Take along all the information you have about the dog's background, feeding habits, and any vaccinations that have been given. Take a stool sample from your dog so that it can be analyzed for the presence of parasites (worms). It's a good idea to write a list of the questions you have about the care of your puppy, so you won't forget anything. The vet will check your dog's general health, give the needed vaccines, and give you advice about caring for your new pet.

Maybe you named your puppy before you took it home, or maybe the dog will suggest its own name by some special habit. If your dog has been registered under a kennel name, this can't be changed. But you can always choose a short, easy-to-say nickname. If you use the nickname every time you speak to the puppy, you will be delighted with how quickly it responds with a general wiggle of pleasure. A distinct two-syllable name is best because the dog can distinguish it easily from other words.

The next step in teaching acceptable behavior, housebreaking, is not so simple, but if you go about it the right way, it should not take too long. Exactly how long depends on you and the individual puppy, but mostly on you. The easy part is that the dog just naturally wants to please, and all you have to do is make it understand what is expected. So make up your own mind just where you want the dog's "bathroom" to be, and always show the dog that same place.

A method of housebreaking that has gained popularity despite its seemingly inhumane appearance is crate training. A crate is a metal shipping cage that can be bought at a pet store or borrowed from someone who no longer uses theirs. Consult your pet store or veterinarian about the appropriate size crate for your dog. Using a shipping crate as a way of keeping your puppy in a confined area for short periods of time, especially when you are not around to watch it, will facilitate housetraining, minimize the possibility of household destruction, and provide a comfortable and familiar place for your dog to call home. It is important that a dog not be forced into a crate either as a form of punishment or neglect. Since a dog's tendency is to not soil its sleeping area, keeping your puppy in its crate will help it learn to control its need to go to the bathroom. As soon as you let the puppy out of its crate, bring it outside immediately to relieve itself. Place an old towel or blanket in the bottom of the crate, and slowly introduce your puppy to its crate. You can make going into the crate more appealing by placing a few pieces of dry dog food in the crate and petting and praising your puppy while it is inside. If you feed your puppy in its crate as well, the dog will link pleasant experiences with being in its crate. The way to stop a puppy from barking while in its crate is to go to the crate, clap your hands, and firmly say "No barking." If you respond every time it barks by letting it out, the dog will learn that that is the way to get your attention and be released. If used correctly, your crate will be a a safe haven for your dog, who will learn to go in on its own without your having to ask it to.

If yours is a city dog, or a country puppy in cold weather, you'll probably be training it to newspapers. Always keep them in the same spot, and always have them spread out and ready. Never put them in a box or a pan, as for a cat. Remember that a puppy urinates frequently, maybe twenty times a day, and it will probably have three or four bowel movements a day. When a young puppy is ready, it's impossible for it to wait, so you will have to take charge. Immediately after eating and after each nap, take the puppy to the newspapers or the spot you've chosen outdoors. Do the same when the puppy acts uneasy, and very quickly when it squats. Whenever it is on the paper, tell your puppy how good it is and that you are pleased. The first time the dog goes to the paper of its own accord, and every time until it is finally a habit, spare no words in your extravagant praise. If you have not caught it in time, show your disappointment. Point to the spot and say, "No!" Take the dog to the right place, and pet it there. If you make yourself clear, your puppy will catch on. Young puppies are easily distracted, so help your pet to remember by having it near the papers at the right time. Don't scold it for a mistake you didn't notice right away. The dog will have forgotten all about it, won't connect the scolding to anything it has done, and will be confused.

Never yell at a puppy or whip or strike it. Confine your punishment to scolding. An older, trained dog that has deliberately disobeyed may be given a quick swat on the rump or nose, but only if you can't control it any other way. Remember that you are trying to teach your puppy, not punish it. Never use the old unpleasant method of rubbing your dog's nose into its mess. That's only more confusing. It's enough to just show it to the dog. If you live in the country or have a safe yard, you can of course train your puppy to go outside instead of taking it to the paper.

Once the puppy is housebroken, you can begin its training outside on a leash. It's a good idea with a city dog, however, to continue using a paper at least certain parts of the day. It's easy to keep clean, and you will be glad that it has become a habit if the weather is bad or if the dog is sick. Never allow your dog to use the sidewalks, buildings, or parked cars for its bathroom. A city dog should get used to using the curb from the first. Actually the first few times you take your puppy outside, it will be so dazzled that it won't use anything at all. It will probably wait until it's inside again, where it feels safe. Be patient, keep on explaining and showing, and the time will come when the dog will tell you it's time to go out.

Before leash walks start, you will avoid some tangles and confusion if you start the leading process calmly at home. It's simple to accustom the puppy to a collar. Select an adjustable size, and fasten it tightly enough so that it cannot slip off the dog's head, yet loosely enough so the dog won't choke. You should be able to slip two fingers under it easily. Put the collar on the puppy for a little while each day, and use a lot of praise, saying how nice it looks. Your puppy may try to paw it and shake it off at first, but you can distract it with play and more praise. It won't take long before it will get used to a collar if the fit is right and it is not so wide as to rub its shoulder or ear. An older dog often becomes so used to its collar that it seems almost embarrassed without it. And every dog out of doors should always wear one, with the license attached. In most communities now, this is the law. Its enforcement has helped control rabies and reduce the number of stray dogs. As an added precaution, it's a good idea to have your name and address attached to a tag on the dog's collar, too.

Once a young dog feels at home in the collar, you can begin leash training. For the first few times, simply snap the leash onto the collar and let the puppy drag it around as it plays. Take it off after a while, but put it back on later and let it alone with it. Very soon the dog won't mind at all, and eventually it will bring the leash to you of its own accord by way of letting you know it's time for a walk. Even though the leash is going to be a means of control, you don't want the dog to be afraid of it. Actually, you don't want the dog to be afraid of anything. You want it to obey because it enjoys pleasing you and not because it fears punishment. A dog's strong desire for your company and approval is a marvelous trait, and you will want to develop it in your pet. In all training, praise for doing the right thing is reward enough and your disapproval is the only punishment. If you want to strengthen the praise with something to eat, you may, provided your dog isn't so terribly good that all these rewards spoil its digestion. But you must realize that the dog's pleasure is partly in your having given a special treat and not entirely in the taste of it.

You and your dog will learn to talk to each other in ways that can't be understood by anyone else and can't be equaled. But that will be a special sort of language. For everyday training, you will need to devise a code that the dog will understand quickly and precisely. Always use the same words for commands, praise, or disapproval. "Stay," "Sit," "Come," spoken clearly; "Good dog," said with enthusiasm; and "Bad dog," said in a deep voice are common signals. Never raise your voice to a dog. Its hearing is much more acute than yours, so that it hurts its ears to hear you shout; and it is much more impressive to see a dog respond to a quiet command.

Don't be afraid that teaching your dog absolute obedience will change its personality. There will be lots of free play time. Actually you will develop its personality much more completely if you educate your dog than if you let it run wild. A dog doesn't want to be a nuisance — it wants to be liked — so show it how to make friends.

FURTHER TRAINING

A dog has to remember many things while it is being trained. The first few months should be spent in getting acquainted with you, in being housebroken, and in starting to come when you call. When the dog is about nine months old, teach it to heel — that is, to walk at your side with its shoulder in line with your knee — to avoid confusion and pulling and panting on a leash. When the dog walks on your left side, hold the leash in your right hand, across your body. Your left hand is then free to pat the dog and to shorten the leash for greater control in an emergency. This is a comfortable and companionable position for both you and the dog. While teaching, you must be firm, patient, and consistent, and give frequent short lessons. Use the command "Heel," and start walking in the right position. When the dog dashes ahead, say, "Heel," again, slow your steps, and give a sharp, little jerk on the leash to bring the dog to your side. When the dog lags behind, hasten your steps and give the command again to bring the dog into line. Once the dog is in the right place, look down and give a lot of praise. It takes time, but sooner or later your dog will enjoy answering the heel command without any leash at all.

Some people like to use a training choke collar and a flat leather leash of a convenient length to help the dog understand more easily what they want. If a dog lunges ahead in an ordinary collar, there's a steady, uncomfortable pull on its throat, but the dog may still go prancing on ahead, leading *you* instead of the other way around. A slip-chain or choke collar put on the right way, which any pet shop will show you how to do when you buy it, acts as a sudden check and command. The second the dog obeys and stops pulling, the chain loosens. As long as the dog is walking in the right direction, it's comfortable. The flat leather leash is preferable during training because you can get a good grip on it. A round leash will slip through your hands, and a chain leash will slip and hurt and clank unpleasantly. After your dog has learned the proper manners, use any kind of collar and leash that is most comfortable for you and your dog.

It's most important during the lessons that you watch your dog closely and talk so that all the dog's attention is focused on you. A dog won't even notice commands if it is absorbed in the luscious smells of a city street. Timing is very important. It is the same with everything you do. When you are riding a bike, for example, you don't wait to veer until you are a few inches away from a tree. You look ahead and steer to avoid trouble before you are on top of it. So be alert, and steer the dog away from trouble.

A good watchdog barks only when something unusual happens. Constant barking is not only annoying, but it is a sure sign that you have not been fair to your dog and taught it all it should know. Every time your dog barks unnecessarily, say, "Quiet," very firmly, and put your hand gently around its muzzle. A dog can't bark when its mouth is closed. The yapping habit can grow quickly, so take time to train your dog every single time it barks when it shouldn't. Never let it go one single time. This, of course, is true of all training, and it is the reason you must have patience. Never lose your temper. Just go through the regular commands firmly each time they are needed. Your dog will learn much more quickly if you don't panic and act angry.

There will be times when you need to leave your dog alone, so for its own good as well as that of the neighbors, you'll want to make sure your pet is comfortable being alone and will not bark and whine the whole time, leading your neighbors to think that something is seriously wrong. While it's just a puppy, leave the dog alone for a while each day, with its papers, bed, and a bowl of fresh water. A puppy needs to rest anyway. You know how much a human baby needs to sleep, so remember that a baby animal needs quiet as well. Too much excitement and exercise are as bad as none at all.

After your dog is trained to a collar and leash, if you need to leave it alone outside and have no fenced runway, don't tie it on a short leash. You can rig up a high wire between two poles and clip the dog's leash onto that, which will allow the dog to run back and forth. Pet shops also sell a kind of metal stake that has a swivel top. When the stake is put firmly in the ground and the leash is hooked to the swivel top, the dog can run around without getting the leash tangled. Make sure there is no fence the dog can jump and no obstacle on which the leash can catch and strangle your pet. When you leave, speak reassuringly so the dog will know it's not being punished. Say that you are coming back. It will soon learn to recognize that phrase. If the dog seems very uneasy, leave a glove, scarf, or anything that belongs to you. Make sure the dog has shade, drinking water, and a place to lie down comfortably. A dog may learn to behave well when it is tied up or left alone, but it will never grow to like it, so be sure to make a fuss over your pet every time you return to untie it.

A grown dog running loose outside will take care of its own need for exercise. But few communities allow dogs to run loose, and you will have to see that a house pet gets enough exercise to keep it healthy and slim. This is one reason for having a small dog if you live in the city. If you have time to walk miles each day with a big dog, that's all right, but just remember that exercising must be done every single day. A little dog, of course, can keep well on less exercise. Besides the daily walks, you can have fun with your pet by playing indoors. Bouncing a rubber ball and letting the dog chase it and bring it back is a game easily taught. Just signal the dog to bring it to you, and wait until it does. Don't grab for it. Always throw it again and praise the dog when it fetches the ball. Frisbee is a favorite game for many dogs. And it's not hard to teach a dog to jump over a stick. Hold the stick close to your side at a reasonable height and step over it yourself, calling the dog to come and play. You can show a dog how to play hide-and-seek, and invent any number of other games. Do this all you can. It's fun for both of you. But be careful not to play too hard right after the dog has eaten or when the weather is very hot.

The matter of calling the dog to come to you is as important as any part of its training. Never call the dog to you to punish it. Always pet and praise the dog for coming. If your pet comes almost all the way and then darts off before you take hold, never keep grabbing for it. The whole thing gets to be a fine new game that it will play every time, and you will grow tired of it long before the dog does. It can be dangerous for a dog not to come when it is called. Don't keep nagging at your dog, trying to get it to run back when there's no point in coming and when it's having a harmlessly good time nosing around by itself. Teach the "come" call in short, frequent lessons, as you did with heeling. Fasten a long rope to the slip-chain collar and let the dog run loose on it. When it's about ten feet away, call its name and order, "Come." If it doesn't come to you, pull on the rope with a little jerk, and order, "Come," again. Repeat that until the dog naturally stops and comes to you when called. Of course, as always, praise the dog, pat it, and make a fuss when it obeys so it will be glad to be with you. Naturally the jerk on the rope or leash should never be so sharp as to hurt the dog. Just make it a quick, positive motion to remind the dog what is expected.

To teach a dog to sit down when you tell it to, stand directly in front of the dog, using the leash held rather short. As you say, "Sit," pull up the dog's head gently and press your hand down flat on the end of its back.

To show the dog what you mean when you say, "Lie down," press down on its back and gently lift his paws, forcing its body down. Always remember that your dog wants to please you, and your job is to show it patiently what your words mean. After all, you can't understand the dog's language, so you shouldn't expect that it will learn yours without practice. A dog will think your word means nothing if you sometimes let it get away with disobedience and are sometimes cross. Until it is fully trained, don't try to give orders when there are too many distractions. Wait to give the command when you have the dog's full attention.

Both you and your dog can learn commands easily if you take an obedience training course. Many 4-H clubs and community adult education programs offer these courses. Experienced trainers will show you exactly what to do, including how to give hand signals as well as spoken orders. Have no fear that you will break your pet's spirit by proper training. A dog always enjoys your praise and is proud of each new accomplishment. If you have a purebred dog, you may be able to train it well enough to enter obedience trials in which the American Kennel Club awards a C.D., which means Companion Dog, and later a C.D.X., meaning Companion Dog Excellent. All breeds of dogs are capable of earning these awards if you do your part. More highly specialized training is needed for the U.D., or Utility Dog, and the U.D.T., or Utility Dog Tracker. There are reliable places where you can send your dog for all sorts of training, from ordinary housebreaking to hunting skills. This is far better than no training at all, but it's much more satisfactory for you to learn to teach your house pet at home.

Dogs like to show off, so teach any tricks you want to. But remember that by far the best trick of all is to have a well-mannered dog that will sit when told to, come when called, refrain from chasing the neighbor's cat, and not jump, with shrill barks and scratchy claws, on your visitors. Although it's your own dog, your whole family and close neighbors are affected by everything your pet does. Don't allow any annoying habits. Perhaps you don't mind if your dog digs in a flower bed, buries bones behind sofa cushions, or yaps at the delivery truck, but other people mind, so be reasonable and try to make your pet popular with everybody.

"Everybody" includes other animals. A farm dog would have a glorious time charging around a chicken yard, taking delight in the squawks and flutters. But a dog can be taught to take the responsibility for guarding chickens, or whatever else you train it to watch. Dogs and cats seem to be natural enemies. So many cats have been chased by so many dogs that a kitten automatically arches its back and hisses at its first sight of a dog, even when it is so little that you have to put your ear practically to the ground to hear it hiss. But dogs and cats can become friends, and this is much more satisfying than the same old chase. Orphan puppies have been nursed by motherly cats. One particularly self-assured cat had so much confidence in a neighbor's cocker spaniel that she lay back and allowed the dog to wash each of her newborn kittens. Now and then she'd reach out a paw and give her approval by patting the dog on the head. You could almost hear her say, "Good dog."

Family mealtimes present another reason for good training for your dog. Even if *you* like to have your dog at your side as you eat — drooling, whining, and looking sad over every morsel that goes into your mouth — the rest of the family may not. If you want your dog to be popular, train it to stay away from the table. Put the dog in another room, or tie it if necessary, and above all, don't get too softhearted and occasionally slip it some food. All dogs can assume tragic expressions, but don't give in while you're teaching. Some people shouldn't even try to raise a cocker spaniel because they aren't strong enough to resist the sad act a spaniel can put on.

FEEDING

Meal training will be easier and kinder if you feed your dog before you eat. A dog's meals should be given at regular hours, but never immediately before or after strenuous exercise. Your dog's food is very important to its health. There are various opinions on what a dog should be fed, but veterinary scientists have done so much research on the subject that you can rely on the food requirements they have established. Reliable companies have used this information to produce commercial diets that are best for dogs. The basic diet for your dog should be a good commercial brand of dog food, which can be supplemented with some meat or cheese now and then, but these extras should never be more than half of a daily meal.

When you first get a puppy, find out what food it has been eating, and don't change that diet for a few days until the puppy is well adjusted to you and its new home. If you find that food is not the best for a puppy, change the diet over several days, gradually decreasing the old food and increasing the new.

There are three basic kinds of commercial puppy foods to choose from: dry foods, which include Puppy Chow and kibble; semimoist foods packaged so they need no refrigeration; and canned complete dog food. Select the type that is most convenient for you, or a combination of all three. Never feed an all-meat canned food to a puppy unless you mix it with another type. Puppies fed an all-meat diet tend to develop growth and digestive problems. The main requirement for puppy food is that it be at least 20 percent protein and that it be easily digested so that your puppy can eat it without developing diarrhea.

Feed your puppy four times a day until it is three months old, and then feed three times a day until it is mature, which is at ten or fourteen months. Always provide plenty of fresh water. Milk is not essential for your puppy, but it is good food for growth. If it causes diarrhea, discontinue it. Gradually increase the food as your growing puppy requires it. Specific amounts are difficult to prescribe because each pup is different, so ask a veterinarian or determine for yourself what your pet needs. When your dog is mature, reduce the feedings to one or two a day. Most dogs enjoy meals twice a day.

It's always tempting to give a dog snacks from your own food, but it's not really kind. The dog is happy and contented on a regular balanced diet and will remain much healthier without "people food." Don't give your dog bones of any kind, but especially not chicken bones, because they crack and shatter easily into splinters that can puncture the intestines. Bones can catch in the dog's throat and cause choking, and hard particles can gather in the colon and cause a painful illness.

If a puppy has no toys to play with and chew on, it will use your shoes and furniture as teething rings. You have to teach a puppy not to destroy things by saying "No" severely when you catch it in the act and even giving a single slap on the rump with your hand or a folded newspaper. When you take away the forbidden object, give your puppy one of its own toys. Play with your pet for a while, showing that now it is a good dog.

Puppies, and even grown dogs, have a lot of curiosity but very little judgment as to what should be swallowed. Loose marbles, small balls, bells attached to toys, nails, safety pins, a needle and thread — anything at all will be happily gulped down, so be careful what you leave around. Anything painted with lead paint is particularly dangerous for your dog. Dogs, as well as children, develop lead poisoning from chewing on painted wood objects, peeling paint, or plaster. Be certain that your dog doesn't chew on such things. Rubber toys can be dangerous, too, because bits can be chewed off and swallowed. One of the best toys is rawhide, because it is safe and tough to chew on. If you have an old pair of blue jeans, cut off a leg, tie it in a knot, and your puppy will love to shake it and play tug-of-war with you. And for straight, concentrated chewing, nothing is more satisfying or safer for your puppy than a large dog biscuit.

Even after your puppy is fully grown, keep up the toy habit and play with your dog. You may be surprised at how a grown dog will guard its toys and often keep them in a special place, perhaps burying them in its bed. If you keep one toy apart, your dog will be excited when you bring it out, knowing that this is a special playtime for both of you.

SLEEPING

As your puppy grows and becomes housebroken and well mannered, you'll allow it more freedom in your home. But it's still important for your pet to have a clean, private place of its own to sleep. Don't share your bed with your dog, because a dog never sleeps straight through the night as you do, and its stirring around will disturb you. A dog with a thick coat can sleep comfortably outside as long as you provide a dry, draft-proof kennel and good bedding. But a dog that's kept in the house must also be free from drafts. A pillow with a washable cover makes a nice bed that is raised off the floor a bit. Cover the pillow with a blanket so the dog can enjoy turning around on it and arranging it to suit itself. It's bad manners for a dog to use all the chairs and sofas, leaving hairs behind and no room for people to sit. But if you conveniently can, it is a cozy habit to let a dog have its own chair and join the family circle for a quiet evening.

GROOMING

Keep your dog clean, especially if you want it to be comfortable — and welcome in the house. This is one of the easiest things you have to do for a dog, and one you will both enjoy. A dog loves the attention of being brushed as well as the way it feels. While you are brushing, you can have a good time talking to your pet. You can brush your dog on the floor perfectly well, but if there is a table handy, it's easier to have the dog stand on that, especially while it is learning how pleasant a grooming can be. Naturally if you go at the dog suddenly and roughly and pull harder than you like your own hair pulled, any dog will try to get away, the job won't get done, and nobody will have a good time.

First find out from a pet shop or groomer what brush and comb are best for your dog's type of coat, and use those. Both you and your puppy will gradually get used to these grooming sessions until you have learned to do a good job and the dog feels comfortable, too. Grooming takes the dirt out and keeps the skin and hair in good condition. Occasionally rub a smooth-coated dog with a few drops of oil. Brush your dog every day, and when you think it's necessary, give it a bath. It's easier, of course, to keep a smooth-coated dog well groomed than one with a long coat, so bear this in mind when you select a dog. Certain breeds, such as poodles, are better groomed by professionals, who can trim them to look as good as they deserve to.

When you get ready to bathe your dog, fill a tub with lukewarm water up to the dog's elbows, and put a towel or rubber mat in the bottom to prevent slipping. Talk constantly and reassuringly all the time, because most dogs don't like baths, and you want to keep your pet from being frightened. Use the mildest soap. Pet stores carry soaps made specifically for dogs. Don't use shampoos made for people because they will dry out the dog's skin too much. With a damp cloth, wash the dog's face first, being very careful not to get soap in the dog's eyes and ears. Some people like to put cotton in the ears and a bit of Vaseline around the dog's eyes to keep water from running in, but that's not necessary if you're careful. Don't ever dump water over the dog's head. Finish the rest of the bath as quickly as you can, and make sure that you've rinsed off all the soap. When you take the dog out of the tub, you may be fast enough to give the dog a quick towel-rub first, but be prepared to step back and let the dog have a good shake, because you won't be able to stop it. Once that's done, finish drying the dog with a towel. If it's a hot summer day, let the dog run outdoors, but if it's not, keep it indoors for at least an hour.

Along with the daily brushing, check your dog's eyes. If they ooze a bit at the corners, wipe them gently with a tissue or cotton dipped in a boric acid or warm salt water solution. Also check the ears, because infections are not uncommon. After you've been grooming your dog for a while, you'll become familiar with the smell of your dog's ears and with the small amount of wax that accumulates there. You should wipe out the ears occasionally with mineral oil on a cotton swab. If there is a foul odor or an excessive secretion of brownish wax from either ear, have the dog checked by a veterinarian.

Some small daily grooming chores will make your dog a more welcome part of the family. Nobody wants a ragged, dirty dog tracking mud through the house. In bad weather keep an old towel handy, and when you bring the dog inside, dry its coat and wipe its paws clean.

SPAYING AND NEUTERING

One of the most important decisions to make about your dog has nothing to do with training. Unless you are ready to take on the enormous responsibility for breeding your dog, raising the puppies, and finding good homes for them, it's very important to have a female dog spayed or a male neutered when it is about six months old. These are simple operations that will leave your dog unable to produce young. They are always done under anesthetic, by a veterinarian. Neither operation changes your dog's personality, although a male dog will be less likely to want to roam or fight. The number of unwanted dogs in this country is a national disgrace. The lucky ones are taken to an animal shelter, where they at least have a chance to find a new home. But millions of unwanted dogs are simply dropped by a roadside and left to starve. A responsible dog owner won't let that happen.

If you love your dog well enough to give it the simple training and care that has been suggested here, you will have a pet you can feel proud of. The more time you spend with your dog, the more you will grow to understand each other until you have a bond of affection that lasts a lifetime.

2. Cats

JUST about everybody likes kittens — they are so lively and fun to watch as they play, and they look so soft and relaxed when they are sleeping. But lots of people don't like cats. A child who likes all animals said, "You can't love a kitten as much as a cat because you haven't had time."

It does take time to know a cat, and the cat is perfectly able to wait. Any cat will go on right on thinking deep cat thoughts and pursuing cat pursuits whether you like it or not. But if you conduct yourself in a manner pleasing to the cat and you are accepted, you can feel proud, because cats are particular. That doesn't mean they're not affectionate. They are just reserved and independent. Once a cat loves you, that love is strong, and as proof, the cat may settle warmly on your lap and purr. When the cat feels like hunting, it will not only catch a mouse but will present it to you and expect praise.

Cats are definite in their minds about the right time for everything. There are no doubts as to whether this or that will please you. If a cat wants to rest on your lap, it does so. Suddenly the rest is over, and the cat will spring down gracefully. It's washing time.

You can't change a cat's nature, any more than you can change any animal's, but cats do seem to have more of a sense of pleasing themselves than of pleasing you. Because cats like comfort so much and are so direct in securing it, it may seem as though they care more for their homes than for the people in them. But this is not so. They seem to want both security and freedom, and if they are treated with courtesy and affection, they will know very well who provides this well-being, and they will make themselves at home where the family lives.

ADOPTING A KITTEN

If you have decided to have a cat in your family — and it really is a family decision — get a kitten and watch it grow up, unless a grown cat pays you the compliment of adopting you. Don't make the mistake of bringing a kitten to your home too soon, even if you feel tempted to. Every young animal needs to be with its mother for the proper length of time. The mother animal knows instinctively just how long this should be and does not try to prolong it. In general, the more intelligent and highly developed the species of animal is, the longer the young stay with the mother.

Not only does the mother cat give milk that is more healthful than any you can supply for the kitten, but she also knows how to train her young in things they must know. It is not fair to your kitten to take it away from its mother until it is about eight to ten weeks old. If you do take it younger, you can probably keep it alive, but it will not have had the right start. Maybe its bones will not be as strong as they should be. And surely it will not have had a happy, easy time of learning how to be a proper cat. Kittens need to play with their brothers and sisters in order to develop their muscles and learn to defend themselves. The mother teaches them to move quietly, to stalk, and to hunt. She washes the kittens and teaches them to wash themselves. Have you ever watched a mother cat teach her kittens how to climb a tree? Over and over again, she will climb a few feet up, urging the kittens to follow. They do this readily, but then the mother starts down backward, looking over her shoulder and hooking her curved claws into the tree trunk. Over and over, she shows her kittens how to do this harder thing.

The kittens are usually born in a dark place. At first their eyes are closed, and when they open, in about ten days, they are a hazy blue color, but the kittens cannot yet see. They can't see clearly until they are about three weeks old. By this time they can walk in a tumbling fashion out into the light, and their pinpoint teeth are coming through. All this time the mother will nurse them, and she will prefer that people do not handle them but only admire them from a distance. She will quite rightly expect praise for what she has done.

After the kittens have been walking for a few days — a complicated trick for them because their stomachs are apt to be so full that they drag on the floor — it is time for them to start being weaned. For that, you heat a mixture that is half milk or condensed milk, half water, plus a teaspoon of baby cereal, and put it down in a saucer. The kittens, of course, have no idea what this is for, so they have to be shown. To do this, dip your finger into the warm milk and let the kitten lick it off. Gradually bring your finger nearer the saucer until finally the kitten's tongue is right in the milk. Some kittens are quicker than others to learn, but after a few days, they all pass through the sneezing stage when their noses instead of their tongues go into the saucer, and they will no longer drag their feet and elbows through the milk. As soon as they have learned to drink, you can add a little lean, raw, scraped beef or strained baby foods, both meat and vegetable. Always warm it. Never serve it icy cold.

The weaning has to be done before the kittens leave their mother, of course, because she will continue to nurse them while they are learning to eat and drink from a saucer. But it's good to know about this early care in case you ever raise kittens yourself. Besides, if you have an idea how your kitten was treated while it was with the mother, you will find it easier to let it grow up naturally and gradually and to keep it from feeling too strange with you at first. By two or three months, a kitten will be completely weaned, although it would still be nursing its mother for comfort and out of habit if they were together, even if it no longer needs to.

FEEDING

You will be feeding your kitten four times a day, and that's enough. Gradually cut down on the number of feedings, giving more food each meal, until, by the time it is six months old, your kitten is having two meals a day. That's what it should have for the rest of its life.

Don't let anyone persuade you that your cat will become a better mouser if it is hungry. It's true that an overfed cat may become fat and lazy, but the right amount of food will keep it in good health. A healthy cat will be a better hunter, even if it's to be a barn cat, living where its duty and pleasure is to keep down the mice. Individual cats vary as to the exact amount of food they need, but about half a cup at a time is average. Always keep clean, fresh water where the kitten or cat can get it, and offer milk if it seems to want it.

Different cats vary about many things, including preferences in food. If you want your cat to have a well-balanced diet and also be easy for you to feed, encourage it to eat a variety of foods while it is young. All cats are carnivores, but a total meat diet may be too high in protein for an older cat because it puts extra work on the kidneys. For these cats, add some bread, potatoes, or pasta to their food now and then. Some cats enjoy green vegetables, especially green beans, as long as these don't amount to more than half their food. You can also give your cat a chopped hard-boiled egg or the separated yolk of an egg once or twice a week, but don't give a cat raw egg white. Some cats like milk, but others get an upset stomach from it.

Most commercial cat foods, both canned and dry, provide all the nutrients a cat needs each day, and you can feed these as its total diet. But a male cat should not eat a lot of dry or canned food that has a high ash content, because it may contribute to forming a urinary blockage. Check the label on any commercial food to make sure that it is low in ash.

Since cats wash themselves so often, they constantly swallow hair, which can become matted into fur balls that can't be digested and are hard to eliminate. Tuna and other oily fish once in a while helps cats get rid of fur balls, but don't feed them a diet high in red or dark tuna because that can lead to a vitamin E deficiency, which takes the form of a painful disease in the fatty tissue. Any sort of mild oil will do the same, and many cats enjoy the taste of a little olive oil or cod liver oil on their food now and then. Never force oil down a cat's throat, because that can cause serious problems. Don't be surprised if your cat eats grass. It contains vitamins, and it also helps the cat bring up fur balls. Don't give your cat bones, particularly chicken, fish, and pork or lamb chop bones, because they splinter easily. Animals need salt, so don't forget to sprinkle a little on meat each day or on other food you may be cooking for your cat. You don't have to add salt to commercial cat food.

KITTEN CARE

Before you bring a kitten home, plan to have everything ready so that you can make your pet feel at home. It ought not to have the whole house to roam over at first, because it will seem so huge and frightening. Select the place where you want to keep the litter box, perhaps in the bathroom, and make that the kitten's headquarters until it is old enough to remember where to find its pan. Fix a nice soft bed, out of drafts. Cats love the cozy, protected feeling of boxes. A box laid on its side, to make a little cave, and lined with a blanket is ideal.

Naturally you won't want to make a lot of noise welcoming the kitten home, because cats like quiet sounds. And you won't want to pick up the kitten until it seems ready. Just let it poke around and investigate its room, and watch to see what it does. After it has examined things for a while, when you wiggle your fingers on the floor, you can be certain that the kitten will come over to see what's going on. Let it smell your fingers and play with them a bit. When you see that it is ready to make friends, pick up the kitten gently. Never, even when it is entirely used to you, grab it suddenly, but let it see what you are going to do. Never squeeze hard, but hold it gently. Don't pick it up by the scruff of the neck, as the mother cat does, but take the kitten carefully in both hands. Never let the hindquarters dangle, because that's uncomfortable and can injure a young kitten.

Kittens like to be cuddled, and they are used to caresses from their mother, so let your kitten get comfortable in your arms, and rub it gently on top of the head and under the chin. Never ruffle the fur, because cats like to feel tidy. Pet and talk to your kitten often, and soon it will learn its name. Of course the kitten needs time to itself, but remember that for all its independence, a cat likes to be invited to do things.

Ordinarily you will not have any housebreaking to do at all, since cats are naturally clean. But you will have to make it easy for your kitten to find and know the pan you have prepared. Just remember that a little kitten can't possibly find its litter box if it is given too much space to roam around in. Think how immense even a small apartment must seem to a

tiny animal at first. This is one important reason for keeping
the kitten in just one room when it first arrives. There are
many kinds of litter boxes available at pet shops. A plastic pan
with high sides is best, with a layer of kitty litter on the bottom. There are many good deodorant and highly absorbable
litter materials made for litter boxes, and the cat will follow
its natural instinct to cover a mess it has made.

The chances are the kitten will find this pan for itself. If
not, when it uses the wrong spot, pick up the kitten and put it
in the pan. Sometimes you can catch the kitten in the act of
using the wrong place and move it to the pan in time. Don't
be too severe or you will frighten it instead of teaching it what
to do. Once the litter box has been used, try leaving a small
amount of soiled litter when you clean the box, as a reminder.
You'll only need to do this for a few days, because once a cat
has settled on a certain spot, it is reliable about returning to
it, and you will want to keep the box clean. Scoop out the
feces daily, and flush them down the toilet. Change the litter
as often as necessary. Many cats will not use a pan that needs
cleaning. It is particularly important to show your kitten the
proper place right away, because if the training is badly man-
aged, the cat can become as determined about the wrong
place as the right one.

Once your kitten shows that it is completely at home, it
can — and will — investigate the whole house. At this stage,
make sure the door to its own room is always open. There is
really no use in trying to keep your cat out of certain rooms.
It will understand you readily enough, but it won't obey. A
kitten's curiosity is so strong that it just can't resist seeing
everything. A closed closet is a challenge, and sooner or later

it will get in to explore it. A kitten can't resist half-open bu-
reau drawers, and it will crouch down in the farthest corner
of your room and watch to see when they are left open. The
only thing to do is to be very careful not to lock your kitten in
when you don't mean to.

You have to decide if your cat will be an indoor pet or one
that is free to go outside as well. Some veterinarians suggest
having the claws of an indoor cat's front paws removed to
prevent the cat from clawing and scratching furniture. But
before you decide to have this done, check with more than
one veterinarian so you thoroughly understand the conse-
quences. It's true that an indoor cat is safe from dogs and
cars, but if a declawed cat ever does get out of its house, it
can't climb a tree to escape a dog. It has no protection. In
England, it's against the law to have a cat declawed.

Even if you live where it is not safe for your cat to go
outside, you may want to let it out occasionally while you
stand guard. At first the cat will go cautiously out the door,
slowly investigate, and suddenly dart back in. After a time or
two of this hesitation, it knows the smell and location of its
own territory and will be less likely to get lost. If your cat lives
where it can go outdoors safely, it will be happier, and you
will save yourself a lot of time if you cut a small swinging door
so that it can come and go as it wishes.

Kittens play practically all the time when they're not sleeping. If yours ever gets too rough with teeth or claws when
pretending to fight your hand, don't pull away. Just hold your
hand perfectly still, and the kitten will let go. Be sure always to
do this, not just to save your hand, but to teach the kitten to
play gently while it is still young. Otherwise it's likely to be a

problem when it is older and its teeth and claws are really strong. Grown cats play a lot, too, and like to have you play with them. Their games are all on the stalk and pounce principle, and they are very clever at them. A soft rubber ball that doesn't make too much noise is fun, and as it bounces, any cat can catch it on the fly with its paw. Small pieces of paper, especially crinkled, rolled cellophane, are fine for throwing. A cat will bat the paper, stalk it, and sometimes even bring it back to be thrown again. Cats don't retrieve as dogs do, as a way of pleasing you, but may bring something back with dignity in case you may want to throw it again. A light stick that makes a pleasing sound or a string dragged across the floor are wonderful cat toys. It's even better if you tie a wad of paper to the string, to be batted around as it swings when tied to the back of a chair. Some kittens will climb to the top of a chair and try to undo the string. Most grown cats love to play with catnip, either dried or fresh, although some get over-excited. Cats can be taught tricks, but it is far easier and better to let them think up their own tricks to entertain you. They always seem to know when you are talking about them. Perhaps it's not the words themselves, but the tone of voice you use, so be careful what and how you say things.

CAT CARE

The independent nature of cats has led them into trouble because it has often been misunderstood. For example, people take a kitten to a cabin or resort for the summer, and then because it seems so capable, they leave it to shift for itself when they return to the city for the winter. This is horribly cruel, and in most places it is against the law. A jungle cat's skill and intelligence give it a good chance of survival, but a domesticated cat, accustomed to food on its plate, cannot adapt as easily as some people suppose. There's usually not nearly enough food to hunt, nor has the cat learned to be an expert hunter. Used to human companionship and protection, a deserted cat is desperately lonely. Every summer on college campuses and in summer resort towns, thousands of cats are abandoned. Some survive and become successful feral cats (a feral animal is a tame one gone wild), but most fall prey to starvation, illness, cars, exposure to extreme weather, or as food for hawks, dogs, or other large predators.

Most of these abandoned cats have not been spayed or neutered, which makes life even more difficult for them as they breed and have to raise the kittens. One of the most important things you can do for your cat is have it spayed if it's a female or neutered if it's male. These simple operations do not make cats fat or lazy or change their personalities, but they do protect them. A spayed female is less likely to have mastitis and infections of the uterus, and a neutered male won't roam and get into fights that can leave it badly hurt. When you take your kitten to the veterinarian for its first checkup, you can find out more about this important protection for your pet.

Cats have a dignified manner, and they seem shy about their interest in people, but that seems to make them particularly interesting pets. You can take your choice — having a cat in your house its whole life, being fed and kindly treated and yet never really known or understood because you haven't taken the time to watch its subtle, expressive face or respond to its small advances. Or you can pay close attention and have more companionship with your pet. Cats can be trained, provided they understand and approve of what is expected. But cats hate to be scolded, and they never forget a punishment, especially a spanking.

So if you don't want your cat to sit on the table when you eat and daintily fish choice bits of meat from your plate with its paws, you must teach it that the game is not worth the disapproval. But you have to play fair and recognize that there are certain cat rules that must be obeyed, too. For instance, claws have to be sharpened. When a cat wakes up from a nap, it has to stretch and pull. This doesn't amount to much with a cat that's out of doors most of the time. That cat will work its claws on a sturdy tree trunk. But a housebound cat will need a scratching post that can take the shredding, unless you don't mind having your furniture torn apart. A log or a sturdy, high post covered in carpet and set in a firm base makes a good scratching place. If there happens to be a convenient spot in your house, you can nail strong burlap to the wall, and your cat will learn to reach up and sharpen its claws on that.

Hairs on your lap and on furniture can be kept at a minimum if you groom your cat daily. Use a brush and a fine-toothed comb. Give a final rubdown with terry cloth moistened with witch hazel. If you start this when your cat is young, and do it gently, grooming time will become a pleasant, conversational time for both you and the cat. Never, except under the most unusual circumstances, bathe cats. They like to watch water dripping from a faucet or running in a brook, but they hate to get wet, even though they can swim. Soap and water are bad for their coats. Their skin is too delicate and should not be allowed to become too dry. But occasionally your cat's hair and skin may get so dirty that a bath is necessary. Do not spray water onto the cat, but gently pour it on while holding the cat in a small amount of warm water. Use a very mild soap or baby shampoo and rinse it out well. Avoid getting water into their eyes. Be very careful what sort of flea soap or ointment or powder you put on them, because they lick themselves so thoroughly that they might swallow a poison that could be safely left on a dog's coat. And because cats can absorb chemicals through their skins, coal tar or kerosene preparations can kill them.

Most cat owners are pleased to have a pet that is a good mouser, but many are unhappy if their cat catches birds. Naturally this distinction seems unreasonable to a cat. This peculiar idea of yours may be one of the things your cat is wondering about when it stares at you unblinking, then slowly crosses its eyes. Actually, cats, even hungry stray cats, do not catch as many birds as most people think, because birds have the habit of flying away. To lessen the chance of bird catching, don't put your cat outside at night, when birds are asleep. When you do let the cat out, put a tiny bell around its neck, fastened to a stretchable collar, which will slip off if it gets caught on something. Otherwise the cat might strangle. Be sure the cat wears the bell in spring, when birds are nesting, particularly to protect and warn the parents of fledgling birds, which can't leave the nest.

CAT BREEDS

It hardly seems necessary to describe different breeds of cats, since their general characteristics are so much alike yet their individual habits are so varied, depending partly on the amount of attention they have received. At times they all look as though they possess a knowledge beyond human understanding. At rest they are graceful, utterly relaxed, yet aware. Everyone who likes cats at all has a preference between longhaired and shorthaired varieties. Those who like longhaired cats claim they are softer and more beautiful. Those who like shorthaired cats claim they are more interesting to watch because you can see the grace and strength of their muscles as they spring five times their height and land on their feet precisely on a chosen spot.

Most cats are shorthaired "alley" cats that come in every cat color, striped, plain, or spotted. Abyssinians are rare purebred cats with big ears, handsome stripes, a smooth, unusually short coat, and large, intelligent eyes. Siamese are a more popular purebred short-coated breed, with cream-and-coffee-colored coats with a dark face, feet, and tail. Often their eyes are blue and slanted. They have a special and very demanding voice and are said to be highly intelligent. But intelligence is an individual trait; there are smart cats and not-so-smart cats among every breed.

Longhaired cats called Persians can be white, orange, tabby, black, tortoiseshell, or a smoky gray known as "blue." The tabby-marked, longhaired Manx cats, from the Isle of Mann, are famous for having no tails. A new breed called the rag doll will always need the protection of people because it is so gentle. When it is picked up, it goes as limp as a rag doll. It won't protect itself, not even if it's in pain. There are many other new breeds, such as the Scottish fold cat, bred in 1961, that has one ear folded down like a tiny cap. If you go to a cat show, you can see Angoras, calicoes, sphinx cats, hairless cats, and dozens of other breeds.

Whether you choose a fancy breed from a cat show or go to an animal shelter and adopt a cat that needs a home, yours will be one of 58 million cats that share the homes of families in every part of the United States.

3. Small Caged Animals

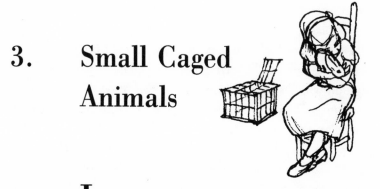

It's important to remember that a cage for any animal should feel like its home, not like a trap. But just to put an animal in a nice cage and thrust food at it at the proper times is not enough. It will be lonely and it may be afraid of this new place, with its new smells and sounds, and strange food. Let the animal get to know you gradually. Greet it by name so that sound becomes familiar and reassuring. Never startle an animal by a sudden noise or by touching it before it knows you are there. You should handle your caged pet, play with it, and sometimes let it out of its cage. When you treat it well and add to its comfort, this little animal, which is so dependent upon you, will come to trust you.

Sometimes when people see a cute animal in a pet store, they want it so much that they buy it before they know what it eats, how long it lives, or how much room it needs. That's not fair to the animal or to you or your family. Read books about the animal that interests you, and ask questions of people who know about the animal. You will want to be a kind, responsible pet owner, so make some promises to yourself. Promise that you'll never hit or tease an animal, especially one in a cage, since it can't get away from you. Always wash your hands after handling your pets, and even if you wear rubber gloves while you're cleaning their cages, wash your hands afterward. This will help prevent diseases from spreading and will keep both you and your pet healthy. Never let little animals run free in the house when your dog, cat, or other large animal is around, unless you are guarding your small pet closely. People might trip over a small animal or accidentally step on it. Your pet's health and safety depends on you.

RABBITS

A soft, lovable baby rabbit given to a child at Easter time often ends up in an animal shelter because its owner didn't know how to take care of it. If you want a pet rabbit, it's a good idea to find out as much as you can about these interesting animals before you bring one home.

A rabbit has the reputation as a quiet, timid animal that would rather hide than fight. Actually most animals survive because they know when it's better to run than to fight, and a rabbit is no different. But don't underestimate a rabbit. If cornered or frightened, a rabbit will scream and will defend itself with big, sharp, front teeth, sharp nails, and long, strong back legs, which can deliver a powerful kick.

There are more than fifty different breeds of domestic

rabbits, ranging in size from the huge Flemish giants to the medium-size English lop-eared to one of the miniature or dwarf breeds. You can choose a brown or gray rabbit with hair so short and thick that it feels like plush, or an albino, which is a pure white, pink-eyed "Easter bunny" kind of rabbit. You may want a cashmere rabbit, with long, fluffy fur, or a silky-haired Angora. Find out about all the different kinds of rabbits at a pet shop or from a rabbit breeder's association, but always choose a domestic breed. Never try to tame a wild rabbit, even a very young one. A grown wild rabbit is likely to die of fright and sorrow if caged, and any young wild creature is extremely difficult to raise.

Many species of wild rabbits live in burrows. Either they dig their own or, like the cottontails, borrow the abandoned holes of woodchucks or other animals. All domestic rabbits have a little of the same tendencies, which is why they enjoy the privacy of a box or small barrel inside their hutch. No matter how much freedom you allow your rabbit, it must have its own hutch for sleeping, eating, and security. A hutch is easily built from wood and wire netting, with a wire floor for cleanliness. Flooring made from one-fourth-inch wire mesh is comfortable for the rabbit's feet yet big enough to allow droppings to fall through to a pan or newspapers underneath. An oblong movable hutch, built on legs to keep it off a drafty floor, is convenient because it can be kept indoors or out, depending on the weather. Rabbits catch respiratory infections or sniffles easily, so you never want to leave the hutch outdoors in cold weather or indoors in a damp or drafty place. A hinged top — so that you can easily reach inside — is a fine idea because you must keep the hutch absolutely clean. The right size hutch depends on how big your pet is and how much of its time it will spend there, but give your rabbit reasonable hopping room. Two compartments are best: a closed-in nesting place and a runway for exercise. An outdoor hutch must be sturdy enough to keep out any neighborhood dogs or cats. It must also be well ventilated, dry, easy to clean, and built to provide protection from direct sunlight and cold winds. You can find a variety of plans for building a hutch in 4-H bulletins or in books on raising rabbits.

When you have a place ready for a rabbit, it's time to choose the one you want at a pet shop or from someone who raises rabbits. To find a healthy rabbit, look for one that is alert, with bright eyes, and a smooth, shiny coat of fur. Although you will always pet a rabbit from head to tail without ruffling its fur, you should make one exception when you make the "fly back" test. Rub one hand over the rabbit from tail to head, and notice if the fur quickly flies back into place and lies smoothly. If it doesn't, the rabbit may be ill. Look at the rabbit's teeth. The front pair of cutting teeth must not be crooked, because these teeth keep growing, and the top and bottom teeth must meet so they can wear away against each other.

Never for any reason pick your rabbit up by the ears! That hurts the rabbit, and it would have a perfect right to reach up and scratch you with its back claws if it could. Support the rabbit by scooping up its body securely with your hand and arm, and steady it by gently gripping the loose skin at the back of the neck. You hold on to that loose skin only to keep the animal still, not to pick it up. Never let any animal dangle. That is an alarming and painful way to be carried. After you've petted and played with your rabbit, or after you've cleaned its hutch, always wash your hands so you don't get any diseases the animal might carry.

Rabbits drink a lot of water. In the wild, they get moisture from eating green plants, but your rabbit will be eating a lot of dried food, so it will need a steady supply of fresh, clean water in a bottle fastened to the side of the hutch. You can use a heavy water dish that won't tip over, but that gets dirty quickly with leftover food and hay. Use a heavy dish for your rabbit's food, too, but not a plastic one, which your rabbit will chew to pieces. Feed your rabbit twice a day, with the biggest meal at supper, because the night is its liveliest time. Fill the bowl to the top either with pellets especially prepared for rabbits, which you can buy, or with whole-grain, clover, or alfalfa hay. Cut the hay into three- or four-inch lengths; otherwise your rabbit will just nibble on the ends and waste a lot. The commercial rabbit pellets made from dried plants, seeds, and vegetables are best because they provide a well-balanced diet, but your rabbit will also love a variety of fresh food every day. Chop up leftover carrots, celery, lettuce, apple, tomatoes, melon, and other fruits and vegetables, as long as they are fresh. Don't feed your rabbit food that is rotting. Offer a few dandelions, plantain, chickweed, clover, and other wild plants once or twice a week, as long as you haven't picked them from a lawn that was sprayed with chemicals. And don't overdo it, because too many greens can give a rabbit an upset stomach and cause diarrhea.

Don't worry if you see your rabbit eating some of its own droppings. It's perfectly natural, and essential. Rabbits are herbivores, which means they eat only plants. But plants contain cellulose, a substance that is too tough to be digested.

Cows can't digest the cellulose in grass and hay, but they have bacteria in their stomachs that do that for them. Rabbits have these same bacteria, too, in pouches in their lower intestines. Night droppings are different from the hard pellets dropped during the day because they contain partly digested food and bacteria. When the rabbits nibble on these night droppings, they are getting extra vitamins and other nutrients that didn't get digested the first time through.

Be careful not to overfeed your pet. If it doesn't finish a meal, take the leftovers away and give a little less next time. Don't give your rabbit in-between-meal nibbles, and don't give it any meat. Fasten a salt lick to the side of your rabbit's hutch where it can gnaw on it when it wants to. You can buy a small salt lick at a pet shop, or you can make one by baking table salt well soaked in water. After it cools and hardens, you can turn it out of the mold or just leave it in the baking dish. It's also a good idea to give your rabbit a small log to gnaw on, which helps wear down its teeth.

Cleanliness is most important to a rabbit's health, and of course a dirty hutch is smelly and unpleasant to have around. The hay, sawdust, or shredded-newspaper bedding should be changed and new bedding put down every day. Don't messily give your pet its food on the floor, but put it in the heavy dish. Wash the dish every day, and scrub the hutch at least once a week. Scrub hard, and use a soap that contains hexachlorophene or a disinfectant solution to do away with all odors. Wait for the hutch to dry before you put in clean bedding and return the rabbit to its home.

Occasionally the two front teeth, or incisors, of older rabbits will grow too long for the rabbit to eat properly. If that happens to your rabbit, take it to a veterinarian, who can trim back the teeth. Don't try it yourself.

If you want to have more than one pet rabbit, it's best to keep two sister rabbits because they will get along well together. An assortment of bucks (males) and does (females) will fight, and they will produce more baby rabbits than you can imagine. If you wish to raise rabbits at all, do it scientifically. A doe can be bred at about six months old, the age depending on the breed, and give birth, or kindle, several times a year. The ideal number for one doe to take care of is six in a litter. It is healthier for a doe not to start a family until she is at least eight months old, and three litters a year is enough. She will usually continue to breed for about four years.

If you start with healthy, purebred stock, one buck is enough for ten does. He should be kept in a separate hutch. The does can be kept together except when they are ready to kindle or when they are raising families. If you get into the rabbit business to any extent, you probably won't be letting your pets hop around the house as much as if you had only one or two, so remember that they need exercise. Your hutches should be large enough to allow plenty of freedom, or you can put your rabbits in a large runway for a while every day.

If a doe is ready to mate, she will seem restless and rub her face against things. When you see her doing this, separate her from the other does, and put her in the buck's hutch for a few hours. She may fight if the buck is brought uninvited to her house, so be sure to take the female to the male. This is the polite procedure for all caged animals, because the female doesn't like anyone intruding in her private territory. After mating, the doe should have nursery equipment, because she will kindle in about thirty-two days. Inside her large hutch put a small box or barrel, open at one end, but with a board nailed across half the open side for greater privacy. There should be a roof so she won't jump in and out of the nest on the babies, which are called kittens. You can also buy nesting boxes at farm supply stores. Keep the doe supplied with plenty of clean bedding, and notice that a short while before kindling, she will add fur pulled from her own chest to soften the nest.

From this point on and for several days after the kittens are born, don't touch the nest or handle the mother or disturb her in any way. She knows by instinct how to raise her young, and if her private plans are interfered with, she will be upset and may injure or even eat her own babies. Many animals do this if nature is interfered with. No one really knows why this awful fact is true, but it is. Some people believe that it is simply an overdone attempt to protect the young. Before and after the kindling, make sure the doe has food, adding plenty of greens, and lots of fresh water. In warm weather, a doe and her litter can take about a gallon of water a day!

Choose a time when the mother is out of the nest to take your first look at the kittens after they are three or four days old. But a week may go by before the mother settles down and lets you look at her litter. You may be surprised to find that brand-new rabbits aren't very good-looking. Only two or three inches long, they are hairless and blind, although they have a good sense of smell so they can find their mother's milk.

The babies quickly make up for their ugly start. At three weeks their fur is grown and is the softest thing you can imagine. Their eyes are open, and they like to nibble soft greens. They still nurse from their mother and need her care for a few more weeks; but in two months your doe will be through with her job, and the young rabbits should be put in a hutch of their own and fed on regular rabbit food. Since they are so active and playful, they are happier if kept together for company. When they are tired, they huddle together for warmth and comfort. You'll have fun putting them out in a safe place for a while each day, letting them play and hop around you. Always remember, though, that they are young and fragile. Handle them very little, and then with special care. A four-month-old rabbit is practically grown up and ready to set out on an adult life of its own.

GUINEA PIGS

Guinea pigs are one of the of nicest pets and the easiest animals to have around the house. Originally these sturdy little rodents came from Central and South America, where they were domesticated from their ancestor, the wild cavy. Long before Spanish explorers arrived in South America, the Incas were raising guinea pigs for food, and even now, guinea pigs run loose in and out of the houses of Indians who live in the

Andes Mountains. Guinea pigs are popular pets all over the world, but they have been so valuable in research laboratories that their name has come to mean anything or anyone taking part in an experiment or trying something for the first time.

Domestic guinea pigs are rounder and thicker-bodied than their wild cousins, with a large head, short legs, and a tail so short that it's hard to tell it's there at all. They scurry along on dainty little feet, but they don't hop or climb much or run. They "talk" in squeaks and squeals, and when they are used to people, they seem to like attention. They like being picked up, petted, and cuddled as you talk to them. There are many breeds to choose from, some with long, soft hair, and others with smooth, glossy coats in patterns called tortoiseshell, Dutch, or Dalmatian. Although they are friendly, your pets would probably be more confused than pleased to be allowed the run of your house. They are most content in a roomy pen with other guinea pig companions. If you decide to get a guinea pig, it's best to get two.

Have a hutch ready before you bring your guinea pigs home. The ideal pen is built on legs, with a fine-mesh floor that is comfortable for their little feet but lets their droppings fall through to papers below. It should have two compartments: one boxed-in for sleeping and lined with wire mesh, the other an open wire runway. As a general guide for space, the box for an adult pair should be a yard square, and the oblong runway a bit longer. Both should have the mesh floors and hinged tops or front doors for easy cleaning. Change the wood shavings or hay bedding every other day, and wash the entire pen at least once a week. If you keep your guinea pigs clean, you will find they are almost odorless, because their feces are dry and have practically no smell. Complete cleanliness is important for your own sake as well as for your pet's health. Your guinea pigs should be kept indoors most of the year, unless you live in a warm climate. They need a constant temperature that never goes below 65 degrees. On warm, sunny days, you can put them in a pen outdoors, where they can graze on grass and get some exercise. Give them things to play with, such as a cardboard tube, a shoebox with a hole at one end to explore, or a ramp to climb.

Feeding is easy, inexpensive, and fun. The guinea pigs get so excited at mealtime that they greet you with high-pitched sqeals and much scuffling. Keep a constant supply of water in a bottle on the side of the cage. Along with pellets from the pet shop, give them hay or mixed grains. Let them nibble on carrot tops, outer lettuce leaves, dandelions, or any kind of uncooked greens, because they need the vitamins from the fresh food. In a sturdy, unchewable bowl, give them all they want to eat every morning and evening. They don't store foods as hamsters do, and they won't overeat. Guinea pigs eat only as much as they need at one time. If you see your guinea pigs nibble on their own droppings, don't worry. Like rabbits, they do this in order to get more vitamins and nutrients, because their stomachs don't digest all the food that went through the first time. Keep a small salt block in their pen, too.

Baby guinea pigs, called puppies, are irresistible at birth; they are tiny versions of the grown-ups. They are born with all their hair and with their eyes open, and in a few days, they explore their home on wobbly feet, ready to sample their parents' food when they are four days old. In three weeks the mother has finished nursing, and the young pups are on their own. If the hutch is not crowded, the father, or boar, can safely be left with the family, although he doesn't help raise his children. If there isn't much room, it's best to move the father to his own pen so he won't hurt the pups. The mother is called a sow, even though these rodents are not related to pigs.

Although guinea pigs are easy to raise and can breed when they are only a month old, the average number of pups born to one sow is under fifteen a year, which is much fewer than many other animals have. It is healthier for them not to have young until they are about six months old, so when your small pigs are just under a month, start to get new pens ready and separate the males from the females. You will find their dispositions vary, but if there is plenty of room and food, a number of animals can be kept together without fighting. They are gentle animals, and the more time you spend with your guinea pigs, letting them get used to you, the more naturally they will behave when you are around.

WHITE MICE

White mice are acrobats, and if you give them the equipment they need, they will invent such amazing stunts that your friends will believe you are a top animal trainer. Actually they are only doing what comes naturally, and the only training you can give is to let them become so used to you that they know you will never startle or hurt them. Mice are livelier and seem more contented if they have company, so it's best to keep two mice rather than one. When you reach into the cage, they sometimes step onto your fingers and hide in your half-closed hand, then run up your arm. Their little feet are tickly, so be sure you like that friendly feeling. You'll scare them if you scream or suddenly pull your arm away.

Before you bring mice home from the pet store, have their cage ready. You can keep them in a cage made from glass, plastic, metal, or wood, but mice will gnaw on wood or plastic unless it is very smooth. And make sure there are no rough edges for them to gnaw on inside a wooden cage. The cage doesn't have to be huge, but it ought to high enough for climbing. If you put two mice in a cage eighteen inches long and twelve inches wide, they should also have a second story, built like a platform and connected by a tiny ladder they can use for a staircase. If you make a swing trapeze and an exercise bar, they can jump from one to the other. They'll enjoy a small log or chunk of wood to gnaw on and roll around. Make a private bedroom for them out of a tiny box with a small round doorway, and hang it on the side of the cage or on the platform. They like to go upstairs to bed. This is their nesting place, which you don't interfere with except for an occasional cleaning. But don't give them a bed. They like to make their own, and they are fussy about it. They will shred rope, clean cloth, or any soft, dry material you leave in the bottom of the cage.

Any cage should have good ventilation, and it should be

easy to clean. A metal cage with three solid sides ought to have a hinged top and a front panel made of fine nylon or wire mesh. This kind of cage will be draft free, but it will allow you to watch your pets and reach inside to clean. Mice are comfortable at a normal house temperature, around 70 degrees, with no sudden or extreme changes. If you use a glass tank, don't put it next to a window, where it would overheat in direct sun.

Mice like to be clean, and they are persnickety about washing and grooming themselves, but they can't clean their own homes. You'll have to do that for them. If you don't keep too many mice, they will have no noticeable smell as long as you clean the cage regularly. But if you aren't faithful about your cleaning duties, your pets will develop a nasty mousy odor, and neither you nor your family will want them around. Before you start to clean, shoo the mice into their nesting box or put them into another container while you work. Take out stale food, and scrub the food dish. Wash the water bottle and fill it with fresh water. Take out the shredded paper, wood chips, or hay they use for bedding, scrub the floor, and put in new bedding.

Add new toys to the cage now and then to keep your pets from getting bored, but don't let it get cluttered with too many things. Mice like to play with wooden spools and twigs. They'll enjoy running in and out of an empty jar and rolling it about. An exercise wheel in the cage will give your mice hours of fun, but make sure it has solid treads so your mice won't catch their little feet in it.

Tiny animals like mice can't go very long without food or

water. If you are going to be away for twenty-four hours or more, make sure someone feeds your mice, or they might starve or dehydrate. They like to eat all day long, so keep fresh food in the cage all the time. Mice love to nibble on bread crusts, uncooked rice, sunflower seeds, carrots and other vegetables, or an apple and other fruits. A dog biscuit is especially good for them, and it will give them a chance to wear down their continually growing front teeth. Don't give them cheese, but once a week you can give them a tiny bit of liver or raw beef. In the wild, mice eat worms, crickets, other insects, and the juicy grubs of insects. You can buy commercial mouse food at a pet store, but you can mix your own from crumbled brown bread, some birdseed, and powdered milk. At one meal a day, you can add a little water and a drop of sunflower oil to make a thick mash that they'll enjoy. Use a sturdy food dish that won't tip over easily, and hang a drip-feed water bottle on the side of cage so they'll always have fresh water.

A mother mouse prefers to raise her own family without any help from anybody, and she is an attentive and meticulous mother. Make sure she has bread soaked in milk as well as her regular food, and don't disturb her nest. The babies are called "pinkies" because they are bright pink when they are born. They have no hair, and their eyes aren't open. As soon as the mother mouse has her babies, take the father mouse and other females out of the cage, because any disturbance will upset the mother. She or the other mice often react by eating the babies. Scientists don't know the reasons for it, but this kind of reaction occurs in many animals.

HAMSTERS

No one ever raised hamsters before 1930, when the first domestic hamster was born at the Hebrew University in Jerusalem. Until then, they had only lived wild in meadows in Europe and Asia, much as prairie dogs live in this country. There were no hamsters in the United States until 1938. Hamsters are wonderful pets, but in their wild habitat, they are an awful nuisance to farmers, because they steal so much grain, hoarding far more than they can eat. They live in a maze of underground burrows, with passages, sleeping rooms, and many storage rooms for food, which they gather at night and carry to their burrows in their huge expandable cheek pouches. Be sure your hamsters stay at home. Don't let them loose outdoors, because you want hamsters to remain as pets in this country. No one wants them to become pests for farmers here.

If you saw a hamster suddenly scurry across the floor, you might think it was a mouse, unless you noticed its short tail and its golden brown fur, set off with spots of black on its head and cheeks. The cheek pouches extend all the way to the animal's shoulders, and they can hold an amazing amount of food. The mother hamster can even carry her newborn pups in her pouches. A hamster has big, dark eyes, tiny pointed ears, and whiskers on either side of its pointed nose. Big eyes and whiskers are clues that a hamster is a nocturnal animal — one that is livelier at night — and this is something to consider before you bring a hamster home. Your hamster will snooze most of the day, but by late afternoon or early evening, it will be very active. New hamster owners are often surprised to hear their hamster running in their squeaky exercise wheel in the middle of the night. Of course you can wake up your hamster during the day, but remember that no one likes to be wakened suddenly. Don't just reach into the cage and pick up a sleeping animal, but talk to it softly until it yawns and stretches. Offer it a sunflower seed or a bit of food, and then when it is wide awake, pick it up.

Before you bring a hamster home, get a comfortable cage ready. Hamsters like to live alone, one to a cage. A covered metal or glass cage is best, because your hamster will gnaw its way through wood or plastic. Like other rodents, they have sharp, ever-growing front teeth. A small, cozy cage about two feet square is big enough for one hamster, as long as you take that hamster out of the cage for exercise once in a while. But you may want a larger cage if you're going to keep an exercise wheel and other toys in it, too. Pet stores sell all kinds of cages for hamsters, but you can make one yourself from a large fish tank with a screened cover.

You'll need a water bottle attached to the side of the cage, as well as a food dish too heavy to be tipped over. The bottom of the cage should be covered with material that will absorb moisture, such as wood chips or shavings, excelsior, cat litter, dried grass, hay, or sand. If you provide some soft paper or extra bedding, your hamster will make a storage place and hide food there (the German verb *hamstern* means to hoard). Put a small box inside the cage for a sleeping room, where the hamster can retire, or where you can shut it in if you need to. A stout piece of wood will make a good place for your hamster to exercise its teeth.

Hamsters are clean and free from odor, so you won't have any trouble on that score as long as you hunt around for the hoarded food and clean it away before it spoils. You'll find that a weekly washing and bed changing is enough if the cage bottom is made of mesh with a pan or newspaper underneath to gather dirt that drops through. If the cage has a solid bottom, though, you'll need to scoop out wet litter every day, because a hamster's droppings are dry and odorless, but the urine is not. Once your hamster has chosen its "bathroom" corner, however, it will always urinate in that same spot. So it's easy to take out that wet litter every day and replace it with fresh. When you do the weekly cleaning, make sure you also scrub the food dish, water bottle, and your hamster's toys.

For food, you can buy commercial hamster food or use poultry-breeding pellets, which are inexpensive, nonfattening, and contain protein. Add to this some apple or potato peelings and fresh leafy vegetables. Feed your hamster once a day, and it will follow its natural instincts to hide away some of the food to nibble on during the night. Notice how much the hamster eats in twenty-four hours, and be guided by that in how much you give. One small cupful a day will be plenty. Hamsters drink very little water in their natural habitat because they get liquids from the foods they eat. If the vegetables you feed it are juicy, your hamster may not drink water, but keep fresh water in the bottle anyway.

You can raise hamsters easily if you want to, but just make

sure you don't find yourself with too many hamsters and no homes for them. There is no excuse for raising them by mistake, because it's quite easy to tell the difference between the sexes by the time the hamsters are two weeks old. A female hamster can start having babies when she is only eight weeks old, and it takes her only sixteen days to have a litter of eight or more. A month later, she is finished raising that family and is ready to start another. After the seventh litter, one every seven weeks, the hamster mother is through having young, although she may live two or three more years.

Hamsters protect their own territory, and if you put a male into a female's cage, she will fight to protect her territory. But if she is ready to breed, she won't fight if you put her into the male's cage. Some breeders solve this problem by keeping a third cage used only for mating, which neither hamster "owns" and won't try to defend. Give the mother extra shredded paper or bits of soft cloth from which she can make a nest to suit herself.

The pups need no special care — the mother will attend to them, but she must not be bothered or annoyed, and she must be alone. Do not leave the male hamster in the cage with her. The pups are naked, blind, pink, squirmy little creatures, but within three days, their skin darkens and they start to grow hair. For the first few days, all they do is sleep or drink their mother's milk. They begin eating a little solid food before their eyes are open, and by the time they are two weeks old, they can see perfectly and are running around. Then you can pick them up gently and treat them as individual pets. Always support a hamster with one hand so it will feel secure, but if it's really squirmy, you can also hold on to the loose skin at the back of its neck. When the babies are between three and four weeks old, put them in their own cage away from the mother, and separate the males from the females before they are two months old, or they will breed and you'll have more families than you know what to do with.

GERBILS

Gerbils are bright-eyed rodents that are every bit as friendly and curious as hamsters, but they have slightly different habits. These sand-colored desert animals are four or five inches long, with tails the same length, and weigh about three or four ounces. They have short front legs and longer, strong hind legs that allow them to leap about twenty-four inches, which is a long way for such a small animal. Sometimes they are called sand rats, desert rats, or antelope rats. In the wild they live in burrows in the sand, with many tunnels and exits to the surface. The first gerbils were brought to the United States by a scientist in 1954 from Mongolia, and they are still useful laboratory animals for psychological and other studies. It didn't take long before these gentle, intelligent animals became popular pets.

Before you buy gerbils, you should have their cage ready and know what food you'll need. Gerbils are social animals. They love company, and they will be much more contented pets if you keep two females together or two males. Like other rodents, they'll need a cage that can't be gnawed through, and it must be at least twelve inches high because gerbils like to leap. It should have a small box or dark glass jar to use for a sleeping room. Give them paper (but not newspaper because the ink is poisonous to them), cloth, or leaves and grasses, and they will make their own bedding. If you are a good carpenter, you can build a house for them with several levels and rooms to explore. This might be made of hardwood with a front of wire or glass that opens easily for cleaning.

Because gerbils are burrowing animals, they will be happiest in a cage that has a floor covering deep enough to tunnel into. If you use a glass tank, you'll be able to watch them as they dig. Fill the tank to a depth of four inches with a mixture of peat moss, sterilized potting soil or compost, some chopped straw, and a bit of charcoal. Tamp it down and cover that with a layer of hay. Make sure the gerbils have a few toys, such as a log to gnaw on or an empty cardboard tube from a roll of toilet paper, because they like to keep busy.

In the wild, gerbils eat seeds, roots, greens, and insects, but you can give them commercial gerbil food, varied with dog or cat biscuits, birdseed, and their favorite snack, sunflower seeds. They also like nuts, apples, leafy vegetables, and root vegetables such as carrots. They love melon, both the seeds and the flesh, but you can give them almost any raw fruit or vegetable you would eat. But they don't need much! An apple core with a bit of flesh still on it is plenty, not a whole apple. Take uneaten food out of the cage every day, and put in fresh. There is very little water in their desert habitats, so gerbils survive on moisture in the food they eat. But in captivity, they quickly learn to enjoy a drink of water, so it's important to keep a water bottle attached to the side of the cage.

Gerbils have very little body odor, so it's easy to forget that their cage must be kept clean. Aside from removing leftover food each day and keeping the water bottle filled, you'll need to clean a wire or wooden cage thoroughly once every two or three weeks. Put the gerbils safely in another box, and then wash the whole cage and put in fresh bedding. If you have made a deep earth floor in a glass tank, you can clean out wastes daily, but you'll only have to empty out all the dirt and scrub the tank every two or three months.

If you decide you'd like to raise gerbils, you'll need a breeding pair of adults. Gerbils are monogamous, which means they stay with one partner for life. If one of the pair dies, it is possible that the other will refuse to accept another mate. In any case, they have preferences about each other among themselves, and if two fight, they should be separated. If a friendly pair mate and have pups, usually about six in a litter after a gestation period of from twenty-four to twenty-nine days, the father can often be safely left in the cage. Don't disturb the babies for the first week or so. Like other rodents, the mother may get so upset that she will kill her young without any reason that makes sense to us. Left to herself, the mother will take complete care of her newborns, which will be pink, hairless, toothless, blind, and deaf. But they grow fast, and three weeks later, they will look just like their parents, except smaller. You can wean them from their mother about that time by putting them in a cage of their own and feeding them as you do their parents. Unless you want your gerbils to have another batch of babies right away, which is not healthy for the mother, you must separate the male and female at this time.

Gerbils seem to have as much fun when you play with them as you do. They like to run into your hand and up your arm. They like to come out of the cage to explore and poke around in different size boxes and cardboard tubes, but be careful that they do not get lost or fall off ledges. One gerbil may be more bold and curious than another, and you'll begin to see how different each animal is. The more you get to know your gerbils, the more fun you'll have.

4. Caged Birds

CANARIES

Canaries have been bred in cages and aviaries for so many centuries that now they are domestic birds, unsuited to life in the wild, but well adapted as home pets, provided, of course, that they have proper care. Their natural habitats are the Canary and Madiera Islands, off the west coast of Africa. The wild canary is a small yellowish-green finch, hardy, friendly, and easily tamed. They are hard-billed, seed-eating birds, and they build their nests in open branches. The male's natural, cheerful song is not nearly so varied and elaborate as that of the domestic canary.

Variations in song, color, and plumage (feathers) have been developed by selective breeding since the early sixteenth century, so that now there are dozens of different types of canaries and many ranges of singing ability. The most common canaries are yellow, but there are also white, green, blue, cinnamon-colored, light red, and mottled varieties. The more red in a canary, the more valuable it is. A canary called the roller, which was bred in Germany, has a song that sounds like a trill or roll. These birds sing from their throat, with the beak almost closed, and they can be taught to sing elaborate melodies beautifully. The chopper is an English canary with a less controlled song, but wild and free in sound. The chopper sings with his head thrown back, his beak wide open.

A bird's song is its way of communicating. A male bird sings to let other males know that he's there, defending his territory, and he also sings to attract a mate. Females seldom sing beyond cheerful chirps and simple trills. Like many other birds, a canary's song is often imitative. He will sing better if he hears music, and once he has mastered a particular trill, he will practice that and remember it. The song of another bird will inspire him to sing, but you can encourage him yourself by singing or whistling to him, or by playing tape, radio, or piano music.

If you want a songbird, be sure to select it carefully. Go to a reliable store, and be wary of a bargain. Take time to listen to the different songs, and select a bird that has a voice you like. Inspect the bird before you buy it. It's not easy to cure a sick bird, so you want yours to be alert, healthy, and in good feather. All birds molt, which means they shed their feathers and grow new ones periodically. Canaries usually molt in the summer, but don't buy one while it is molting, because it needs special care, and it's a poor time to accustom it to new surroundings. November and December are good months in which to select a bird, but if you live in the north, make sure the bird is kept warm in a draft-proof container when you take it from the store. If a bird is on a perch with its feathers all puffed up, don't buy it, because it may be sick. Birds fluff their feathers to help retain heat. Its eyes and nose should not be runny, and its droppings should be black and white, and not green and runny.

You can buy a wide variety of cages at the pet store, but the three most important requirements for your pet's cage are that it be large enough, that it be placed where there is no draft, and that you keep it clean. An old-fashioned round cage doesn't allow much space for hopping. It's best to use an oblong, flat-topped cage, with perches spaced so that a bird has room to stretch its wings. A foot-long cage is often used for one bird, but a cage two feet long and two feet high is much better. If you use a brass cage, make sure you keep the brass in good condition, because if it corrodes, as brass will without care, your bird may peck at the lumps, which are poisonous. A painted cage can also be a hazard in case the bird eats flecks of paint, which may contain lead. Plastic cages are durable and easily kept clean.

If you are a good builder, you can make a cage that will cost less than any you can buy. A breeder would build a large cage called an aviary, which consists of a covered house and an open flight cage made of fine mesh. Since a draft is much more dangerous for your bird than cold weather, you may want to avoid the wire birdcages, and make yours of a wooden box turned on its side, the front covered by fine galvanized mesh. The mesh front must be fitted with a door and openings for two hooded porcelain or plastic cups, one for drinking water and one for seed. The door should be constructed with grooves so you can slide it up and reach the bottom of the cage for the daily cleaning. You can keep papers on the floor, but if you are skillful enough to make one, it's even better to have a metal tray that slides in and out to make cleaning easier and more thorough.

Place wooden perches near enough to the water and food cups so that your bird can reach them easily, but don't crowd the cage with perches. Put them at several different levels. Strong twigs with smooth bark left on are comfortable for the bird's feet, but even if you use the smooth wooden perches usually supplied with birdcages, make sure you use various thicknesses so your bird doesn't always need to grasp exactly the same position. Avoid sharp edges. It will be an added comfort to the bird if you supply one flat perch that is wider than your bird's foot, so that it can sometimes roost without having to curl its claws. Some cages come with a swinging perch, but not all birds like that motion, and you may want to remove the swing and replace it with another regular perch.

Canaries sleep soundly through the night. A bird won't fall off a perch when it's asleep, because it has tendons in its feet that lock the muscles in place as the bird settles down. The feet don't unlock until the bird stands up. You'll know when your canary is ready to retire because it will puff out its feathers, and sometimes it will stick its head under one wing and stand on one leg. At daybreak, your canary will be lively again, and hungry.

It takes just a few minutes a day to keep your bird's cage clean, and it is absolutely necessary. The bird's water must always be fresh, and both water and food cups should be washed every day. Take out the perches and wash those every day, too. Never put a wet perch back in the cage, because it might chill your bird. It's a good idea to have a double set so that you can always give your canary a clean, dry perch. Once in a while, sand the perches so they stay smooth and clean.

Most canaries enjoy a bath every day, except when they are molting. Put a shallow dish of water at room temperature in the bottom of the cage. Your canary will splash water everywhere, so do this before you clean the cage. Or you can buy a special enclosed plastic bird bath, where the bird can splash to its heart's content and shake the water from its feathers without splattering the whole cage. If your bird seems hesitant to bathe, you might try luring it into its tub by sprinkling some seeds or floating a piece of lettuce on the water. If that doesn't work, you should spray your canary lightly with warm water about three times a week in summer and once a week in winter.

To absorb moisture and waste, cover the cage floor with a thin layer of bird litter, which is usually made from shredded corn cobs, instead of gravel. Birds need small bits of gravel to help them digest their food because they have no teeth. The food goes directly into the crop, where it is softened by digestive juices, and then passes to the gizzard, where gravel and muscular contractions grind it into a soft, digestible mass. But too much gravel can clog the gizzard, so it is best to put a small amount of bird gravel in a food dish now and then instead of on the cage floor. You can also cover the cage floor with plain paper toweling, but not newspaper because the ink can make the bird sick if it shreds and eats the paper.

The main item of your canary's food should be a good quality of mixed canary seed, which can be purchased at any pet shop. This is a mixture of six parts of a long, light brown

canary seed, especially grown for birds, and four parts rape-
seed, which is round and reddish. You can buy various seeds
and mix your own bird food, but the commercial mixtures are
easier to use and they have the right amounts of nutrients.
Keep a cuttlebone on the bars of the bird's cage. Your canary
will use it to sharpen its bill, and more important, will eat
little bits of it, which will supply the necessary calcium and
other minerals. The white, chalky cuttlebone is taken from a
small squid called a cuttlefish. An occasional eggshell, dried
in the oven, will also provide calcium for your canary, as will
some oyster-shell grit added to the regular food. You can buy
bird biscuits for an extra healthful treat. Like most seed-
eating birds, wild canaries also eat some insects, so it's a good
idea to add a little protein to your canary's diet in the form of
mealworms or the mashed yolk of a hard-boiled egg, especially at molting time. Some breeders add a bit of cayenne
pepper to the bird's seed as a "color feeder." The color of
some birds' feathers are affected by the foods they eat. Fla-
mingos, for example, become pink when they eat shrimp.
The cayenne pepper will give a yellow canary's feathers a
deeper yellow or orange color.

Avoid overfeeding your canary, because it's as unhealthy
for a bird to get fat as it is for humans. Most experts suggest
no more than a tablespoonful a day, and usually less. Throw
away the leftover seed each day, and put fresh seed in the
cup. Soon you'll get to know how much your bird needs. Canaries love a section of peeled apple or tangerine wedged
between the bars of the cage, where they can peck at it, and
they need some greens as well. A couple of times each week,
offer your canary some fresh, well-washed watercress, dande-

lion (both flower and leaves — taken from a lawn that has not been sprayed with chemicals), bean sprouts, or lettuce. Bacteria and mold settle quickly on the cut surfaces of fruit and vegetables, so make sure you take any leftovers out of the cage every day. Never give your canary sugar or a sweetened cracker.

When you approach the cage, whistle, chirp, or talk softly to your pet so it won't be startled but will get used to you. Don't put your hands up over the top of a wire cage, because it's frightening for a bird to feel closed in or cornered. Touch the cage from the bottom up. One of the best ways to make friends with your canary is to offer a green leafy food from your hand. If you stand quietly while the bird pecks at a leaf tucked into the wire, it will gradually learn to associate such treats with your presence. It may even learn to hop on your finger and take a treat directly from you.

It's upsetting to a bird to have its cage moved around often, so carefully select a convenient spot where there is sunlight and a reasonably constant temperature. Don't put a cage in front of an open window, because drafts can chill a bird, and constant, direct sunlight can overheat it. If the cage is large enough, the bird will get enough exercise. But if your pet seems listless and bored, offer it some new things to play with, maybe a bell hanging from the top of the cage or bits of short yarn to unravel.

You will add to your pet's pleasure and yours if your canary becomes tame enough to have a daily flight in the room. Naturally you must be sure that doors and windows are closed, that the stove is off, and there are no flames burning in a fireplace. Never pick the bird out of the cage, but just leave the door open. It will come out when it is ready. Don't leave the bird alone. Sit quietly and watch it fly. When you want to put your canary back in the cage, you don't need to catch it. Remember that the cage is its home, its own territory, and it will return when it's ready. By mistake a canary was once let out of a New York City apartment window, and nothing was seen of the bird for three days. But the owner hung the bird's cage outside, with the door open, and at last the canary found its way back, probably just as relieved to be home as its owner was to see it.

Handle your canary as little as possible. All birds have hollow bones. A small bird is very fragile, and it's awfully easy to squeeze too hard by mistake. Its hollow leg bones are especially easily broken. If for any reason you have to catch any bird loose in a house, never chase it, because it may panic and injure itself. Instead, pull the drapes or shades or somehow darken the room, or wait until evening and turn off the lights, because the bird won't fly in the dark. Then locate the bird with a flashlight, and pick it up very carefully when it is still. Grasp it gently from above, holding its wings down and leaving its head and legs free.

Once in a while, you may handle the canary this way to check its toenails. They need to be cut before they curl uncomfortably and scratch the bird. You can learn to do this with a small, sharp scissors. If you look at the bird's nails, you can see a thin, red line, which is a blood vessel. If you cut below that, you won't hurt the bird, just as you don't hurt yourself when cutting a fingernail as long as you don't touch the quick. But until you feel confident in doing this, it's best to take the canary to a veterinarian, who knows exactly where to trim.

Even if it's not the kind of pet you can handle much and cuddle, a canary singing in the house will give you many years of joy.

FINCHES

Besides canaries, there are many other members of the large finch family that can be caged and kept as pets without your worrying that they are longing for their freedom. They have been raised and housed in cages for so many centuries that there is no reason to suppose that they even know about open spaces. As long as they are well fed and comfortable, finches are content and unconcerned with the past or future. Early paintings, hundreds of years old, depict children holding the end of a string on which a tame finch is tethered by the leg. Present-day cages are certainly more comfortable for the birds than that.

In fact, finches are such fascinating pets, and there are so many kinds, that after success with one caged pair, you may be tempted to build an aviary and try to keep different kinds of finches together in the larger space. It's best, though, to start with one pair of a kind that is especially easy to keep and inclined to make good parents.

Before selecting yours, give yourself the fun of looking at

the various finches in a zoo, a pet shop, or in a fully illustrated bird book. There are far too many to mention here, but take a look at the tricolored parrot finch. Both male and female have bright blue faces, red tails, and green bodies. The cordon bleus have French-blue heads, throats, and breasts; greenish-brown wings and backs; and bills that are crimson, tipped with black. The males are further decorated with a crimson spot on each cheek. The society finch is a less gaudy kind, but a good variety for you to start with because it is gentle, full of personality, and easy to raise. Some are entirely white, but most are mottled either tan and white or brown and white, and the combinations of these colors are arranged so that there are no two birds exactly alike in pattern. It's impossible to be sure just what the fledglings will look like, but they will all be pretty.

The general care of finches is just the same as the care of canaries, except that they should have less green food and the standard seed mixture is more varied. A finch mixture can be bought ready-packaged, or you can measure out your own, using two parts canary seed, four parts small white or yellow millet, one part large red millet, and three parts large yellow millet. Your birds will enjoy sometimes picking their own millet if you give it to them on the stalk, just before the seeds are ready to fall. They, too, will need small amounts of fine gravel or some kind of grit that will help them grind their food.

Finches like company, so it is best to keep them in pairs. You'll have to depend on your pet shop or breeder to sell you a pair of the society finches, because it takes experience to tell the male from the female. As soon as they are used to their new home, you will notice the difference in their personalities. The female has a brief, restrained song and appears to be talking to herself when she sings. The male has a more elaborate, but still simple, low song, which he uses to woo his mate. As he sings, he spreads his tail, throws out his chest, and dances for her pleasure, peering around often to make sure she is looking.

If you want to raise finches, hang a large dried, empty gourd in the cage, or a closed wooden nesting box with a small opening near the top. Though the society finch has been domesticated through long years of crossbreeding with other finches in China, its ancestors all used hollow logs for their nests, and a caged finch has retained that instinctive memory when choosing a nesting site. Line the box with flannel, and spray it with a safe insect spray. In the cage leave short strands of wool, bits of feather or hair, and perhaps a loosely woven bit of burlap, which the finches can unravel and use to build their own nest.

Both birds share in building the nest. After the eggs are laid, one a day, they take turns brooding by day, and at night they crowd into the nest together. Occasionally as many as five eggs are laid, but normally there are three. Usually the parent birds will not start to incubate, or sit on the nest, until all the eggs are laid. From then on you can count on fourteen days for hatching. Both parents busy themselves feeding the fledglings, and during this time they need additional food, because like many birds, they swallow the food themselves, then regurgitate it down the throats of the young. That's why baby birds stretch their heads straight in the air and leave their mouths gaping open. A lot of food is needed, so add to the regular finch-seed mixture ground hard-boiled egg yolk and a commercial fledgling food, which consists of unleavened, unsalted cracker crumbs or crumbled toast.

When the fledglings, which were nearly bare when hatched, have feathered out and grown too big and strong for the nest, they will come out of their own accord, and you will begin to see what their final mottled feather design will be. The parents will continue to feed them for a while, but you should help out by putting fledgling food in a dish on the floor. About six weeks after the first egg was laid, your finches will be ready to start another family. After removing the old nest, wash and sterilize the gourd or box, set it up again with a fresh lining, and provide new material for the new nest. Wait until the second clutch of eggs has been laid before you put the first fledglings in their own cage. By this time they will be able to eat by themselves, and their parents will be busy incubating the new eggs. Keep on feeding them the fledgling food, but also give them the finch-seed mixture. When you notice that plenty of the seeds have been hulled and eaten, you will know that the babies are ready to go on a regular adult diet.

Even though society finches are exceptionally good parents and will want to nest at any time of the year, remember that raising a family takes a lot of energy, so don't keep your birds at it too steadily. Three or four clutches a year are plenty. No matter what sort of birds you are raising, it is better for their well-being to refuse them a nesting place even though they appear to be asking for it. Too much activity wears out the parents, and the later babies may be weak. Many species of the same family of birds can be crossbred, but in some cases this produces "mules," which are perfectly healthy but infertile birds. So it is not wise to try this until you have more experience.

BUDGERIGARS

All animals communicate in one way or another, but it takes a lot of study and patience for a person to even begin to figure out their language. When we watch an animal's facial expressions and body language, we often miss what it is trying to tell us. Probably we expect them to express themselves as we would, instead of concentrating on their ways. In any case we are fascinated when we find a pet that can actually speak our language in words we know.

Certain groups of birds can do this. Just as songbirds imitate each other and learn a tune from hearing a person sing, some birds can learn to copy human words distinctly. Parrots, parakeets, crows, and mynah birds as well as other members of the starling family can learn to speak by imitating a word repeated often. There is no truth to the idea that these birds can talk better if their tongues are slit. That's a cruel thing to do to a bird. It's difficult to know whether these birds really know what they're saying. After years of research, scientists now know that parrots can understand many concepts, so until they study these smaller birds more fully, we can't assume what the birds do or do not know. But be careful what words you teach, because your pet will remember them, and often choose an embarrassing time to speak up.

Budgerigars, which are native to Australia, can become good talkers with large vocabularies. Their name means "pretty bird" in the aboriginal language of their region. They are more commonly called budgies, and that name seems to suit their friendly ways. With a lot of attention and conversation, a single bird will become totally tame and appear to develop real affection for the family. These birds look very much like miniature parrots, with their long tails and strong, curved beaks, although parrots' tails are short in proportion to body size.

Budgies should not be confused with lovebirds, which are a different species and have different natures. Lovebirds should be kept in pairs because their favorite pastime is to sit side by side and cheek to cheek in what seems to be consuming love for one another. They, too, are related to parrots, and although they are small like the budgies, their bodies are thicker, and their tails are short, wide, and blunt.

Wild budgies are green, with wing and tail feathers tipped in black. The tail is blue, and the throat, cheeks, and forehead are yellow. On each cheek there are three black dots and a splash of blue. The males and females are marked exactly alike, except for one sure sign, the cere mark, which is a narrow band across the nostrils. In the adult male this is bright blue, and in the female it is brown. It is impossible to tell the sex of the babies, because they are all hatched with a dull blue cere mark, which turns brighter as the male grows older, and in the female turns first white, then tan, then brown. Fortunately identification doesn't matter, because if you want a special pet that you can teach to talk, it's better to have only one budgie, and there seems to be no difference in the natures of male and female or in their abilities to learn.

If several budgies are kept together or with other birds, they will not learn human words, but instead will imitate high-pitched bird sounds, which appear to be easier for them than the low human voice. You will find that they also pick up other sounds around your house besides the words you want to teach.

In pet shops you no longer see budgies with only the original colors. By careful mating, it has been possible to develop a large range of colors, and you may see pale yellow, chartreuse, or light blue. Some are a cobalt and turquoise combination flecked on the upper body in a pattern like that on a Plymouth Rock chicken, but all of the budgies have the same blue or brown cere mark. Pick your favorite color. There is no difference in their intelligence or talking skill, and you will find these birds are easy and fun to raise.

If possible, buy a young bird, one that has been out of the nest only about four weeks. The average clutch laid by the female is between three and seven eggs. After hatching, the young stay in the nest, where both parents feed them for four to six weeks. A young bird will be easier to train than an older one, and since budgies are hardy, you should have no trouble raising one if you learn what it needs before you take it home.

The cage can be either oblong and flat-topped or cylindrical, but it should be large enough for them to stretch their wings, with enough perches for climbing. Budgies are active climbers, and they will use their strong bills as well as their claws on the wires of the cage, so be sure the bars are strong, unpainted, and rustproof. Perches should be of very hard wood and round, without any edges that your budgie can whittle away, and they should be different sizes, which is better for the bird's feet. The bottom tray should be removable for easy cleaning. A small platform at the door encourages your budgie to come in and out when it is ready for the freedom of your room. And eventually you will need two open dishes set firmly in the side of the cage for seed and water.

When you first bring a young bird home, however, it will feel confused, and it will be too much to expect it to find unfamiliar dishes. Birds have sharp eyesight and hearing, but little sense of smell. Scatter bird litter in the bottom of the cage for cleanliness. Don't line the cage bottom with paper, because the bird may tear it and swallow bits. Put a small, very shallow water dish on the cage floor. If your budgie doesn't find it right away, put a small, clean sponge in the pan, and the bird will get a bit of water by pecking curiously at the sponge. Expect your budgie to be alarmed and eager to escape at first when you put it in its new cage. As long as the cage is in a quiet place, and of course free from drafts, the bird will soon adjust to its new home.

The seed you feed your budgie can be purchased at a store, or you can mix it yourself. For a young budgie, mix one part canary seed, two parts white millet, and one part cracked oats. For an adult budgie, mix three parts canary seed, one part white millet, and three parts cracked oats. Your budgie may prefer one kind of seed and pick that out, leaving the rest.

Another important part of the diet are fresh greens and fresh fruit. Two or three times a week, offer your budgie small amounts of dandelion greens (picked from a lawn that's not sprayed with insecticides), carrot or celery tops, spinach, broccoli, or lettuce. Once in a while treat your budgie to grapes or a slice of apple, orange, or banana. If you start these foods when the bird is young, it will eat them regularly and will get the necessary vitamin B in its diet. Make sure you provide a cuttlebone, for sharpening its beak, and grit for its gizzard, either on the floor or in a cup.

Some budgies like to bathe in an open dish, but if yours doesn't like to, put wet lettuce leaves on the cage floor, where it can roll in them, then remove the leaves when the bath is over.

There is no special time when your young budgie should be ready to use the seed and water cups, or when it will be ready to come out of the cage and fly around the room. These stages depend on the individual bird but even more on you and on how quickly you have made the bird feel at home. Never startle your budgie, but as you talk quietly, slowly put your hand into the cage, near the bottom, and let your pet get used to you and to sitting on your finger. Eventually the bird will become so tame that it will easily come out of the cage and join the family circle, going first to one person and then another for a little attention. Never chase a bird, but let it come to you. If you must catch your budgie, do so in a darkened room, where it will not move or fly. You'll be able to find the bird in the beam of a flashlight, and then you can gently pick it up and put it back in its cage.

It's not likely that your budgie will pick up its first words by itself; you'll have to teach the words deliberately. The earlier you can start, the easier it will be, but don't start before you are sure that the bird is used to you and trusts you. Stand by the cage and repeat often and clearly two simple, one-syllable words, such as "Hi, Bill." Do this many times a day, the oftener the better. At first there will be no result at all, but if you continue with the same words in the same tone, eventually you'll hear your bird repeat them. The bird will seem to be pleased at this accomplishment, and you won't have any trouble showing how pleased you are, too. Go back to this phrase now and then to be sure it is fixed in the bird's mind, but start adding new words, one or two at a time. After those first words, the rest come more quickly. If you are a patient teacher, your pet will learn to talk a lot and won't be shy to talk in front of other people. Professional trainers sometimes put a cloth over the cage while they are teaching, so that the budgie will have no distractions and will concentrate better. Perhaps this method works because of the way birds learn in the wild. As the young birds imitate the calls of their parents, they may be hidden by leaves and not see their bird teachers.

Boredom can be a very real problem for any caged animal, and even though your budgie will often fly free in your house, you won't always be there to let it out, so put plenty of things for fun and exercise in the cage. Your budgie may enjoy a swing perch and a good supply of wooden toys, as well as a bell to ring. A bird can be pretty destructive, so you'll need to replace these toys now and then. Buy a box of jointed toys and use your imagination to build different shapes for your pet's amusement. Budgies love to climb a ladder and swing a tiny dumbell. Give it a cloth to play with, but make sure it is square and strong and not easily ripped. Don't give it a long, narrow strip that could get wound around the bird's neck, or a stout thread or rope, because the bird can get caught up in that, too. Once you have taken a budgie as a pet, make sure you are never so busy that you neglect it and it feels lonely. These birds will enjoy their toys more with you standing by to watch, and they seem to thrive best in the hubbub of active family life.

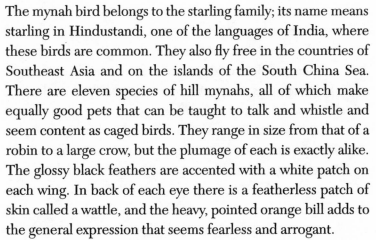

MYNAH BIRDS

The mynah bird belongs to the starling family; its name means starling in Hindustandi, one of the languages of India, where these birds are common. They also fly free in the countries of Southeast Asia and on the islands of the South China Sea. There are eleven species of hill mynahs, all of which make equally good pets that can be taught to talk and whistle and seem content as caged birds. They range in size from that of a robin to a large crow, but the plumage of each is exactly alike. The glossy black feathers are accented with a white patch on each wing. In back of each eye there is a featherless patch of skin called a wattle, and the heavy, pointed orange bill adds to the general expression that seems fearless and arrogant.

Mynah birds like to listen to music and quickly learn to whistle a tune. They never seem to tire of practicing over and over any words you repeat. Pitch your voice rather high, because that seems more natural for the bird. At first the sound comes out blurred, but shaped like your word. Then after some practice, the bird can say it perfectly, even imitating your tone and expression. If you are a good teacher, your mynah will soon learn to say whole sentences. After it has mastered a sentence, you can start it, and instead of repeating it after you, the bird will complete the sentence for you. You can also teach it intelligent answers that make the bird appear to be answering difficult questions. For example, you can say, "Where is the handsome bird?" and the mynah can learn to answer, "At home in the nice cage."

As with all talking birds, it's best to have only one mynah if you want it to learn human speech rather than bird chatter. The cage for one bird should be quite large, at least four feet long, and high enough for a brief flight from floor to perch. After your mynah is tame and comfortable with you, you can let it out into the room, but a mynah is not a climber and acrobat like a budgie or a parrot, so it will fly around but be less companionable outside. Since it feeds mainly on fruits, a mynah's droppings are untidy and not easily wiped away, which is another thing to consider before you let it fly free indoors. Its cage will need to be cleaned at least once a day. Because its natural home is in the tropics, a mynah must not be allowed to get too cold — about 72 degrees is right — and of course place the heavy cage on a secure base in a spot free from drafts. A mynah loves to bathe and will splash around at a great rate when you give it a shallow tub.

Mynahs are heavy eaters, needing at least three meals a day. Most of the food is green and would spoil if left overnight, which means you must remove the leftover greens from the cage every day. There should always be bird litter on the floor and a fresh cuttlebone or crisp eggshells available. Fruit is a mynah's favorite food, so give the other things it needs in the morning, when the bird is especially hungry and you can be sure it will eat them. The main breakfast should be toast or a commercial mockingbird food. Into this stir grated carrot and mashed hard-boiled egg, seasoned with several drops of cod-liver oil. For lunch the bird should have more toast, stirred with diced banana, small bits of apple, or grapes. Supper is most fun for both you and the mynah. Offer another helping of toast, and perhaps one or two mealworms, and all the fruit the bird seems to want. A mynah will let you know with great squawks which fruits it likes best. It's funny to watch the bird's pleasure in a grape, which it will snatch and swallow, and then go off to its perch to enjoy the taste in silence. The grape won't go all the way down; you'll see a lump in its throat. But soon it will bring up the grape again, roll it around in its bill, and swallow it a second time. Take the time to give your pet fruit from your fingers, as a way of making friends. If the bird pecks at you, scold it and watch its face. You can't tell what it's thinking or even how much it thinks, but you can't misunderstand the bird's expression that seems to say, "So what?" You'll never be bored with a mynah bird in the house.

PARROTS

Parrots are amazing, intelligent animals that live thirty or forty years, and often longer in captivity. The Bronx Zoo had a parrot that was sixty years old. The choice of a parrot as a pet must be a family decision, partly because it will be living with you for a lifetime, and partly because it is not the kind of pet that can be tucked away in a corner of your room like a quiet little hamster or goldfish. Parrots can be loud and messy, and they are always members of the family.

Since 1993, it has been illegal to capture wild tropical birds and bring them into the United States, which is a good thing for both the birds and people who want them for pets. Parrots sold in pet stores are those that were hatched from captive parents, and they are much more contented to live in a house than a bird taken from the freedom of its home in a rain forest. Parrots mate for life, and they enjoy and thrive on companionship. Young parrots learn by imitating their parents, just as human babies do, which is why it's so easy to teach a parrot to speak.

At first a parrot will listen and memorize and sometimes mumble the sounds, but it doesn't take long before it repeats the words and tones exactly. One parrot, who used to spend his days in the back window of a New York apartment, amused himself by listening to the noises he heard in the adjoining backyards. Next door two children often played outside, and although the parrot never came close to them, he soon began to screech out their names as if calling them in for supper: "Mabel!" "Tommy!"

At one time scientists thought that parrots didn't understand the words they learn, but now we know that they do. At the University of Arizona, when Dr. Irene Pepperberg taught an African gray parrot named Alex to speak, she discovered that he definitely knew what he was saying. Alex learned words by imitating Dr. Pepperberg, just as a baby parrot would imitate its parents. He also learned to select different objects by size, shape, color, and material. In one test Alex is shown a tray full of objects such as toy plastic cars, wooden blocks of various colors and shapes, keys, a rock, and a piece of red cloth, for example. When asked to find the blue, square, wooden object, Alex looks at each thing carefully, touches it with his beak and tongue, and finally he picks up the blue, wooden block. Shown two identically shaped plastic keys and asked, "What's different?" Alex gives the correct answer, "Color." Dr. Pepperberg and other scientists now agree that parrots are similar to chimpanzees in their ability to think and understand. So having a parrot in your house will challenge you to keep your pet from being bored.

Parrots have a sense of humor, and they do great imitations of loud, chortling human laughter. A parrot that lived in a country house had the good fortune to spend his summer days outside on a low limb of a tree. One day a duck meandering by was startled by something and flew up a few feet. As the duck passed under the tree, almost brushing the parrot with her wings, the parrot let out a loud, "Wow," and strutted up and down the limb, laughing and repeating, "Wow." The joke lasted him for the whole morning, and he had a good time over it.

There are more than three hundred species of parrots, and about one hundred of them are facing extinction because the tropical rain forests, which are their habitats, are being destroyed. Among this colorful group of birds are the cockatoos, with their elegant crested heads. They make interesting pets, although they aren't as talkative as other parrots; and neither are the more delicate lories, which have long, divided brushlike tongues that can reach deep into the blossoms of tropical plants to get pollen and nectar. The African gray parrot or one of the familiar green-bodied macaws, with their brilliant head and tail markings of yellow and blue, can be taught to whistle, sing, and talk better than any of the others, but they also need the most space.

A parrot should not spend the entire day in a cage, because it needs exercise. Even so, the cage must be large enough for the parrot to stretch its wings without touching the cage bars and to move around without brushing its tail feathers against the perches. The ornithology department at Cornell University suggests these cage sizes for birds: two to eight cubic feet for small birds, twelve to eighteen cubic feet for medium-size birds, and twenty-four to thirty-two cubic feet for large birds. For example, a cage of eighteen cubic feet might be three feet wide, three feet high, and two feet deep. A large flat-topped cage allows your parrot to climb all over it, using both beak and claws, so the bars must be sturdy, unpainted, and rustproof. A parrot has four strong, limber claws, two pointing forward and two backward. It can hang upside down or reach sideways with one foot anchored while the other foot reaches for something. Its hooked beak acts like a third foot when it's climbing.

Cover the bottom of the cage with bird litter, not paper, which can be shredded and swallowed. Perches should be of various thicknesses and very strong so they won't be whittled away. One perch should be suspended for swinging. Hulls of seeds and droppings should be cleaned out every day, and the cage kept sanitary with thorough weekly scrubbings. A removable bottom tray makes this easier. Your parrot will constantly clean and preen its feathers, and while it may not take a bath, it will enjoy a shower of lukewarm water from a spray bottle once a week or more often in the summer.

Keep the cage out of a draft, but never put it off in a lonesome corner. Remember that your pet likes company and likes to be busy. Give the parrot toys to play with, a bell to ring, a piece of wood to whittle. It should be kept indoors where it's warm, but in summer put the cage outdoors for a while each day. Be sure your pet can't reach any plants that have been sprayed with insecticides. Some parrots don't like it if you put a cloth over the cage at night because it's frightening for a bird if it can't see its surroundings. You'll have to see whether your parrot wants this cover at night or not.

Parrots like a variety of foods, but especially nuts. Their strong beaks can easily break open the hardest of nuts, and their tongue is as agile as a thumb in digging out the nutritious meat. Keep clean, fresh water in an open dish attached firmly to the bars of the cage so it can't be spilled. In a similar dish keep a supply of sunflower seeds, large canary seed, unhulled rice, and a variety of other seeds. Provide some cuttlebone or toasted eggshell for extra minerals. Your parrot will love chunks of apple, orange, banana, and other fruit, as well as a green and a yellow vegetable every day. Many parrots enjoy corn on the cob, too.

You can show your affection by talking softly to your parrot. Say its name, and keep whistling the same tune or saying the same sentence, often letting it come out of its cage. A parrot will climb out of the cage if you open the door, but it probably will like the extra attention of having your help. After you are friends, if you put your hand slowly and fearlessly into the cage, the parrot will raise one clawed foot high and step carefully and deliberately onto your finger. Let the bird keep to its habits. If it is used to having you put your left hand in, palm up, a parrot may give you a harmless peck if you offer your right hand with the fingers in the wrong direction. Birds seem frightened by an open, upturned hand. A parrot can give a hard, nasty bite, but only if it is startled or threatened in some way. Don't ever grab for your pet or try to catch it in midair.

It won't be long before your parrot begins to take an interest in all household matters and very likely will lord it over your other animals.

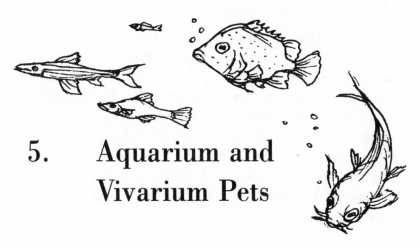

5. Aquarium and Vivarium Pets

FISH

If you realize that there are nearly forty thousand known species of fish in the world, each with its own shape, colors, and habits, you'll have an idea of how fascinating it can be to care for and learn about any one kind. Watch your aquarium through a magnifying glass, and you will find out all sorts of interesting things about your pets, whether they are ordinary goldfish or rare tropicals. You can see more accurately if the sides of your aquarium are straight, because a curved glass distorts the shapes slightly. Even casual watching will show you how even individual fish of the same species vary, some being more aggressive than others.

First of all you must know that it is not true that fish have no feelings. They have nerve centers connected with their brain and their spinal column, and they can feel pain — less pain than we feel, but still pain. Their eyes, which are protected by a membrane, don't close, but they see colors, which dogs and many other animals as well as some people cannot do. They have skeletons, blood vessels, and balancing devices, as we do. Even though they live underwater, fish need oxygen. Instead of pumping blood to lungs that take oxygen from the air, a fish's heart pumps blood to gills, which take the oxygen from the water. Water goes into a fish's mouth, over the gills, and out of the gill slits you can see on the side of a fish's head. Close to the surface of the gills are tiny blood vessels that exchange the carbon dioxide in the fish's bloodstream for oxygen, which is dissolved in the water.

PREPARING YOUR AQUARIUM

Before you select your fish and bring them home, set up your aquarium and make it ready for them. The size of the tank will depend upon the kind and number of fish you will have. You may want to start with one or two goldfish in a small tank, but the same general rules apply, no matter what fish you choose to raise. First clean the glass thoroughly with a salt solution, then rinse it and let it dry. Pour into another bowl or pail as much ordinary tap water as you'll need to fill the tank, and let it stand uncovered for a day and overnight. The chlorine will escape into the air. Buy fine or medium-size gravel for the tank bottom, but before you put it in, rinse it thoroughly by letting tap water run through it until it runs clear. Then put about an inch-and-a-half layer of gravel on the bottom of the tank, sloping gradually toward the front of the tank to about half an inch. The dirt and debris will accumulate in this low spot, making it easier to clean. Don't pour all the water into the tank at once because that will churn up the gravel. The easiest way to add water is with a newspaper. Fold two or three sheets of newspaper to fit loosely inside the tank, and lay them carefully over the gravel. When you pour the water on the newspaper, it doesn't disturb the gravel or any decorations you may have arranged. Then pull out the paper.

Now you are ready to plant your greenery. You can find a wide variety of water plants at a pet store; choose the ones you think are prettiest. But the main purpose of having plants is decoration as well as providing a natural-looking habitat where fish can hide if they want to. Many fish experts believe that plastic plants are better because they are cleaner, they don't die and decay, and the fish don't nibble on them. These experts also suggest using a minimum of plants and other plastic decorations, enough to give fish a place to hide, but not so many that you'll rarely ever see the fish.

If you do use plants — plastic or real — root them in the gravel in a semicircle with the taller ones in back so the fish have plenty of room to swim. Pet stores sell a huge variety of little bridges, castles, divers, and such for fish tanks, but whatever you use, make sure they are clean, with no residue of soap or cleaning fluid. When your aquarium arrangement has settled for a few days, and your live plants have taken root, it's time to bring home your fish.

In order to keep your fish healthy, you need to know about their natural environment so you can keep the aquarium as near the natural condition for each species as possible. Do not start out with expensive, delicate fish that need highly specialized conditions. The following basic needs are the same for all fish.

Don't overcrowd the aquarium. A safe general guide for space is one gallon of water for each inch of fish, not counting its tail. So if you have three one-inch goldfish, you'd need a tank that holds at least three gallons of water.

The more oxygen in the tank, the healthier the fish will be. For that you'll need an aerator, which you can get at a pet shop. An aerator is a gadget that pumps bubbles of air into the tank and keeps the oxygen-rich water circulating.

Keep the water at a constant temperature that is right for your species of fish, and never allow a sudden change of even a few degrees. Even though your fish might be the kind that can stand a wide range of temperature, the change must always be gradual, just as it would be in a large body of water outdoors. Your fish will thrive only if the water is about the same as it would be in their natural environment. A temperature of 75 degrees is comfortable, although all but most delicate tropical fish can stand a five-degree variation, as long as the water has cooled or heated gradually. Don't try to guess at the water temperature, but keep a thermometer in the tank. Pet shops sell floating thermometers and others that stick on the outside of the tank, which are easy to read.

The surest and easiest way to keep the water at a constant temperature is to buy an electric heater and a thermostat for the aquarium. Fish are very sensitive to sudden change because they are cold-blooded, which means they have no constant body temperature but rather take on the temperature of their surroundings. If you move them from one aquarium to another, be sure the temperature of the water is exactly the same. A sudden change can kill them. If humans should get steaming hot and then run outside in freezing weather, it wouldn't feel very good, but it wouldn't kill us because we are warm-blooded. Our body temperature stays the same, no matter what the temperature is around us.

Fish jump, so it's a good idea to fit a nylon net over the top of your aquarium, or a sheet of glass if you use an aerator. Besides keeping the fish in, it will keep a cat out. A glass also helps by cutting down on evaporation, but in the summer this evaporation cools the surface, so at that time a net has an advantage.

Constant, direct sunlight may cook your fish, so don't put your aquarium in a sunny window. But fish do need eight to ten hours of light, as we do. A tank has to stay in one spot because it's too heavy and awkward to move around, so the answer is artificial light. Don't use a regular incandescent bulb, because it will give off too much heat, and that will upset the balance of temperature in the water. A purple or blue fluorescent light works best, because it will light the tank with a nice color, without heating it or encouraging the growth of algae. You can buy these lights as separate fixtures or built into a tank cover. Your exact needs will depend on the size and position of your aquarium, so before you buy, get advice at a pet shop.

CARE AND FEEDING

When you bring your fish home, don't just dump it in the tank. Suspend the small carrying container in the big aquarium until the water in both the tank and the container are the same temperature. Never pick up a fish with your hand, because you might break the thin film that covers the scales. This film protects the fish from fungus and infections, which are difficult to cure. Let your fish swim out of its plastic carrying bag when it is ready, or use a soft fine-mesh net that is big enough to hold your fish without rubbing its sides.

The daily care of fish takes very little time compared to the hours of pleasure you'll have watching them. You'll be surprised at how quickly fish learn to come up for food when the shadow of your hand passes over the surface of the tank or when you tap the tank with a fingernail. The species of fish you start with will thrive on an assortment of store-bought dried foods, such as finely ground meal made from beef, shrimp, fish, and liver. But live food such as brine shrimp is a treat. Watch and judge the amount your fish need, giving only what they finish in a few minutes. It is tempting and easy to overfeed, so be careful not to do that.

Normally you should feed most fish once a day — tiny fish twice a day — at a regular time, but don't worry if you have to go away and skip a weekend, because they can live for a while on the plants and invisible particles of food in the water. Too long without food will weaken fish. When the temperature is high, their metabolism rate increases and they need more food. If you are not sure how long you'll be away, you can buy an automatic fish feeder that fits on the side of the tank and dispenses food at set times. Some people like to always put the fish food in the same spot, in a floating feeding ring that keeps the food from scattering and gives all the fish a better chance of getting enough to eat.

There will always be some uneaten food, as well as fish feces and bits of decayed material in the tank, which must be cleaned out as often as necessary before it contaminates the water. To do this, you can learn to use a hand siphon, which will suck out all visible dirt that will accumulate conveniently on the sloped gravel at the front of the aquarium. If you can buy one, a filter works even better than the daily siphoning because it continually pumps water through a filter that traps the dirt. If enough of the water is exposed to the air and if you haven't too many fish for your space, this daily cleaning is enough, and you'll hardly ever need to change the water. Just add more as it evaporates, always using water that is within two degrees of the temperature of the tank and that has set for twenty-four hours.

Despite your cleaning, a green film sometimes appears on the sides of the fish tank, especially if it is near a window where it gets too much sun. The film is a harmless mass of minute plants called algae, which grow in water everywhere. Some fish vary their diet by picking at the algae. If the sides of your tank become thick with algae, you can get it off with a long-handled plastic scrubber. Don't use soap, and make sure your hands have no soap film on them if you put your hands in the tank. Water snails in the tank also keep the algae under control.

GOLDFISH

Goldfish are members of the carp family. Originally they came from China, but it was in Japan that they were developed by selective breeding into the many varieties we have now. They are raised for sale in this country in great quantities, but people in the United States didn't see a goldfish until 1850, when P. T. Barnum displayed them at his circus. They were so popular that by 1865, New York City pet stores were selling goldfish by the thousands. And now, more than 60 million goldfish are sold each year in this country.

When you go to a pet store to buy goldfish, it may be difficult to decide which ones you want because they come in so many shapes and designs. Most of them are gold, but some are white, black, or silver, and others are red. Some are plain, but some have long, fanlike tails, and others have big bulgy eyes. One called the lionhead has a swollen bumpy head that looks like a raspberry.

It is easier to keep goldfish than tropical fish, because they are hardier, and in the natural state, they can stand a much wider range of temperature than fish that come from warmer waters. Once they are accustomed to an outdoor pond, goldfish can live there very well, even in winter when the pond freezes over, especially if it has a natural dirt bottom instead of a concrete one. Although goldfish seldom grow more than a few inches long in an indoor tank, the same fish living out of doors will adapt itself to the space provided and may grow over a foot long. Their hardiness doesn't mean you can be careless, however, and any change you make in the temperature of their water should be gradual. The most comfortable range is 55 to 65 degrees, and if you want to breed goldfish, which is fairly easy to do, you must keep them at a peak of health with a constant temperature of about 60 degrees.

Since goldfish are hardier than tropical fish, you won't have to buy all the devices that you'd need for more delicate fish. But you do have to remember to provide an adequate supply of air, no overcrowding, the right food, and daily cleaning. You don't have to buy an oblong tank, although that's always best. You can use a rounded bowl or a wide-mouth jar, provided you don't fill it to the brim but only to its widest portion, which will allow the most surface exposed to the air.

To feed your fish, you can buy several kinds of inexpensive prepared goldfish foods. Feed sparingly, using one kind one day, and another kind the next, so that your fish will have all the varieties of food they need. You may want to vary their diet even more by occasionally giving your fish bits of crumbled dog biscuit, hard-boiled egg, lettuce, liver, or fish eggs, which are called roe.

It's fun just to care for your goldfish and watch them, but you might like to raise them to sell to other people. If you look into your aquarium with a magnifying glass, you may find that jellylike eggs have been hatching without your knowing it. Your grown fish may have eaten up all the eggs before they hatched, or they may have eaten the tiny baby fish before you knew they were there.

At the moment your fish are ripe, which means ready to spawn or lay eggs, you will be able to tell the sexes apart if you look closely. The female's body will enlarge, and the male's fins and gills will be decorated with tiny pearl-like bumps. He will chase her and fertilize the eggs as she scatters them behind her. When he leaves her alone, you can be fairly sure that spawning is over and there are at least five hundred eggs, which sink down and stick to plants or pebbles in your aquarium. It takes only from three to six days for the eggs to hatch, so you had better take out all your adult fish and start a new tank at once, or the babies — which are called fry — will be eaten up. Once hatched, the fry will come to the surface, and they should be fed finely powdered goldfish food, rolled hard-boiled egg yolk, infusorian, or sifted daphnia (these last two are living organisms, which can be purchased in a pet shop or cultivated at home). The fry don't look like much of anything at first, but by the time they are six weeks old, they are miniature, fully shaped goldfish. As they grow bigger, you can give them coarser food, just as long as it is small enough for them to swallow.

TROPICAL FISH

Tropical fish are fascinating pets because there are so many different kinds. Each species and crossbreed is a different shape and color, and their habits and needs are different, too.

They come in an amazing variety and combination of colors and designs, with the male of each species more highly decorated than the female. Even within a species there may be slight differences. For example, the male guppy, so much smaller than his mate, is splotched in iridescent rainbow colors, but each individual male has its own pattern. No two are exactly alike. The breeding habits of each species are so interesting that most people are never content just to keep tropical fish without raising young.

You may want to raise gourami, a species in which the male takes care of the eggs. He blows a nest of mucus bubbles close to the surface of the water and adds tiny bits of plants to it. As the female spawns, the male fertilizes the eggs, then catches them in his mouth and deposits them in the bubble nest. He guards the eggs from bigger fish, catching any eggs that drop out and spitting them back into the nest.

The Egyptian mouthbreeder is another fascinating fish. The female lays her eggs in a hole, and after they have been fertilized, she scoops them up in her mouth and carries them there until they hatch. Even after they've hatched, she allows the tiny fry to swim in and out of her mouth, hiding there for safety until they are about two weeks old and too large to fit in. During this time she will not eat and grows gaunt and thin. The larger mouthbreeding fish have a similar system, except that it is the male that carries the eggs.

With more than five hundred kinds of tropical fish to choose from, and more being imported and developed by crossbreeding all the time, you'll have an interesting time trying to decide which fish you want to raise. Some are rare and expensive, but there are plenty of others you can afford and will find easy to keep.

Each species has two names, the common and the scientific. Both names often describe the fish in some way. The scientific names are Latin, and they tell the exact classification, giving the dominant characteristic of that group, and also sometimes honoring the person who discovered the fish. From the common names you can sometimes guess at once something about the fish. The neon tetra has startling bright color marks like small neon lights. Though easy to keep, neon tetras are difficult fish to raise because conditions must be exact and everything in the tank sterile. The merry widow fish is related to the neon, both being characins, which are especially active fish. The keyhole is a mild-mannered, easily raised fish in the family Cichlidae; it is splotched all over but always has one definite dark spot on its side, shaped like a keyhole. Also in this family is the Jack Dempsey, which was named after a famous fighter. This fish is large for a tropical fish and brilliantly colored, but each pair should be kept by themselves because when they are together, they attack each other in wild, ferocious fights.

The natural location or habitat of the tropical fish found in fish stores is well known, and an experienced ichthyologist (a person who studies fish) can tell you the exact aquarium conditions and breeding needs so you can see for yourself which kinds can be kept together and what equipment you'll need to buy.

The relationships between the different species are complicated, and so are the Latin names, but you don't need to bother with these until you've had some experience keeping tropical fish. It's enough to remember that all fish are divided into two basic groups: the egg bearers and the live-bearers. The eggs bearers you know about through goldfish. Live-bearers lay no eggs. Their young are protected longer within the female's body, and they don't hatch until they are fully formed. One mating with the male is often enough to fertilize several broods of a live-bearer's fry.

Guppies. The scientific name of the common little guppy, a popular tropical fish, is longer than the fish itself: *Lebistes reticulatus.* The first word means "pot" and describes the fe-male guppy — a fat, round-bodied fish, about an inch and a half long. She is a grayish-green color, dark on top and blending to light on the belly. The second word means "netlike" and refers to the shiny, uneven color marks of the smaller, slender, inch-long male. For a long while, scientists were confused by the fact that the bright rainbow colors of the male blend differently in each fish. Several times, when they found a new blend, they thought they had discovered a new species of fish, and they gave it a new name. At one time the scientific name was *Girardinus Guppii,* in honor of two scientists, Charles Girard and R. J. Lechmere Guppy. By chance and use, the word *guppy* stuck and has become the common name of the fish.

Guppies are easy-going fish, and they can live comfortably in a temperature range of 65 to 85 degrees, provided there is no sudden change. The ideal temperature is 75 degrees. If you keep on hand four or five kinds of prepared fish food and alternate the kinds you use, your guppies will thrive on a balanced diet. They do need some fresh greens, but they can get them by nibbling on water plants. Although it's not necessary, it's good to vary their diet with live daphnia, live red tubifex worms, tiny bits of fresh lean meat, and small pieces of lettuce. Since the fish are small, always give them finely ground food.

Guppies produce many young, an average of fifty every five months, so your chances of raising fry are reasonably good. You can plainly see when the mother is going to have a family, because the dark spot on her light-colored stomach grows larger and more distinct. As soon as her body swells, prepare a second aquarium — a small one — and plant it heavily with greenery so the fry can hide away from the mother, because she will eat them as soon as they are born if she can. When her stomach spot has grown steadily darker and you think she is ready to drop her young, put her in this small aquarium by herself. After the birth is over, put the mother by herself in still another temporary tank for a week or so before you transfer her back to her home aquarium. The female guppy needs this rest period so she won't be worn out with too frequent breedings.

Keep the new fry in their hatchery tank until they are full-grown, which will be in about eight months. The more space you give them and the more live food they eat, the stronger they will be, so it's better to give away or discard half the fry than to stunt their growth by overcrowding. Feed them exactly as you feed the adults, only powder the food while the fish are too small to swallow and digest larger pieces. Newborn guppies can eat micro-worms, which you can buy in a yeast-paste culture and can easily renew once a week by seeding the new culture with a teaspoonful of the old.

Zebra Fish. The egg-laying zebras are tiny, trim fish, under two inches long, and as you'd guess from the name, they are striped black and white — although the stripes go lengthwise instead of around as they do on a four-legged, land-dwelling zebra. Their scientific name is *Brachydanio rerio,* and they come from Sri Lanka. Since this island nation is just below India, and not in a completely hot tropical area, the natural temperature range is great, which means the fish can live in water from 60 to 85 degrees if the change is not sudden. The best temperature for breeding zebras is about 75 degrees.

Zebras will live peacefully with other small species, and they will be well nourished on the same kinds of prepared foods you give the other fish, with an occasional treat of daphnia. If you have several zebras, you will probably get eggs, but in order to hatch them before they are eaten by the parents or other fish, you'll have to transfer them to another tank.

Prepare the nursery tank — or wide-topped bowl — ahead of time so the water can stand for a few days. There's no need for gravel or plants, but the bottom should be covered with a layer or two of marbles to provide resting and hiding places for the eggs, which will sink to the bottom and roll around there, without sticking to anything. Before you put the marbles in, clean them as well as the tank or bowl with salt water, then rinse them with fresh water. The water in the tank or bowl doesn't have to be deep; four inches is enough. Keep the tank or bowl in sunlight for a few hours each day, which will encourage the growth of algae, but don't let it overheat. And don't bother to clean the algae from the sides because it will be healthy food for the fry.

Watch your zebras carefully to see when they are about to spawn. Then pick out the one that is fatter than the others. If its tail fin shows a yellowish cast, it is probably a female full of eggs. She'll also be especially active, because she'll be constantly chased by thin-bodied males. If you put a good, lively female with several fast-swimming males into the nursery tank, she will drop so many eggs that it won't matter that some are eaten before landing safely on the marble bottom. The males follow the female closely and fetilize the eggs as they drop. When the female is through spawning, she will be as thin as the males, and you will know it's time to put all the adults back into the home aquarium.

The eggs will hatch within two to ten days, developing faster in warmer water. Newly hatched fry do best on live foods, algae, and infusorian. As they grow, add brine shrimp, and by the time they are a month old, you can give them powdered prepared food as well. Their growth depends upon their diet and care, but they should be fully matured within four to six months, and ready to be added to your larger aquarium.

WATER SNAILS

Water snails are fun to keep with your fish, about three of them to a five-gallon tank. They are useful because they eat up extra food, and more important, they slide across the sides of the aquarium, eating the green algae that collects on the glass. They scrape the algae off with their radula, which is a bony ribbon covered by many rows of hard curved "teeth." A complex group of muscles pulls the radula back and forth in the snail's mouth, the way a cloth is pulled over a shoe when polishing it.

A snail's shell is permanently attached and grows with the animal. For protection and rest, a snail pulls its body into the shell. To move, it pushes out a big, flat membrane and crawls along on a slimy secretion by contracting and relaxing this "foot." A snail's eyes are on the tips of two flexible stalks or tentacles.

There are many kinds of water snails that will live well in an aquarium. The shell of a ram's horn snail is reddish in color and shaped like a rolled-up horn. If you keep ram's horn snails in your aquarium, you may find, with a magnifying glass, their tiny, colorless eggs bunched on the stem of a plant. Put the whole plant in a small jar of water and watch the eggs hatch in ten to forty days, depending on the temperature of the water. If you find two bunches of eggs, put them in separate jars, one cool and one warm, and keep track of how much sooner the eggs in the warm water develop and hatch than the eggs in the cooler water. If the eggs stick to the side of the glass, let them hatch where they are, because you can't scrape them off without injuring them. When they hatch, the snails will be tiny and horn-shaped. You won't have to feed them because they will find food too small for you to see on plants and the sides of the aquarium. Keep the baby snails in their own tank until they are too big for a fish to swallow.

A Potomac snail is larger, rounder, and smoother than a ram's horn, with a shell striped in brown. This snail does not hatch from an egg but is born from a grown snail. At birth it is smaller than a pea, but its shape, shell, foot, feelers, and radula are fully formed and will grow as the snail grows.

If you find baby snails, put them in a separate jar before your fish eat them, and use your magnifying glass to watch them grow up. Snails are hermaphrodites, which means that both sexes are combined in the same animal, so you don't have to worry about getting a pair to mate. One snail can handle the whole process.

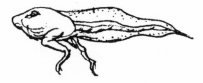

TADPOLES

Tiny tadpoles, also known as polliwogs, are fun to keep in a separate aquarium, but if you put them in with your goldfish, they are likely to be eaten. Even though they look nothing like their parents, tadpoles are either baby frogs or toads.

Frogs and toads are amphibians, a group of animals that begin their life in the water and become land animals when they are adults. Like insects, their bodies go through several changes, called a metamorphosis.

For a few weeks early in spring, you'll find frog and toad eggs in ponds, marshes, and ditches. Frog eggs look like a mass of soft gray jelly, dotted with black beads. Toad eggs come in a long chain, like a string of black jelly-coated beads. Don't take all the eggs, but scoop up a handful along with plenty of the pond water to put in a bowl at home. Add a few pieces of pond weeds, too, in order to keep the habitat as natural as possible. Cover the bowl with a screen if there is a cat in the house, and don't put it on a windowsill, where it may overheat in the sun.

In a few days, you'll see the black dots inside the eggs changing shape. First they'll look like a fat comma, and by the time they hatch about ten days later, they will have distinct heads and tails. They'll have feathery gills on either side of the head, which supply them with oxygen, and they'll hang on to a plant with a sucker where their mouth will be. Tadpoles don't need a mouth right away because they still get nourishment from the leftover yolk of their eggs. When their mouths do open a day or two later, the tadpoles eat plants and algae. If you float a lettuce leaf on the water, they will nibble at the edges of it. They will also eat fish food.

The first big changes you'll notice are the knobs just under the tail, which will become the hind legs, and the disappearance of the gills. At this stage, the gills are inside the tadpole's head, like those of a fish. In five or six weeks, you'll see that the knobs have sprouted into legs. Soon after that you'll also see the shorter front legs appear, and then the head begins to look like that of a frog. This strange half-frog, half-tadpole, which still uses its tail for swimming, also uses its legs to move through the water with a sort of jerky, froglike motion. By this time your tadpoles will have developed lungs. They no longer breathe under water, but stick their broad faces, with their round, blinking eyes, out of the water to take in air. Now they need a landing place, such as a small raft or rock in the bowl. They also need tiny bits of meat or flies to eat. They have become carnivores. Frogs and toads have amazing long, sticky tongues fastened in the front of the mouth. When they see a juicy insect, they flip out their tongue almost faster than you can see it. The insect sticks to the tongue and is pulled back into the frog or toad's mouth. If you watch a frog swallow, you can see that its big, bulgy eyes blink to help push the food down.

As soon as your tadpoles have turned into frogs or toads, they need more space and live food, so don't try to keep them any longer, even if you've given them a wooden raft to jump onto. It's kinder to put them back where you found them, and much pleasanter to think of them living a regular frog or toad's life than to watch them cooped up where they can't move freely.

There is one exception to putting a tadpole in with your goldfish. The bullfrog tadpole is big enough to avoid being eaten by little fish, and you can keep it longer, because it remains a tadpole for two years before it becomes a frog.

Although you raise frog and toad tadpoles the same way, in their adult forms they have significant differences. Frogs leap with long hind legs; toads have shorter legs and just hop.

Most frogs have smooth, moist skin, whereas toads have dry, bumpy skin. Most frogs live in the water. Although toads lay their eggs in water, they live on dry land, especially in gardens, where they earn their living by eating insects.

SALAMANDERS

Like frogs, salamanders are also amphibians, animals that begin their life in water yet spend part of their life on land. There are many kinds of salamanders, each with different characteristics, from the five-foot giant that lives in Japan to the two-inch red-backed salamander you can find under logs in damp woodlands. A salamander is shaped like a lizard, but that's the only similarity. A lizard is a reptile, with dry, scaly skin and claws on its feet. Salamanders have smooth, moist skin, and their toes are soft.

If you find a land salamander, pick it up gently and carry it home in a jar or box lined with damp dirt or moss. But if the salamander you find lives in a stream or pond, put some of the pond water into the container. If you don't know what kind of salamander you have, the first thing you should do is look it up in a field guide to amphibians or in a book about salamanders.

You can make a comfortable home for a tiger, spotted, red-backed, or other land salamander in a glass tank at least two feet long, with a few inches of soil on the bottom. Into this, sink a "swimming pool" made from a plastic, ceramic, or any rust-proof pan. Keep it full of fresh water. To make a more natural-looking habitat, plant some moss and a few ferns, and add a chunk of bark or arrange some flat stones into a cavelike hiding place. A glass top on your vivarium will keep the moisture in and will prevent the salamander from getting out. Salamanders that live in the water will need a tank filled about half full of pond water on top of a one-inch layer of sand. Add some rocks or a log or an island of dirt and moss to hold a food dish.

When your salamander gets used to its new home, it will begin moving around in search of something to eat. In the woods, a salamander makes a meal of slugs, spiders, worms, and insects every day or two. Try to catch flies and other insects or tiny worms for your salamander, but you can also tempt it into eating tiny pieces of raw meat or fish if you stick them on the end of a thin stick and wave it around so they look alive.

A salamander isn't the kind of pet you can play with and handle a lot, but if you do pick it up, do it gently. Never grab it by the tail, because its tail will come off in your hand! Don't worry, it will grow a new one, but it's never quite as graceful and long as its first tail. In winter, your salamander will be less active, and it may not eat as often. It may even burrow into the dirt and hibernate for several weeks. The more you know about a salamander's habits, the more prepared you'll be to keep it healthy. If you are going to be away for a long time or if you think your salamander isn't thriving, be kind enough to take it back to the woods where you found it.

TURTLES

If you have a turtle for a pet, it's not likely to be the small, green, half-dollar-size aquatic turtle that your parents may have had when they were young. It is now against the law to sell any turtle smaller than four inches. Far too many baby turtles were dying, many before they even got to the pet stores.

But turtles can be wonderful pets, and there are many kinds to choose from. Before you go shopping or hunting in the woods for a turtle, get a guidebook with colored illustrations that will help you identify the turtles you see. Or look at the turtles in the zoo. Read as much as you can about the ones that interest you, so that you will know what kind of cage to get ready and what food your turtle will need. Do you want an aquatic turtle, or one that lives on land? Will it be easier for you to maintain a tank or a dry pen?

Turtles are reptiles, with dry, scaly skin and a protective shell that grows with them. Like all cold-blooded animals, they regulate their body temperature by moving into and out of heat. They have not changed much since they first appeared on earth 175 million years ago, with their dinosaur cousins. Turtles are smaller now than they were in the age of dinosaurs, but their habits are much the same.

Sometimes people get confused about the difference between a turtle, a tortoise, and a terrapin. Any reptile with a shell is a turtle. *Turtle* is the general name for this whole group of animals. You're right if you call a Galapagos tortoise a turtle. But it's not right to call a snapping turtle a tortoise. A tortoise is a turtle with stumpy hind legs that spends its entire life on land. In England, water turtles are called terrapins, but in the United States, we limit that name to one species, the diamondback terrapin.

As a general guide, remember that turtles that live mostly in water have flat shells, whereas land turtles (tortoises) have a more rounded top shell. They all eat much the same sort of food — a wide variety of meat and plants — and .all the young are born from eggs. The female turtle uses her hind feet to dig a hole, usually at the water's edge. In this nest she buries many leathery round eggs and leaves them to hatch by themselves. Newly hatched turtles have soft shells, and many enemies. Raccoons, big fish, snapping turtles, birds, and many other animals scramble to eat the young turtles almost as fast as they leave the nest. Fortunately the baby turtles don't need to eat for many weeks, even months, and many of them survive because they can stay hidden underground until their shells harden.

A turtle cannot live without its shell. It is permanently attached. The top shell, called the carapace, is an extension of its backbone and ribs. Don't drop your turtle, because a broken shell can kill it, and so can a shell that's been painted, because it prevents the shell from growing. If ever you find a turtle whose shell has been painted, no matter how pretty you may think it is, be sure to scrape the paint off carefully with a knife. A turtle's shell is both protection and camouflage. Pulled tight into its shell and remaining perfectly still, a land turtle is safe from almost any predator. And a brown water turtle striped with green may be safe because its coloring makes it almost invisible among underwater plants.

One of the tortoises you can recognize most easily is the Eastern box turtle, because its top shell is raised and rounded, and there is a hinge on its undershell, which opens when the turtle wants to come out and closes tightly when its legs and head are pulled in. The box turtle's markings are mottled, and when it is closed and lying in a bed of forest leaves, it could be easily mistaken for a stone. If you live in a region where there are box turtles, you can bring one home and keep it in the garden. Don't pen it up in a box, because it likes lots of space, and it also needs some water or swampy ground and some leaves to hide under. As a garden pet, a box turtle will feed on slugs, worms, grasshoppers, beetles, and a variety of insects, as well as the juicy parts of plants. You can also offer extra treats, such as chunks of apples, grapes, bananas, strawberries, and other fruits and vegetables. Cars are the biggest danger to a turtle in your yard, and it's a good idea to put up a low fence around the garden to keep your turtle from wandering into the driveway. Before someone starts up a power mower or other garden equipment, make sure your turtle is safely out of the way.

If your family doesn't mind, you can bring your box turtle in the house in winter and let it roam around. It is a clean animal and no trouble at all. It may hide under a radiator or in some dark corner, and just come out and walk around now and then. When it does appear, it will be hungry, so offer small bits of raw meat to take the place of insects, or give it crickets and mealworms you can buy at a pet store. Fill one shallow pan with fruits and vegetables and another with fresh water. Even if no one minds having your turtle loose in the house, it's a good idea to build a large pen for your box turtle as a home base, where you can feed it and where it can stay at night and when you're not home. Turtles need a lot of sunlight, so you'll want to have an ultraviolet light that shines on part of the pen all day, leaving part of the cage cooler. If you keep your turtle in a pen outdoors, don't leave it in the hot summer sun without some shade.

When it is cold, it's natural for your turtle to dig in the soil and try to hibernate. Out of doors, a turtle could hibernate safely, because it would be so cold that its body would hardly function at all, and it could live on its own fat. But indoors, where it is warmer, the fat would be used up more quickly, its appetite would not come back, and it would starve to death while hibernating. So it's best to keep your turtle warm all winter and to keep feeding it regularly.

It's hard to tell how much your turtle knows and whether it recognizes you. Most turtle owners say that their pets show a definite preference for certain people. There is one house tortoise that went its own way for years, impartially indifferent to all members of the family. When its owner grew up and went away to school, the tortoise didn't seem to notice. But always, when its owner comes home for a vacation, her pet makes its slow way into her bedroom and remains aloofly there as long as she is home. Water turtles in a tank will swim to the surface when they you see you enter the room, and they'll learn to take food from your hand. But watch your fingers! Turtles have no teeth, but they have strong, sharp jaws that can give you a painful nip.

If you live in a region where you can find one of the common water turtles, like the red-eared slider (they don't have ears, but two red stripes on the head), the cumberland, musk turtle, or Eastern mud turtle, you can bring one home and put it in a tank. Aside from no cost, one advantage to catching a turtle is being able to return it to its home pond if you find that it doesn't respond well to living indoors. The size tank you use depends on the size and number of turtles it will house. For each turtle smaller than four inches, you need five gallons of water. For larger turtles, you need ten gallons for each turtle. For one six-inch turtle, for example, you would need a ten-gallon tank. Don't overcrowd the tank. Don't put live plants in the tank, because a turtle will make a mess shredding and eating them. The less you put in the tank, the more space the turtle will have and the easier it will be to clean. Never put a snapping turtle in with other turtles, and don't put large turtles in with very small ones, because the small ones will be a quick snack for the large ones. Some water turtles are "clingers." A mud turtle likes to lie on the bottom of a pond, but when it comes to the surface, it clings to a log or rock. Others need a place to climb out of the water and dry off. Before you put a turtle in a tank, read and learn about the needs and habits of that kind of turtle.

Aquatic turtles eat from a slightly different menu from that of land turtles, but none of them can survive on the canned ant eggs that are sold as turtle food. Your turtle will starve if that is all it gets to eat. Aquatic turtles thrive on small goldfish or guppies. Although you can substitute lean dog or cat food, raw shrimp or chunks of fish, these are not as appetizing to a turtle as going after live food. Also feed your turtle fresh spinach and chunks of fruit. Don't feed your turtle in its tank, because it will make an awful mess. At feeding time, put the turtle in another container, the size depending on the size of the turtle. You can use a plastic box, a pail, a sink, or a child's swimming pool filled with warm water to a depth that just covers the turtle's head. Aquatic turtles must eat in water because they need water to help them swallow.

Before you buy a turtle at a pet shop, make sure it is healthy. Its shell should be firm and whole, its skin free of sores, and its eyes clear, not swollen or puffy. It should be alert and strong. If it pulls back into its shell when you pick it up, that's a healthy, natural response. When you grasp one of its legs and pull gently, you should feel it pull back with some strength. Don't buy it if its legs feel limp. A healthy turtle can live with you happily for many years.

LIZARDS

If you live in one of the southern states, you probably have seen tiny green American chameleons running around your yard catching insects. In spring, carnivals and pet shops sell thousands of these lizards, which aren't true chameleons at all even though they can change color. These popular pets are anoles (scientific name *Anolis carolinensis*), and they are easy to keep if you understand their habits and their habitat. Many of these delicate anoles die in captivity because they are handled too much or too carelessly. Years ago, it was fashionable to buy these little animals with tiny collars and chains so they could be worn as lapel pins, but humane societies put a stop to that. No creature can survive that kind of treatment for long.

The anole's color change is fascinating, although it's not a dramatic run through the rainbow colors that some people may expect. The anole can change from green to brown and back again, depending upon the temperature, intensity of light, and the animal's mood. Disturbed or frightened, a green anole may turn brown, but it doesn't necessarily change color to match its surroundings. It is true that you will often see your pet change from brown to green when it climbs out on a leaf. As it champs its jaws, and with its tiny pointed teeth chews on an insect it has snared with its long, sticky tongue, you may see its big eyelids turn green as if in great contentment. The color pigment cells in the scaly skin have the unusual ability to alter their shape, and other cells act as filters and reflectors, and so give various color effects. An added color decoration is the throat fan, or dewlap, of the male. This is usually folded down, but when the male is looking for a mate, he puffs the dewlap out into a brilliant red fan calculated to attract a female. But sometimes he raises his red dewlap just because he has found a drop of water on a leaf.

Like all lizards, the anole has five clawed toes on each foot, and with these it can scurry up straight glass walls and move with startling speed. In its natural environment, the anole climbs bushes and trees, usually sleeping through the night stretched full length on a twig, waiting for the morning sun to rise and warm it up. It can even jump short distances from branch to branch. This swiftness and agility has made it easy for many a pet anole to escape. Remember never to seize your pet by the tail, because its tail will break off. It will grow a new one, but it will not be as long or elegant as its original tail. Pick up a small lizard securely and gently around the middle, and don't squeeze.

The best place to keep these lizards is in a comfortable-size box or glass tank at least two feet square, covered by a hinged lid made of fine mesh. Add plenty of plants and twigs they can cling to as they would in the wild. These are social animals, so it's a good idea to keep two or more together. They may scuffle over their territory at first, but they will soon settle that among themselves. Like all cold-blooded creatures, anoles need warmth and sunlight each day. An ultraviolet light placed at one end of the tank will provide both, while the unlighted end of the tank will be a place to cool off in the shade. Anoles don't drink from a dish, but they do need water. If you spray fresh water on the plants at least once a day, the anoles will drink the droplets of water from the leaves.

Your pets will thrive on live insects and spiders, but don't feed them a steady diet of just one thing, such as nothing but flies. The anoles will be healthier if you give them a variety of insects: crickets, grasshoppers, ladybugs, and a few worms. In winter, you can feed them mealworms, which you can buy at a pet shop. As your anoles grow, you'll see them shed their skin several times a year, and they may eat that, too.

There are about three thousand species of lizards in the world, ranging from some two-inch tree geckos to the giant Komodo dragons, which grow twelve feet long. Komodo dragons are an endangered species, but even if you could get one, you wouldn't want it in your house. One Komodo eats a whole goat for dinner! But from this big assortment of lizards, it's easy to find some fascinating pets. A pair of horned toads (which are lizards, despite their name) can live well in a desert vivarium. Many people enjoy keeping green iguanas, if they have room for a large cage. A healthy, well-fed iguana will grow steadily over its lifetime of ten to fifteen years. Before you venture out to buy any kind of lizard, find out as much about these animals as you can, and have the proper cage ready when you bring it home.

SNAKES

A pet must be the right animal, for the right person, in the right place, at the right time. A snake may not be right animal for you right now, but even if you've never thought of owning a snake, it's fun to learn about them. They are fascinating creatures. Many of the ideas people have about snakes are not true at all. Some people think that they were born with a horror of snakes, just as others feel of a horror of cats or mice. But it's not very comfortable to go around with a horror of anything. Far better to have a little knowledge, which will help you to look at snakes with interest, if not with affection.

First of all, snakes are not slimy. If you've never touched one, you may be surprised to find that a snake is dry, and smooth as a peeled hard-boiled egg. Perhaps it's the way snakes coil and twist, and slip silently and suddenly through the grass that gives people the creeps and reminds them of slimy things. Actually, to be able to move as gracefully as they do without legs is quite amazing. Snakes can swim, climb a tree, and crawl along a rope. A snake's skeleton is little more than a skull, backbone, and ribs, covered by powerful muscles and a stretchy skin. Each pair of ribs is attached to a complicated system of muscles, which allows the snake to move each belly plate. The edges of these plates catch on any projection such as a blade of grass, rough bark, or sand. In order for the snake to go ahead, it contracts a rib muscle. This contraction shoves the belly plate backward, and that moves the body forward. The motion is wavelike and continuous, starting with the scales at the head and gliding backward to the tail. In slow movement, a snake's body ripples. Snakes also move by looping and twisting from side to side to get more speed. A desert snake called the sidewinder throws its body in loops.

There are so many kinds and sizes of snakes, each with different habits, that it's difficult to say how fast snakes, in general, move. Because they are so sleek and graceful, and appear suddenly out of nowhere, snakes seem to move faster than they really do. One of the fastest is the western whip snake, with a top speed of three miles an hour. Almost anyone can walk easily at three miles an hour, so you can see that you could get away from a snake if you wanted to, and most snakes only prowl at a speed of one quarter of a mile an hour anyway.

In their natural habitat, snakes hide away when they can, and you normally won't see many kinds. But if you go to a zoo, you can see that the detailed markings on snakes are often beautiful and colorful. If you get an identification book with good colored illustrations, you can begin to learn to identify some of the common snakes in your region, as well as some of the more famous and exotic snakes such as boa constrictors and cobras.

Snakes are not active all the time. Being cold-blooded, they cannot survive in freezing temperatures. More species of snakes live in the southern hemisphere than in the north, but in cold weather they all hibernate. All snakes seek shade when the weather gets too hot, and even in temperate climates, snakes take frequent rests to conserve energy, especially while they are digesting a big meal.

All snakes swallow their food whole, and even though they have strong digestive juices, it takes time and rest to digest hair, skin, flesh, and bone. Snakes' jaws are hinged in a way that makes it possible for them to swallow an object much larger than their own head, and their skin stretches to make room for the food. The lower jaw is not in one solid piece like ours, but in two separate sections, connected by an elastic tendon that can stretch to open the mouth very wide. Each part can move sideways so the snake can close one side of its mouth and leave the other side open. The upper and lower jaws are also connected in a way that allows them to pull apart with amazing freedom of motion. As snakes move their jaws alternately, the food is drawn into the mouth and held fast by the sharp teeth that curve inward.

Nonpoisonous snakes have fewer teeth than poisonous snakes. The bite of a nonpoisonous snake leaves a harmless horseshoe-shaped mark from two rows of teeth in the lower jaw and four rows of teeth in the upper. A poisonous snake's bite leaves two definite punctures from a pair of sharp, hollow fangs that inject the venom. Extra fangs are folded back and protected by tissue in the roof of the mouth. If a fang breaks, a new one moves into place. Besides the fangs, a poisonous snake has four rows of teeth, one on either side of its top and bottom jaws.

Some people used to believe that a snake's forked tongue was its stinger, but that's not true. As the snake's delicate tongue moves in and out of its mouth, it picks up dust and invisible particles in the air and carries them back into its Jacobson's organ, on the roof of the mouth. This organ both tastes and smells, telling the snake about its surroundings and if it has found food.

All snakes are carnivores, and their biggest role in any ecosystem is the control of rats, mice, rabbits, and other small, fast-breeding mammals. A farm without a few snakes around can be quickly overrun by mice, which can eat huge amounts of stored grain. Water snakes eat fish, frogs, and other aquatic animals. Some snakes climb trees and take eggs and hatchlings from birds' nests. On the other hand, snakes have little means of defense against people and other animals that prey upon them, except for escape or camouflage. But even without legs or claws, snakes can capture their own food with amazing speed. A garter snake simply slides up to its victim and bites it, only loosening its hold on a struggling mouse or frog long enough to juggle it around in order to swallow it head first. A constrictor, such as a python, boa, or king snake, strikes fast and throws its body around its prey. Constrictors do not crush their prey or break its bones, but only squeeze it tighter and tighter until the animal quickly suffocates. Others, such as the bull snake, throw a coil around their prey and pin it to the ground for easy swallowing. All these means of capture happen in seconds.

Venomous snakes, of course, kill by injecting venom, which is stored in venom glands on either side of the head and connected to the hollow fangs. Only four kinds of snakes in this country are venomous. Learn to recognize the coral snakes, copperheads, water moccasins, and rattlers, and do not walk carelessly where they might be found. If you know what the poisonous snakes in your region look like and how they act, you won't have an unnecessary fear of the harmless snakes you may meet.

Every snake literally crawls out of its old skin when it is outgrown. The entire body is covered by overlapping scales, something like shingles on a roof. There are no ears to get in the way; a snake can't hear, although it does feel vibrations. Even the eyes are covered with transparent scales. A snake can't close its eyes because it has no eyelids, but the eyes are well protected by these transparent scales. When a snake has grown too big for this complete armor, new scales form underneath. The top layer becomes dry and dull, and the scales over the eyes look cloudy. The snake rubs its head against the ground, much as you might wiggle uncomfortably in clothes that are too tight. Finally the old scales at the head split, and the snake crawls out, leaving its old skin behind in one piece, like an inside-out sock. A young snake sheds more often than an adult.

Some snakes are viviparous, which means they are born alive. Others are oviparous, which means they hatch from eggs. Snakes mate as other animals do, and the female of an egg-laying species lays her fertile eggs in the warmest spot she can find in sand, a hollow log, or under a shelf of flat rocks. The number of eggs varies with the species, but they are all oval and feel like leather. Because they are hidden, the whitish-gray eggs don't need to be camouflaged with spots and colors as birds' eggs do. Most female snakes leave the eggs at once, but some lie coiled around them until they are hatched. The hatching takes from four days to four months, depending on the species and the temperature. Warmth, of course, speeds the hatching. Baby snakes have a small, sharp egg tooth at the end of their snout for cutting through the leathery shell. When they hatch, snakes are fully formed miniatures of their parents, complete with scales, tongue, teeth, and fangs, and venom if they are venomous. They fend for themselves and need no care from the mother.

Snakes born alive are also precocious — completely equipped to take care of themselves. Instead of a shell, these baby snakes develop inside a thin protective membrane. The mother snakes pay no attention to their newborns and don't protect them in any way. The number of young produced by live-bearing snakes and the length of time it takes to give birth vary with the species.

Snakes are interesting pets, and you can buy small boa constrictors, pythons, and other exotic species at pet stores. But they are expensive, and most herpetologists (people who study reptiles and amphibians) recommend keeping a local species, especially if this is your first snake. When you find a snake yourself, you know where it lives, and knowing that helps you make a good home for it. Then if it doesn't eat for eight or ten weeks in the warmer months of the year, you can take a local snake back to its own habitat, where you found it.

Sadly, many snakes refuse to eat in captivity and die of starvation. You must be willing and able to supply the small live animals your snake likes best and to let the snake capture them for itself and swallow them whole. If they are hungry enough, sometimes snakes will eat raw fish or meat if it's waved around to give the impression that it's alive.

Garter snakes are probably the most common species, and they are found in almost every part of the United States, Canada, and Mexico. Many people don't like them because they give off an unpleasant odor if they are agitated, but if you handle a garter snake gently, that won't be a problem. If you are uncertain about picking up a garter snake, you can easily find species such as the tiny red-bellied snakes and DeKay's snakes. These are easy to keep because they eat worms, slugs, and crickets. King snakes, corn snakes, and rat snakes are hardy pets, easily tamed, and contented to eat mice or newborn mice called pinkies, which you can raise or buy at a pet shop.

Do not keep a poisonous snake! That would be foolish. The two most important rules in snake keeping are these: Don't ever scare anyone with a snake, and always handle a snake gently. If you frighten people, you keep them from getting to know and like snakes. And if you handle a snake roughly, you'll hurt it, and it may respond by biting you. Never let a snake dangle, and don't grasp it tightly behind the head. That's the way you might pick up a poisonous snake, but it's not the way you hold a harmless snake. When you pick up a snake, don't squeeze it, but support it with one hand and let it wind around you arm, or move through your hands in a hand-over-hand technique, as if you were climbing a rope.

A snake doesn't need a fancy cage. You can add decorative plants if you want to, but it's not necessary to duplicate a snake's habitat. One expert emphasizes that snakes do surprisingly well in a plain box with a pan of water to soak in, a branch to climb on, an object to hide under, and something to crawl through when it's ready to shed. What a snake does need is the right temperature, humidity, food, water, and a clean cage. The less cluttered the cage, the easier it will be to clean.

You can use a large fish tank covered tightly with a screen, or you can use a wooden box with ventilation holes bored in the sides and covered by screening. The front of the box should be a glass or fine-mesh sliding panel that will enable you to see your pet, reach in to take it out for exercise, and to clean the box. Snakes are escape artists, and they are strong. It's surprising how easily they can lift screens off the top of a cage, even when the top is weighted down. They can flatten themselves and squeeze through cracks so narrow you'd never guess they could get out. Often you'll find the escapee lying on top of the cage, keeping warm against the aquarium light, or under a radiator, or curled up in a bedroom slipper.

Being cold-blooded, snakes need a source of heat. They like to bask in the sun, but never put the cage in the direct sunlight unless there's a cool, shady place the snake can crawl into when it gets too warm.

Read as much as you can about snakes in general and your kind of snake in particular. And always be willing to let your snake go back to its natural home if it doesn't seem to be thriving. If you have a boa, python, or other tropical snake that isn't doing well, you can give it to a zoo.

It's unwise to capture any wild thing unless you are absolutely certain you can take care of it. In most states, strict conservation laws forbid taking wild animal pets and for good reason. You may find a baby animal alone and think it needs your help. But many animal mothers leave their young unattended for a while, perhaps to go off and find food, and instead of rescuing an orphan or an abandoned baby, you may be taking that animal away where its mother can never find it again. The general rule is to wait and see. If you see a baby animal alone, leave and return a few hours later, or perhaps the next day. If it is still there, maybe it does need help. But check with a conservation officer or a wildlife rehabilitator to see if it's a species you can keep.

When you walk in the country, it's fun to turn over old logs and explore under rocks, but you may be destroying some creature's home when you do that. Be a considerate, intelligent explorer. If you turn over a rock, put it back in place. Don't leave destruction behind you, and be careful about putting your hands into holes and crevices you can't see into. Nature sanctuaries ask visitors to follow this good rule: Take nothing but pictures; leave nothing but footprints.

6. Wild Animals and Birds

Oₙᴄᴇ in a great while, a wild animal, if captured when young, becomes a moderately happy pet, but most die young in captivity, even if properly cared for. Luckily there are laws in most states forbidding people from this unintentional act of cruelty.

It would be wonderful fun to have a monkey, for example, but the fun would not be worth the sight of that sad little face when it was ill, and it is terribly hard to keep a monkey healthy away from its natural climate. Besides, it is such a bright, inventive, and active animal that you can't possibly let it have much freedom in your home. Out of curiosity it would destroy too many things.

There is another way of making a pet of a wild animal, if you have the patience to try it. You know that you have more pleasure from your dog, cat, or other domestic pet if you understand it and expect from it only what it is in its nature to give. So why not take this same attitude toward whatever wild animals happen to live in your neighborhood? You will have to seek them out, because at first they will be wary of you. After all, it was their territory first, and you and your house and roads are the intruders. An animal will hide if it can, since it won't want you to interfere with the way it lives. So what you have to do is show an animal that you are not going to catch it or hurt it, and that you want only to watch it and offer it an extra supply of the right kind of food.

WILD BIRDS

If you put out grain and suet for birds and watch them feed, you will learn to recognize the birds that live year-round in your region and those that are just passing through. Bird-watching is such a popular pastime that it will be easy to find books that identify birds and tell you what to feed them. You can also get help from the National Audubon Society, a nature center, a natural history museum, a 4-H club, or the Scouts.

Different kinds of birds need different foods and different shelters for protection and nesting, but they all need water to drink and to bathe in. So if you want birds to stay around your yard, make a birdbath. A natural hollow in a rock filled with fresh water will do, or you can buy a bath on a pedestal — it doesn't really matter, as long as it is shallow and out in the open. Don't put the bath too near a hedge or any sort of cover that could hide a cat or other predator. But if you see a hawk or some other predator catch a bird, remember that it is not doing something terrible. Many animals are omnivorous, which means they eat both meat and plants. Others are carnivorous, which means they eat only meat. All carnivores prey on other animals. We, too, prey on other animals for meat, even if we don't kill them ourselves. Don't expect an animal to show a human being's kindness. Just make sure that you yourself are always kind.

Birds will visit your yard if there is natural food for them, such as berries, seeds, and fruits from trees, shrubs, and flowers, but you can encourage birds by putting out grain, suet, and other food. The seeds of vegetables are good eating, so in the fall leave some vegetables in the garden to go to seed. Don't cut down sunflower heads that are packed with seeds, and don't trim hedges and vines right after they flower, because they will provide late summer berries, which birds enjoy. Wherever green plants grow there will be insects, which are a rich source of protein for birds.

Most of the birds that eat at your feeders will not nest in your yard. Birds are territorial, which means they stake out a claim and defend that territory to keep it for themselves. When a male robin returns north in spring, he finds a place to build a nest, often in the same place he built a nest the year before. He sings his loud, cheery song to let other robins know he's there, and he will drive out other robins who try to settle too close. Such behavior makes sure that an area doesn't get overcrowded with birds of the same species, and that there won't be too much competition for the same kinds of food.

Learning to recognize different kinds of birds is fun. Serious bird-watchers even keep a "life list," to record when and where and how many different species of birds they see in a lifetime. Imagine how many different birds you'd have on a list if you start when you are young. There are many excellent bird books to help you identify birds, and you may also want to start your own book in which you draw a picture of each bird, showing its size, the shape of its tail and bill, and its coloring. You may want to add notes about the weather or anything the birds are doing that day. You don't need any special equipment, although it's helpful to have a pair of binoculars.

You can also learn to identify birds even if you can't seen them. Most ornithologists (scientists who study birds) and many amateur bird-watchers can identify a bird by hearing just a few notes of its call. You can learn to do this, too, if you listen to tape recordings of birdcalls.

The flight pattern of a bird is also a clue to tell you from a distance what bird you are seeing. Each sort of bird has a different flight; some are jerky and darting, some fly in smooth, straight lines, and others swoop and soar. As new birds arrive in the spring, you may wonder how far they have flown, and in the fall you'll wonder where they will go. You'll see big flocks gathering for flight and sometimes moving in formation, as the evening grosbeaks and other finches do. Some kinds travel individually, but at the same season, such as the brown thrashers. You will seldom see the scarlet tanagers arrive, because they travel at night, flying from the south to north with the aid of southerly winds.

If you live in the north, the robin will be among the first birds to arrive in your yard in spring. It's easy to recognize a male robin's rust-colored breast as he tosses his head to pull an earthworm from the soft, spring ground. About two weeks after the male robins have flown north, the less colorful females arrive. Male birds have far fancier feathers and better voices than the females, which suits their job of strutting and singing in order to attract the best mate.

If the male has started to build a nest, his new mate may decide to tear it apart and rebuild it in her own way. But once the eggs are laid, many male birds bring food to the mother while she is nesting and help feed the fledglings after they have hatched. Brightly colored male birds seldom sit on the nest at hatching time, which is just as well because they would attract the attention of predators.

Meadowlarks, blackbirds, and phoebes will come with the robins, and bobolinks aren't far behind, singing high in the air as they travel. They fly several thousand miles from Argentina, and back the same way, over Florida, at the end of summer.

No matter what part of the country you live in, you will see the greatest variety of birds in spring, summer, and fall, if you look for them. These are your main times for watching them. There is not much for you to do in the way of feeding during these seasons, with one exception. You can lure the smallest bird of all, the hummingbird, to drink sugar water from a feeder instead of flying to a flower for nectar. You can buy inexpensive hummingbird feeders or find plans to make one that you can tie to a bush. Red food coloring added to the sugar water is sure to attract these tiny birds, which can hover like helicopters and suspend themselves with wings that move so fast they look like glass instead of feathers. You may even hear the humming sound that is made by the beating of its wings. A hummingbird's long, thin, straight bill is made to dip into deep blossoms, and it will drink from your feeder just as easily.

In cold weather, birds may really use your help. If you put out food for them and watch, you will be surprised at how many kinds are wintering around you. The chickadee, which chirps out its name — *chick-a-dee-dee-dee* — so cheerfully, is the friendliest of all. You will often see its tiny head, with its black cap, black bill, and white cheeks, pecking away at the dinner you have provided.

Charles R. Smith, the director of public education at the Cornell University Laboratory of Ornithology, says that birds are very good at finding their own food and do not have to be fed. And if you start feeding them in winter, you do not have to feed them every day for the rest of the year. People who just want to offer an occasional handful of seeds should feel free to do so, he says, without feeling guilty. On the other hand, if you enjoy watching birds and want to encourage them to visit your yard regularly, you should keep a feeder well stocked all winter.

Feeding stations can be all shapes and sizes and made of anything from a recycled plastic jug to an elaborate shelter costing fifty or sixty dollars. Feeders can be hung from a tree limb, put on a pedestal, or attached to your window ledge. The window ledge is best for you because the birds become so tame they don't mind if you sit still inside and watch closely. Naturally any sudden motion or noise will frighten them off. If there is a vine outside your window, birds will be especially quick to find your winter feeding station. If you are lucky, one pair may remain in the spring to build a nest, then teach their young to fly by practicing from vine to ledge. Timid birds can be taught to feed near your house if you suspend a feeding platform on a pulley and gradually, each day, haul it a little nearer.

Keep the snow brushed off, of course, but don't put a low roof over the station, because birds don't like to fly into closed places. It's best not to put bird food on the ground because predators can easily catch ground-feeding birds, and the food might attract rats and mice. Especially do not scatter bread crumbs on the ground because the bread can get moldy, which can make the birds ill.

Different kinds of birds are attracted to different kinds of food. Juncos, sparrows, finches, grosbeaks, cardinals, and other seed eaters like a mixture of sunflower seed, finely cracked corn, and white millet. Chickadees, woodpeckers, nuthatches, and other insect eaters eat the seeds, but they also like suet. If you just stick out a lump of suet, a squirrel or raccoon or blue jay is likely to snatch the whole thing. You can buy a readymade suet ball, or buy kidney suet at the supermarket and hang it up it in one of those orange mesh bags used to package onions.

Squirrels have performed some amazing acrobatics to get food from bird feeders, but a squirrel is not a thief. Wild creatures have to eat what they can find. If your food disappears before the birds can get it, watch carefully to see what animal took it, and then give that hungry creature some extra food for itself. Place the feeder farther away from your house if you don't want those other animals around.

Wild woods, open sunny meadows, and low bushes are

natural nesting places for different kinds of birds, but a well-trimmed lawn is not. However, birds might nest in your yard if you build wooden houses for them. Any old wooden box won't work. Orioles, for example, won't go into a box. They don't like to be enclosed. They weave an elegant, bag-shaped nest that hangs from a limb and rocks in the breeze. A killdeer nests on the ground, and nothing would persuade it to live in a birdhouse. Your most likely tenants will be birds that nest in holes and that would look for hollow tree trunks to hide their nests. Wrens, swallows, and woodpeckers will use a house if it is placed in a tree or on a high post. You may be lucky enough to attract a bluebird if you nail its house on a fence post not far from a hedge.

The decoration and trim on a birdhouse makes no difference to a bird, but the size and shape of the house does. A general one-size-fits-all kind of house won't work. You must make a particular kind of house for a particular kind of bird. For example, a wren needs an opening one inch in diameter, but the opening for the larger bluebird must be one and a half inches across. The National Audubon Society has house plans for different birds, and there are plans in many bird books as well.

Keep in mind a bird's territory and its need for food and shelter, and don't put up too many birdhouses. Three to an acre is about right. Build the house from wood, because metal would get too hot in summer. An inverted metal cone around the pole beneath the box will keep away predators that can climb. Hinge the roof, because at the end of the season you must clean out the old nest, although you must never disturb it or the eggs any other time. The opening must be small and near the top of the box so the nest will be private. Plan the house for one family only. Like most rules, these last two have exceptions. Purple martins, and in this country only martins, are sociable birds that like to live apartment-house style, one family in each room. They like the doorway cut low to the floor so they can peer out and visit and keep watch while they warm their eggs for hatching. You will attract the bird you want if you know what kind of food it eats, what it needs for nesting material, what kind of shelter it prefers, and the height at which it feels safest.

Even if you don't build a birdhouse, you can make nesting easier for any bird by putting bits of yarn or hair or feathers or straw on a bush or branch. Use short pieces of yarn or string, not more than three or four inches long, so the bird won't get tangled in them. Birds use all sorts of things for building — twigs, moss, leaves, and whatever they can find for soft linings. Robins and other thrushes pack their nests with mud, so if there isn't much spring rain, make a small mud pile somewhere on your lawn. (Later in the summer the dust will make a nice bathing place. All birds enjoy a good dust bath, especially at molting time.) Of course, most nesting takes place in spring, but you may find nests all summer because some birds have several clutches of eggs a season, particularly if the first clutch is destroyed or doesn't hatch for some reason. Certain birds — cedar waxwings, for instance — do not build at all until July or August, since they count on raising their families on autumn berries.

Once in a while, a baby bird falls from its nest. If you find one, don't try to take it home, because your chances of raising it are very slim, and in most states it's illegal to cage a wild

bird or any other wild animal. First, try to return the bird to
its nest. Be sure it's the right nest; compare the nestling you
have found to the others in the nest. The parent birds will
take care of the returned baby bird. There is no truth to the
old idea that birds will desert a nest that has been touched by
human hands. Birds have little sense of smell, and unless they
see you bring the baby bird back, they probably won't even
know you were there.

Sometimes you can't find the right nest or for some reason
you can't put the bird back in its nest. In that case, if the bird
seems big enough and well fledged enough to fly (which
means it has enough feathers), leave it on a low, protected
limb. If the bird is still there hours later, or if it is too small to
fly, you can take it home. Or call a nature center, museum, or
zoo to get the name of a wildlife rehabilitation center that
might take the bird or tell you how to care for it.

The most important thing to provide for a fledgling is
warmth as soon as possible. In its home nest, a baby bird gets
warmth from the other nestlings when the parent birds are
off the nest. Out of its nest, a baby bird quickly gets cold and
easily gets pneumonia. Put the bird on a covered heating pad
set at low heat or on a hot water bottle. If you don't have
either of those, use two glass jars full of hot water. Fasten the
lids tightly, wrap each jar in a towel, and place them on either
side of the bird.

A fledgling bird's legs are too wobbly too support it, but in
its cup-shaped nest, the bird is held upright so all its weight
doesn't fall on its chest. It's important to give your fledgling
this same kind of support. Don't use an old bird's nest you've
found because it might be infected with mites or other

disease-causing organisms. A plastic berry basket makes a good substitute, and it's easy to clean. (A mother bird always keeps the nest clean, so you'll have to take over that job.) Line the basket with pieces of paper towel. If you use cotton to fill the nest, cover it with paper towels so the bird won't get its toenails caught in the cotton. Nestled between the hot water bottles, the bird will be warm and secure in its basket-nest.

Parent birds have no way of bringing water to their young, so you won't need to do that either, unless your fledgling has been without food for some time. Then you can add a bit of sugar to warm milk, and give small amounts to the bird with an eyedropper. Milk is mammal food, but the bird will get nourishment from it, too. A hungry bird will open its mouth for food, but the fledgling may be too frightened to do that. Don't force the beak open, but gently squeeze on both sides of the base of the bill with your fingers. When you are sure the bird can swallow, begin to feed it tiny bits of solid food, especially anything high in protein such as lean, raw ground beef or canned dog food. The kinds of foods you add to this menu depend upon the kind of bird you have. Don't force a bird to eat worms, because not all birds are worm eaters. Chopped raisins, chopped hard-boiled egg yolk rolled into small pellets and softened with cod-liver oil, and baby cereal is a good mixture for seed and fruit eaters as well as insect eaters. You can also use bits of apples, grapes, bananas, or cherries, but peel these first in case they have been sprayed with poison. Cardinals and chickadees especially like a bit of peanut butter mixed with fruit.

If your fledgling is weak, feed it a small amount every fifteen minutes for a few hours until it seems stronger. After that, feed it every half hour for a while, and finally every hour, starting about seven in the morning until seven at night. Mother birds don't feed their young during the night, and you won't have to either. But during the day, you must stick to your job because if you forget to feed it for even an hour and a half, the bird might die.

As soon as your fledgling is strong enough to hop out of the nest you've made, you'll know your job is almost done. When it flies as high as the top of a door, it's definitely time to release the bird outdoors. Don't let it try to fly in a room where the windows have no curtains or shades, because it may fly into the clear window and injure itself. It's cruel to keep a wild bird when it is able to return to its natural habitat. It needs a chance to develop strong wings by exercising them. Let the bird go free where you found it, if that's possible. If there are cats in your neighborhood, or you don't think it's safe for other reasons, take the bird to a secluded place in a park or in the countryside. Your bird will quickly learn to take care of itself, and you will have the satisfaction of knowing you have it given a chance to live on its own.

PARK BIRDS

In any city or town park, the first birds to greet you will be pigeons and sparrows. And you might want to come prepared with some bread crumbs or popcorn for them, because they'll be on the lookout for it. They seem to keep a sharp eye out for human beings and flock around you if you so much as pause and reach into your pockets. The scrub pigeons, mostly gray, but tan too, and many mixtures of colors, strut and bow and coo and are quite bold about snatching the biggest pieces. The common sparrows are quicker than the pigeons. They fringe the outskirts of a pigeon flock, shifting on their dainty feet until they spy an opening, then fly in and away with the smallest crumbs. English sparrows originally came from England, where they were mostly berry eaters, but in the park habitats of their adopted land, they have developed a taste for insects and so are useful birds.

Many parks have duck ponds. The resident ducks are usually fed by park keepers, but even if they're well fed, the ducks will waddle out to greet you, especially if you give them string bean ends or bread crusts. If the ducks are swimming out too far in the pond when you arrive, you can lure them near shore by throwing bits of food out to them. They will duck and gobble and paddle their way in, following your throws. Since they get their natural food — the shoots of water plants, and insects, and small fish — close to the surface of the water, they will dive down, leaving pointed tail and the backs of yellow webbed feet to mark the spot.

At the edge of some park ponds, you'll see a sign: Please don't feed the ducks. If so, it's important to obey that rule, because it was made to protect the ducks from serious illness and death. Not all the bread, popcorn, cereal, and other food that's tossed on the ground gets eaten by the birds. Much of it spoils, and when ducks peck at the rotting food, they pick up the bacteria and molds that do the spoiling. Some of these organisms cause salmonella and other serious diseases, which can spread quickly through an entire flock.

Even if you don't feed the birds, you'll find that it's fun to watch them and learn to tell them apart. Ornithologists (people who study birds) have divided ducks into two general classes: the surface feeders and the diving ducks. Divers get their food from the bottom of the pond and disappear altogether when they dive. When they leave the water for flight, they have to take a few running steps in order to take off, while surface feeders will spring directly out of the water and into the air.

The most common park ducks are mallards, which you can spot by the elegant green head and white neck ring of the male. The female is a modest tan and brown, and her long, rounded bill is orange. Don't count too much on seeing just these colors, though, because wild ducks sometimes interbreed with farm ducks, and park ducks are often an attractive mixture of various sorts. Then, too, your pond may be a resting place for wild ducks, and you may on different days see new flocks that are migrating north to south or back again. Occasionally they decide they like the security of a protected city life and settle down to stay. One lake in Central Park in New York City is a year-round home for a flock of Canada geese. You can recognize these beautiful big birds by their long, black necks, white throat patches, and light breasts.

Ducks, geese, and swans are fascinating to watch at any time of year, but in the late spring they are at their best. Then you can see the mother gliding proudly along, followed by a string of offspring traveling like the tail of a kite and moving just as expertly and fast as the mother. Once in a while you may see all the ducklings crowd on the mother's back and have a ride. At any sign of danger, she may quack them into shore or shallow water, where she can protect them.

Most ducks build their nests on the ground with twigs and grasses, lined with down and feathers from the mother's breast. It's a busy time for the mother, because the father duck moves off after mating with no concern whatever for family life. But baby ducks are precocious, which means that they are ready to do many things for themselves as soon as they peck their way out of their eggs. They can walk and can snap up bits of grass and insects with their bills, and they quickly learn to swim when the mother signals them to follow her into the water. Canada geese also have precocious children, but their family life is different. They mate for life. The male takes turns with the mother sitting on the nest and stays with her while they raise their young together.

CHIPMUNKS

There is something especially right about the sound of the name *chipmunk* for these striped little animals that dart about so swiftly with quick, short, jerky motions. The name comes from the Ojibway tribe of Native Americans, who call them *atchitamon*.

Chipmunks are rodents, related most closely to squirrels. They are about six inches long and have smooth, reddish-brown fur with white stripes outlined in black. When they stand up and settle on their haunches, you can see that the hair on their stomachs is buff-colored. Their lively, big brown eyes are set in the sides of their heads, and their tails stand up in a perky curve.

Chipmunks can scamper up a tree as well as any squirrel to find nuts and seeds, but they don't spend a lot of time in trees, as squirrels do. They prefer the ground, and they seem to like stone walls best. Grain is also a favorite food; they gather and store it in their underground burrows, which are quite amazing. Beginning with a small narrow burrow when it's young, a chipmunk keeps working all its life digging tunnels and adding rooms. By the time it is four or five years old, a chipmunk may have thirty feet of tunnels deep enough beneath the frost line to keep it warm. There may be two or three rooms for storage, a large sleeping room, and the deepest room for a toilet. During the summer a chipmunk packs its storerooms with food. Then when it wakes up from its deep winter sleep, it will find a snack close by. The chipmunk might look around outside on a sunny winter day, but with plenty of food and an indoor toilet room, it doesn't have to go outdoors until spring.

It's not easy to find the entrance to a chipmunk's burrow because, unlike most burrows, where you can plainly see that the earth has been scooped out, it is a clean hole dug from inside, and so small that a clump of dirt can hide it. Chipmunks are clever builders. First they dig a regular sloping burrow for their passageway and living quarters. Next they dig another tunnel and come out into the open through this new passageway, packing down the soil behind them as they emerge. Then they go around and plug up the original hole with soil and smooth it down. Since this construction work is done in spring, grass and weeds soon hide all signs of digging.

Chipmunks have four or five babies in a litter born in spring. Like mice, chipmunk newborns are blind and have no hair, so their mother keeps them hidden in the underground nest of dried grass and leaves until they are about one month old. After the babies are born, the father moves out and digs himself a new burrow.

You may hear chipmunks before you see them. They have a high-pitched *chuck-chuck-chuck* kind of chatter. In spite of the fact that chipmunks move so quickly and are so clever at hiding, it's not a bit hard to make friends with them. If you sit very still for a while each day in a spot where you have seen chipmunks, they will soon get used to you. You may see a chipmunk dart in a zigzag path through the grass and run up a stone wall with a mushroom in its mouth. It may sit upright on a flat rock, tear the mushroom to pieces, hurriedly eat a few bites, and leave the rest to dry in the sun to store later.

After this particular chipmunk has learned that you won't do any harm, you can further your friendship by offering some food. Put nuts, grain, or peach pits on the ground about twenty feet from your watching place, and then settle yourself to wait. Be patient. The chipmunk smells the food and has probably seen you put it down, but an animal must be wary. After a while it may scurry over to your gift and use its front paws to cram the food into its huge cheek pouches. These pouches are so big that they extend all the way to the chipmunk's shoulders, and they hold an amazing amount of food. The chipmunk might glance back with a look that may seem like a hasty "thanks," then dash away with an impudent rear waggle. If you can find a chipmunk's footprints in damp soil, you will see why it has this funny motion. When it runs, its back paws move side by side like your own feet, but its front feet come one directly behind the other.

Each day when you leave food for the chipmunk, you can put it closer to your watching place. If you make no loud noise or sudden motion, it won't be long before the chipmunk will come within a few feet of you and won't be in such a rush to dart away with the food. It might sit up with a very straight back and eat a while. It's fun to answer the chipmunk's chatter in the same sort of language if you don't do it too loudly, which might scare it away. Never touch the chipmunk or try to catch it. Remember that this animal is not your pet, but a friend, and you won't want to do anything that will frighten it or spoil the confidence that your patient watching has built. An animal is wonderful to watch when it is free, but if you hold it in your hand, it may be terrified. If you are bitten, it will be no more than you deserve for betraying your friend.

SQUIRRELS

Squirrels seem to be everywhere — in city parks, suburban yards, and rural woodlands. They need space to rove, trees to climb and nest in, and plenty of nuts, buds, sprouts, and bark to eat. Since gray squirrels do not hibernate, it's easy for anyone living in a city to make friends with them at any time of year, but especially in late fall and winter, when food is scarce. If you sit on a park bench with a pocketful of nuts or grain or fruit pits, it won't be long before a gray squirrel will seek you out. Approaching in an indirect line, with many stops and starts, the squirrel will finally pause within easy smelling-distance. A squirrel's sense of smell is its strongest sense, and it can easily tell if you have a delicious snack. It can even tell the difference between a wormy nut or piece of fruit and a good one.

A sudden noise or quick motion will frighten a squirrel away, at least for a while. But if you move gently, you can reach in your pocket and slowly pull out a nut, then let it roll a few feet away from you on the ground. The squirrel will probably circle around it warily, seize it, and again sitting back on its haunches, turn the nut around and around with its agile front paws. If the nut smells right, the squirrel will bite through the tough shell with its sharp front teeth, which are designed especially for cracking. It's fun to watch the dainty, quick way a squirrel eats, then throws the shell aside. It may take the next nut right from your hand, and you can feel how quick and strong its paws are. Once the squirrel is used to you, it may become aggressive and will even burrow into your pocket without waiting for you to hand it a snack.

You can learn to recognize individual squirrels if you go to the same spot regularly and watch carefully. They almost name themselves by their special traits — some bold, some timid, others scrappy. It's a nice feeling to persuade the more timid squirrels to take food from you. The squirrels will get to know you, too, and will go to you more readily than to a stranger.

When a gray squirrel has had enough to eat, it will take your food anyway and dart off with it, to bury it one piece at a time. Squirrels have no underground burrows or special storage places for food, as chipmunks do, but rather bury it at random and rely on their strong sense of smell to find the stored food later, even under many inches of snow. They don't find all their buried food, but the acorns and nuts that aren't eaten often germinate as seeds and grow into saplings. Squirrels help reforest the land, which is why Native Americans honor these small animals and tell legends of the work they do in providing food for the world.

A squirrel's nest is an amazing structure, much larger than a bird's nest, round instead of flat on top, with a domed roof of leaves and twigs that will shed the rain. Sometimes squirrels remodel an abandoned bird's nest, but ordinarily they build their own. Their summer nest is built in the crotch of a tree, high enough to be out of reach of marauding animals and to catch the summer breezes. It is securely woven with twigs as large as an inch in diameter, interlaced with smaller twigs and roots, and comfortably lined with moss, grass, or shredded bark.

A winter nest is built inside a hollow limb or tree trunk, where it is better protected from the weather. In March or early April, a litter of four or five squirrels is born in this cozy, lined nest. Blind for several weeks, these babies live on their mother's milk. In about six weeks the mother will begin to carry them outside, holding each by the soft belly skin and allowing the baby to hang on to her throat and neck with all four legs and its ever-useful tail. At night, the parents' fluffy tails are spread out on top of the sleeping squirrels like warm blankets. They begin to eat solid food at this age, and soon they become adept climbers.

Squirrels climb with skill and ease with the help of needle-sharp claws that allow them to grasp even the smoothest tree branch. And their long, bushy tail works like a rudder and a balance when they leap from branch to branch and travel across wires to reach a rooftop. Sometimes people put wire netting over attic windows and chimneys to keep squirrels from making their winter nests in the attic. If they decide to gnaw, squirrels can do a lot of damage. If you want to feed birds as well as squirrels, you'll need to use a lot of ingenuity in rigging up a bird feeder that the squirrels can't reach. Otherwise they will take all the suet or grain meant for the birds. It seems that for every gadget inventors have made to keep squirrels out of a bird feeder, some clever squirrel has figured out a way to get around it. They never seem to run out of ways to go wherever they want to.

SKUNKS

If you have a skunk for a neighbor, you probably know about it. Sooner or later your resident skunk will need protection, which means it will shoot out a spray that has a terrible smell. Like all members of the weasel family, the skunk has a pair of musk glands under its tail, but only the skunk can shoot out five or six rounds of this clear amber, oily fluid. If you or your dog are ever so foolish as to get yourself sprayed, you'll know how long this odor lasts and how difficult it is to wash out. Soap and water won't help much. The best remedy seems to be burying or burning your clothes and taking a bath in tomato juice. The acid in the juice is the magic ingredient. After a dog is bathed in tomato juice and dried, it's also a good idea to rub dry oatmeal thoroughly into its coat.

But there is no need to let yourself be sprayed by a skunk because actually, it is a peaceful, harmless, friendly animal that never attacks and only wants to be left alone. If you happen to meet one face to face, don't make any sudden motions. The skunk won't spray immediately but will give you fair warning to get out of its way. First it will stand perfectly still and stamp its front feet. If this doesn't scare you away, the skunk will raise its tail in an angry arch, with the white tip drooping down. If you still don't move out of range, the tip of its tail will bob up and spread out like a signal flag. And that's when the skunk will whirl around and squirt as far as twelve to fourteen feet with great accuracy.

Skunks are black, with white markings. The Eastern skunk has two white stripes down the back, but the spotted skunk found in the South and West has white spots. It seems that an all-black coat would be safer for an animal that roams at night, but the skunk's white markings actually protect it from enemies that have learned from experience how the skunk can defend itself. You're not likely to meet a skunk in the daytime, unless it is very early morning or at dusk. They sleep through the day and come out at night to hunt for beetles and other insects of all kinds, which are the main part of their diet. But skunks also eat mice, earthworms, turtle eggs, fruit, and grain. Many suburbs are being invaded by skunks, because they have discovered that humans leave delicious, easy-to-find leftovers in garbage cans. If you do see a skunk roaming around in daylight, stay away from it, because this unusual behavior means that it might have rabies. Call the health department, humane society, or conservation department; they will capture the animal and find out if it is infected with the dangerous rabies virus.

In the past people sometimes kept young skunks as pets because they are as gentle and playful as kittens, with no danger of spraying after a veterinarian has cut out their scent gland. Fortunately this is illegal in most states now, partly because of the danger of rabies but mostly because of its cruelty. When a pet skunk grew to its full size and wasn't quite as cute or docile as a kitten anymore, people often turned them loose in the woods. But without their scent glands, these skunks no longer had a way to defend themselves, and they became easy prey to larger animals. Skunks, like all wild animals, should live their natural lives and not be caged or kept for our amusement.

OPOSSUMS

Even if you live right in the middle of a big city, you may have more animal neighbors than you know about. The kind you may find depends on what part of the country you live in, but opossums have been moving farther and farther north from Mexico, even crossing the border into Canada. Like kangaroos, opossums have a pouch, but they are the only pouched animals — called marsupials — in North America. Opossums are nocturnal, searching after dark for fruit, worms, insects, and almost any kind of food, including garbage. When you see an opossum in the headlights of a car, its eyes shine dull orange. Sometimes it's mistaken for a huge rat because it has a scaly, ratlike tail. But an opossum is the size of a house cat, and its tail is prehensile, which means it is as useful as an extra "hand" for grasping things.

The female opossum may have two litters a year and up to twenty-four babies in one litter, although many of those do not survive. Each baby weighs only one fifteenth of an ounce, which is so small that a whole litter can fit into a teaspoon. The babies stay in the mother's fur-lined pouch for seventy-five to eighty days, when they are big enough to ride on her back. Then they hang on to her raggedy-looking fur for a few more months until they learn to fend for themselves.

Opossums move so silently on the ground and in trees that you may never even know they are there. If you do meet one, it may try to run away, but its waddling trot isn't very fast. Or it may stand to face you, then open its big mouth to hiss and show its fifty sharp, pointed teeth. An opossum has more teeth than any other North American mammal, but it's not likely to attack or bite you. Actually it may be so alarmed that it will play dead. We've come to call this characteristic tactic "playing possum." An opossum will fall down in an actual coma, lying on its side with its eyes closed and its tongue hanging out. Most of the time this unusual defense works, because a dog, bobcat, coyote, wolf, or other large predator isn't interested in eating flesh it has not killed for itself.

PORCUPINES

A porcupine prefers to remain unseen as it lumbers silently through the woods all through the year, both day and night, seeking vegetable food and enjoying porcupine ways. Unless you know how to look for the signs of a porcupine, you may have no idea that one is around. If you see a tree with bark gnawed off in a ring a foot or two off the ground, you can guess that a porcupine has been there, standing on hind legs and gnawing with its strong, orange, chisel-like teeth. If a rabbit had made the ring, it would be closer to the ground. Bits of bark and debris around the bottom of a tall maple or pine tree are another sign that a porcupine is resting on a high branch after a meal. With long claws on their front paws, these big rodents are good climbers, as much at home in a tree as on the ground.

Porcupines are protected by stiff quills, but there's no need to fear these gentle animals. There are as many as thirty thousand quills on an adult porcupine's back and tail, and each quill is needle-sharp, with microscopic barbs at the pointed end. If a quill sticks into your hand, it slips easily and painlessly out of the porcupine. Some people believe that porcupines can shoot their quills, but it only seems that way. When a porcupine lashes out with its quilled tail, only a slight touch is needed for the quills to stick the attacker; or when a porcupine shakes, loose quills may fly out, as a few loose hairs will when you shake your head.

A porcupine doesn't have to fight. It only has to stand its ground. Any animal that has tangled with a porc, even a bear or a mountain lion, will not be likely to attack again. New-born porcupines know instinctively how to defend themselves. Startled by a noise, a porcupine whirls around with its back to the enemy and covers its face with its front paws. Its back muscles tighten, which raises the bed of quills and the long guard hairs that cover them, the way an angry cat raises the fur on its back. At the same time, the porcupine swings its quilled, clublike tail from side to side. If you're walking in the woods with your dog and you see a porcupine, call off the dog, because it may charge bravely to attack. A dog with a muzzleful of painful quills must have immediate help. Pull out the quills with great care so they don't break and leave the barbed ends in the nose, where they can become infected. You may have to take the dog to a veterinarian for help.

In spite of their prickly reputation, porcupines are fascinating animals that live solitary lives. In spring, after mating, the male goes on alone. About seven months later, the female has one baby (or, rarely, twins). It is born with its shiny black eyes wide open, its teeth in place, and tiny white quills under its black fur. The young porcupine drinks its mother's milk for several months but quickly begins to eat solid food. The mother calls to her little one in a high, singsongy voice, and the youngster waddles after her all summer, learning where to find roots, leaves, and delicious fruits. It may stay in a den with its mother during the first winter, but by the time it is a year old, the young porcupine is on its own.

FIELD MICE

In uncut grass or open woods, mice scuttle silently on minia-ture paths. They live on grain, roots, and other vegetable matter, as well as insects and grubs, and usually build nests and raise their young in burrows or hollow tree trunks. There are 250 different kinds of mice native to North America, and unless their numbers grow too large, they are not harmful. Most of them become food for foxes, coyotes, snakes, owls, hawks, and other predators.

The dull-gray house mouse, which lives in cities, didn't come to this country until the 1600s, when it arrived on ships with colonists from Europe. The best way to keep these pests out of your house is to keep cereal, cookies, and other foods in metal containers with tight lids. If they can't find food, mice will look for another place to live.

The tiny white-footed or deer mouse is the most common of the native mice. With its big black eyes, Mickey Mouse ears, tiny white feet, and chestnut brown coat, it is also the most beautiful of the little rodents. Although they wash and groom themselves carefully, white-footed mice are messy eaters, scattering hulls of seeds and nutshells everywhere. People who close their summer cottages and cabins each winter are used to finding white-foot nests and debris in drawers and cupboards when they return to the house each spring. Outdoors, these mice nest in abandoned birds' nests or hollow tree branches or dig small burrows in the ground.

Some cousin of the white-footed mouse can be found on almost every acre of land from the Arctic Circle south to Mexico. A snow mouse called a collared lemming lives in the Arctic regions. In summer its squat body is yellowish-brown, but in winter its fur turns white, which is good camouflage in the snow. Little pocket gophers live on the western plains, but they are seldom seen because they stay underground in their elaborate tangle of tunnels, which they dig easily with their broad front feet. Pocket gophers carry plant roots in their big cheek pouches and store them underground in their burrows. Tree mice on the West Coast live on pine needles and use them to build nests in the highest branches of tall pines.

If you see signs of any of these little rodents, wherever you live, return to that spot some night with a flashlight and wait quietly. When you hear the pitter-patter of their tiny feet, you may be lucky enough to catch a glimpse of these beautiful little animals in the beam of your light.

WOODCHUCKS

In almost any open field in the eastern United States, you are likely to find chubby brown woodchucks. In some parts of the country, these big rodents are called groundhogs or marmots — or whistle pigs, because they do whistle. They don't hide all day in their burrows, but they do dig them at good vantage points, where they can come outside and sit upright on their haunches to scan the countryside with their sharp-sighted eyes. They are not especially timid, and they don't hesitate to come into the nearest garden for a good meal of new-grown peas. Farmers don't have many kind words for woodchucks, especially in late summer, when the woodchucks are eating every ripening vegetable they can find. These animals need to build a layer of fat almost an inch thick to provide energy during their long winter hibernation. Pennsylvania is the only state with a law against killing woodchucks, for the good reason that their huge burrows provide homes for so many other animals.

We celebrate February 2 as Groundhog Day just for fun. According to tradition, the groundhog comes out of its burrow on this day and looks around. If it sees its own shadow, it scurries back into its winter home and sleeps for six more weeks because spring will be late. But if on February 2 the sky is overcast, with no sun shining to throw a shadow, the groundhog stays outside because it knows that spring will arrive early. No one has ever explained why a sunny day means more winter, while a dull day means spring.

Of course this is only pleasant superstition, but it does remind us that a woodchuck hibernates. During this winter sleep, the woodchuck's heart rate slows from eighty beats a minute to only four or five. Its normal body temperature of 100 degrees Fahrenheit drops to 45 or 50 degrees. Scientists who study hibernation have found a substance in the blood they call HIT, which stands for Hibernation Inducement Trigger. In other words, it's the chemical that is triggered into action in a hibernating animal when the days become shorter and there is less light, or when the temperature drops, or when food is scarce. In extremely dry, hot weather, when food is also scarce, certain other animals fall into a similar deep sleep, which is called estivation.

RACCOONS

Raccoons have been called robbers and bandits, partly because they have a black-mask marking across their eyes and partly because they can't seem to keep their agile hands off anything. Raccoons eat all kinds of food: insects, seeds, berries, birds' eggs and baby birds, turtle eggs and baby turtles, freshwater clams, crayfish, and frogs. They also raid cornfields, orchards, and berry patches, and they are especially good at getting into garbage cans, even those with tight lids. Raccoons are not at all shy around people, especially campers who leave marshmallows and other good snacks lying around.

The German word for raccoon means "wash bear" because of their habit of washing their food, turning it round and round under water with long, limber fingers before they eat it. But even when they are eating dry food, with no water around to dunk it in, raccoons still go through the instinctive washing motions. Their sensitive hands can feel the difference between a stone and a clam in a stream, and that ability to find food by touch leaves them free to keep their sharp eyes open for danger.

If you ever saw a cuddly baby raccoon, you'd know exactly why so many people used to keep them as pets. But if you saw a full-grown raccoon, weighing up to twenty pounds, opening a cupboard or rummaging through a garbage can, scattering food and debris everywhere, you'd also know why it is not a good pet. In most states, it is now illegal to keep a raccoon for a pet because of the danger of rabies, a deadly disease that is spreading across the nation. More animal rabies cases (1,761) were reported in New York State in 1993 than in any other state, and raccoons were the major source of the virus.

Animals with rabies often change their habits. Because raccoons are such adaptable animals, they come in closer contact with people than do foxes, skunks, or any other wild animal. Raccoons are nocturnal, so if you see a raccoon wandering around in daylight, stay away because it may be rabid. A person doesn't have to be bitten to get the rabies virus. It can be transmitted through the animal's saliva. If a dog that is protected by a rabies vaccination tangles with a rabid raccoon, it won't get the disease. But a person with an open sore or cut who touches that dog can get the virus from the raccoon's saliva that may be on the dog's coat.

DEER

Deer are one of the most beautiful, and largest, of all the wild animals, and in recent years, one of the most abundant. By 1900, in the eastern states, deer were hunted almost to extinction, but they have made an amazing comeback. Now there are more deer than there were when the first European colonists settled here in the 1600s.

All species of deer are similar in color, a pinkish tan, dark on the back and legs, and lighter on the throat and stomach. The babies, or fawns, are all a red-brown at birth, and unevenly spotted with white. When lying still, they look like a small patch of earth patterned with sunlight through the leaves of tree branches. As they grow, the spots fade out and they take on the adult coloring.

Fawns are born in spring. A mother deer, or doe, usually has one fawn the first year, and sometimes twins in following years. A few minutes after birth, as soon as the mother has licked it dry, a fawn stands on its wobbly sticklike legs. A young herd animal must be ready as soon as possible to travel at its mother's side at whatever pace she sets.

The females of all deer, except the caribou, have no antlers. Their foreheads are smooth, and their sensitive ears expressive, standing upright and twitching at the slightest sound. The males, called bucks, have powerful antlers, which they use to defend themselves and to battle one another during mating season. On their foreheads are two permanent bony structures, and from these each year a new pair of solid bone antlers grows after the old pair is shed. The first year there is a single spike, and for the next few years often another branch, or tine, is added, until the buck matures with a huge spread, or rack, of antlers. In old age, the antlers begin to dwindle. The bone looks aged, there are fewer tines, and the structure is smaller than when the buck was in his prime. The exact shapes vary with the species of deer, but all antlers make a formidable weapon when the head is lowered for the charge.

Late each winter the antlers are shed and left lying on the ground, where they are chewed by porcupines and other rodents, or sometimes by the deer themselves, providing some of the calcium necessary for growth. Shortly after the shedding, new antlers start to grow from the permanent bases. At first these are just knobs of flesh, covered with hair, but as they lengthen and spread out to their full size, they harden into bone. Even at full growth, the antlers are still covered with short fur, called velvet. If you walk quietly through a woods in spring, you may be lucky enough to watch a lone buck rub his antlers against a tree trunk in an effort to shed the velvet.

In the East you will be most likely to see the white-tailed or Virginia deer. They thrive in woodlands near clearings or open fields, frequently browsing in thickly populated places. Since colonial times, more and more land has been cleared for farms and towns, and that has created perfect habitats for deer. And with no natural enemies, such as mountain lions and wolves, the deer populations are growing so fast that many deer face starvation unless they move into cornfields and orchards and browse in suburban gardens. Deer are strong, fast swimmers, and they do not hesitate to cross large lakes and rivers in search of food.

Where the trees and undergrowth bordering a mountain lake are neatly and evenly cut around the water's edge, it is a sure sign that deer have come out on the ice in winter to feed on evergreen branches as high as they could reach. All deer live entirely on plants and eat about every kind, though they prefer tender new shoots, coming out at dusk to feast on all young plants, flowers, vegetables, or fruits. Like cows, camels, sheep, and other herd animals, deer are ruminants. They take a bite of food, chew it briefly before swallowing, and bring up a partly digested cud later to chew at their leisure. For browsing or grazing animals, this kind of feeding is a protection of sorts because they can grab a bite and run if they sense danger.

The most common type of western deer is the mule deer. These are a little larger and stronger than the white-tailed, and more wary of humans, probably only because they happen to live on open plains and foothills of mountains, where there are fewer people. The rump of the mule deer is white. The short tail is also white, but with a black tip. It always hangs down and is not raised as a signal flag, as with the white-tailed deer. The mule deer's ears are larger — hence the name — and the antlers are forked close to the head, whereas the antlers of the white-tailed have only one main branch. Most of the year mule deer travel in small bands, but in the winter they gather in large herds, seeking low pastures and wooded sloped hills, which protect them from the snow.

Everywhere in this country, deer have been protected by law so they wouldn't be hunted to extermination, as the bison nearly were. But quite the opposite has happened, and rather than fewer numbers, there are so many deer that thousands starve to death each winter. Some people favor feeding the deer, but that's a temporary answer, which doesn't solve the big problem of huge numbers of deer looking for food in smaller and smaller territories. Many people hate the idea of hunting deer, but without any natural predators, there may be no other solution. Deer killed by hunters at least supply meat for the hunters' families. Deer killed by cars serve no purpose, and often people lose their lives in those crashes as well. Communities and scientists are working hard to find answers to these problems.

If you are hunting deer with your camera, or are just walking through a woods, you may stumble across a fawn, but do not pet it or pick it up. The mother deer is probably feeding nearby. Don't try to own a deer. You could pen a fawn and raise it, but the end would be certain sadness for both you and the deer. A grown deer would be miserable fenced in a small area. A need to roam freely is part of its nature, and if it feels confined, it will fight for freedom. Your once gentle fawn, when grown, might turn on you and demand its rights. Even if you were lucky and were not injured by your deer, you would feel like a jailer, building the fence higher and higher as the fawn grew.

Nor can you raise a fawn in captivity and then let it loose when it becomes restless. This would be a sure quick death for the animal, because your protection and care would prevent it from learning to use its instincts for flight and self-preservation. If by remote chance you do find an orphan fawn, and you are certain that the doe is dead and will not come back looking for her baby, call a conservation officer, the humane society, or an animal rehabilitation center. If you live in a remote area where no one is close enough to provide immediate help, you may, as a last resort, take the orphan fawn home. Keep it warm, and bottle-feed it with warm, sweetened whole milk. But in order to obey the law and for the sake of the fawn, you must get in touch with the game warden in your district or the county agent as soon as possible. Best of all, you will have the satisfaction of knowing you have saved an animal's life.

The animals described in this chapter are just a few of the wild creatures around you. There are sure to be many others, and if they interest you, you'll find it easy to learn about them. Develop the habit of walking quietly and noticing little signs. Learn to detect tracks: the human-baby look of the raccoon's dainty pawprints or the line in a dirt path that's been left by the dragging tail of an opossum. Learn which animals hop and which walk as carefully as a cat. Your eye will become quick to pick out the nesting places and feeding grounds and other signs of life. It won't be long before you'll be able to say what kind of animal has passed by without even seeing it. Perhaps this sort of pet, which you can watch and learn to understand, but never own, isn't the most compelling for you. That's all right. The main thing is to be aware of all sorts of creatures, from the tiniest insect up, and to know that each has its place and purpose and that we do not live on this earth alone.

7. Farm Animals

THE dictionary will tell you that a pet is "an animal kept to play with." This book is trying to tell you that to enjoy an animal, you have to know it well enough to play with it in a way it understands and finds natural. You must not force it, but adapt yourself to it. The better you treat your pet, which means the more you suit your treatment of it to its nature, the more pleasure you will have, because it will trust you more and behave more naturally. And that will also be more interesting. No person or animal is at its best when frightened, hungry, or uncomfortable.

This doesn't mean you can't train your pet or discipline it, but only that you do so in the right way, depending on the kind of animal you have. An untrained horse is of no use to anyone. An untrained dog is no pleasure to itself or anyone else. Just don't expect the same kind of pleasure from every kind of animal, any more than you'd expect the same sort of companionship from your parents that you have with your best friends at school.

Farm animals are short-term pets. A baby pig that you

raise on a bottle is one of the most entertaining pets you could possibly have. If one morning you are late with its mash breakfast, your whole family will be startled by piercing, angry squeals. Enjoy a young pig while you can, because when she grows into a sow, she will also have outgrown you to some extent. She'll go into the pigpen with the rest of her kind, and from then on as she grows, you'll be proud that your care has produced a fine animal, which will raise more pigs and eventually go for prime meat.

If you are going to have farm animals, develop a farmer's attitude toward them. Enjoy treating them well and getting them to trust you, but understand that this good care serves a purpose. The best care produces the best and most profitable animal. Besides balanced food and clean and adequate living space, an animal thrives on gentle treatment and learns to take necessary handling by humans as a matter of course. If you are raising an animal for show, your chances in the ring are far better if your animal knows you and is content to let you lead it or show it off in whatever position is most becoming.

If you are going to have a farm pet, you are probably living in the country or the suburbs, and the best way for you to find out about animal care is to join a 4-H club. As a 4-H member, your goal will be to care for an animal entirely yourself. It will be your own project, but you will have the help of an expert who can answer your questions and show you how to find out what you need to know.

You must be at least ten years old to join a 4-H club, but even if you are younger, you can take the first steps toward joining by going to your county headquarters and talking to the people there. Tell them what kind of animal you want to raise, and they can give you some information and arrange for you to talk to a 4-H leader.

This book will tell you something about the fun, profit, and knowledge you can gain from making special pets of some kinds of farm animals. For the selection, care, breeding, and marketing of those animals or their produce, you should turn to the valuable information that your state and federal Departments of Agriculture and your 4-H club can provide.

CHICKENS

If you are going to raise chickens, the first thing to decide is whether you want their eggs or their meat. Collecting and selling eggs might be the best choice unless you or someone in your family knows how to butcher chickens and prepare them for sale. In any case, be businesslike in your dealings. Be reliable in delivering the quantity you have promised and expect to get the current prices. You don't want favors — you just want to supply a real need.

Keep accurate and constant accounts, so that you know where you stand. Keep a chart showing the amount you pay for feed and the amount you take in for each dozen of eggs or for meat. The difference between these two figures will be your loss or gain after you have paid off the amount you invested in the chickens, their housing, and equipment. Even if you give rather than sell eggs or meat to your own family, keep track of the amount and figure it into your accounts. If you work and manage well, you will learn enough about chickens to enjoy caring for them.

If you don't live on a farm that already has chickens, you can ask your county agent or 4-H leader about where to buy baby chicks, what to feed them, and the kind of housing they will need. However you raise chickens, be sure at some time to encourage a broody hen and enjoy the great fun of watching her raise a family. She will make it plain when she's ready to set. She will be so determined and cross if you interfere that you'll have no chance of misunderstanding. Give her a secluded nest by herself, and she will do the rest.

Fertile eggs hatch in exactly twenty-one days, so make sure that your hen doesn't start incubating until the whole clutch is laid, so they all have an even start. If you slip a glass egg into the nest, the hen will be happy until you have as many eggs under her as she can comfortably cover, perhaps from ten to fifteen. She won't care if they are not all her own eggs. She will sit in pleased contentment, both day and night, with one single purpose, that of keeping the eggs warm. Of her own accord, she will get off the nest for water and food, and these should always be close at hand.

If your hen is familiar with you, and therefore gentle, she may let you watch the hatching of the eggs. When the eggs begin to crack, you'll see the tiny bills, each with its temporary point called an egg tooth, peck their way out of the shells, and you can hear the chicks' first faint peeps.

The chicks need no food for the first twenty-four hours. But when they are ready to eat, the hen will leave the nest, walking about and clucking so that they will follow her. Chicks become imprinted on the first moving object they see after hatching. If a chick sees you before it sees its mother, for example, it will follow you everywhere. Don't let this happen, because the chick has lessons to learn from its mother. This imprinting is nature's way of making sure that young birds stay close to the mother and learn from her example how to peck and scratch for food. Like all birds, chickens have no teeth, so they need to swallow bits of gravel and small pebbles along with their food. The stones stay in the bird's gizzard, where they help grind corn and other hard grains.

The other hens will seldom bother the new chicks, unless your space is too crowded. The mother hen watches out for her chicks, calling them to her at night, and gathering them under her wings even in daytime when she senses danger. If a hawk or other predator should try to attack the chicks, the hen will defend them fiercely, and the whole flock will set up a squawking you can hear from quite a distance. Chickens "talk" a lot and have a wide range of tones. You will learn to understand the cackle of accomplishment after an egg is laid, the low pleased clucks of pleasure at finding food, and lots of other sounds.

DUCKS

All domestic ducks are believed to have descended from the wild mallard, although their shapes and colors are now distinct from those of the mallard. The eleven standard

American breeds are divided into three classes. In the meat class, the white Peking, which originated in China, is by far the most practical. The ducks used most often for egg production are called runners. They are tall and thin and of various colors. The ornamental classes are not used commercially. The crested white and black East India ducks, for example, are rare and difficult to raise, and in spite of their trimmings, they are no more attractive and appealing than an ordinary barnyard duck.

Sometimes city children are given ducklings at Easter time, which does not always work out well for the ducks. But if you live in the country or you have a large backyard in the suburbs, you may want to raise a duckling as a pet — or, better still, two for company. When the ducklings grow up, you need not put them in a barnyard if it's all right with your family. The ducks will continue to enjoy your attentions and walk around the yard as if they owned it. At mealtime they may come to the door, quacking their demands for dinner. Any other animals in your yard will soon learn to keep their distance. Maybe your cat or dog can make friends with them, but the ducks will always appear to have the upper hand.

Swimming keeps ducks healthy and clean. That's what their webbed feet are for, and they enjoy being in the water. So before you decide to keep ducks, make sure you can provide a place for them to swim if it is at all possible.

Ducks have such a satisfied air about them that even if you don't want to single out one or two for special pets, you might enjoy raising a small flock for eggs and meat. Besides your pleasure in watching them, you can also manage so they will be self-supporting or even profitable.

Ducks always lay their eggs in the morning. If allowed to roam, they may carelessly drop eggs anywhere in the yard, or even in the water. So in order not to lose any eggs, confine your ducks at night and don't let them out until mid-morning.

PIGEONS

Pigeons are, in some ways, more like caged birds than like farmyard poultry. They have a lot of individuality and definite personalities. They are interesting to watch and easy to care for and train. Since pigeon parents do all the work of raising their young, you will want to keep your pigeons in pairs and learn their nesting habits. Given the right care, each pair can raise about fourteen squabs, or babies, a year, if they are allowed to. But if you don't want to be overrun with pigeons, it's a good idea to replace newly laid eggs with glass or wooden eggs, because the female will be content to sit on the fake eggs for eighteen days.

Pigeons need a lot of flying space and uncrowded, clean living quarters. A protected, draft-proof loft eight feet square is room enough for ten or twelve pairs of pigeons. It should have sand on the floor, which you can rake and keep clean and dry. You'll need individual, comfortably wide perches. Leading from the loft, there should be a wire flight-enclosure outside, measuring eight feet wide and at least twelve feet long and eight feet high.

Even if you are going to let your pigeons fly loose part of the time, you'll want this flight space to confine them when you wish to. You can build swinging trapdoors, adjusting them so the birds can come in but can't push their way out again. The loft can be built on top of a barn, as a separate building on the ground, or anywhere you find convenient. Many cities allow people to build pigeon lofts on rooftops.

You can exercise your birds by waving a pole to make them fly outside. They have a strong sense of their home site, and they will circle around and always come back to the quarters, once they are used to them. Never feed your pigeons before you exercise them. If they learn that they will get fed when they come home, the whole flock will fly to you on call. The only danger in letting them loose is from hawks or accidents. Banding can't protect a pigeon from natural enemies, but a banded pigeon is protected by law in many communities and must be returned to you. Be sure to band your pigeons if you are going to let them fly free.

Banding is useful identification at home, too. All squabs that you want to keep should be banded when they are about five days old. It's easy to slip a numbered metal ring on the bird's leg by pressing together the three front toes and sliding the band over these, then up over the fourth toe. To keep your nesting records straight, you can band again after your pigeons have mated, giving each pair its own color band. You'll need records to show the number and condition of squabs each pair raises, because you'll want to keep only those that are healthiest.

Pigeons usually mate for life. A mated couple seem devoted to each other and jealous of interference. If you crowd your birds, there is likely to be domestic trouble among pairs, but with enough space, each pair will be content in its chosen nest, which the male selects. Your pigeons will be more contented if you breed all the pairs at the same time, so that all are raising their young at once. Each pair should have two adjoining nests, because they like to start a new family before the first is ready to fly. A nesting box a foot square is about the right size. It should be open at the front, with a porch for landing, and a sill two inches high to hold in the young birds. The pigeons will build their own nest, if you provide the materials for them. At a farm supply store you can buy nesting bowls the right size and shape to put into each nest box. If you put long, soft pine needles, tobacco stems, dry straw, or hay in the nesting section of your loft, the birds will use it. Usually the cock carries the material and the hen arranges it in the nesting bowl. When the nest is ready, the hen usually lays one egg late in the afternoon. Shortly after noon, two days later, she will lay another egg. This is not absolutely the rule. Sometimes a weak hen may lay only one egg, and occasionally a hen will lay three eggs. The cock will sit on the nest from about ten in the morning until noon, and then the hen comes to the nest. They bow to each other and coo before they change places, and the hen settles on the eggs, while the cock has his turn at food and exercise.

When the eggs hatch, eighteen days after the first one was laid, both parents begin to feed them pigeon "milk." It's not really milk, but a liquid that forms in a pigeon's crop and is regurgitated into the wide-open mouths of the young squabs. Adult pigeons make this milk only during nesting time, and it is ready about two days before the eggs hatch. After a few days, the pigeon parents add small amounts of grain to the milk, gradually adding more grain and lessening the amount of milk. After a week of this diet, the squabs can digest a diet of only grain. It's a hard job for pigeons to carry enough grain to the nest as is needed for their young for four or five weeks. But by that time the squabs start exploring on their own, and when they are about six weeks old, they are on their own and ready to live in a separate loft.

When your new squabs leave the box for good, brush out the old nest and sterilize the box. You don't want to take a chance of passing along any parasites or disease-causing organisms that might be lurking there.

Two weeks after the eggs hatched, your pigeons will probably want to start their second nest. Discourage this for a week or two so they won't wear themselves out with too much work. The cock will assume most of the responsibility of the second nest, but the hen will help. Both parents will take care of their two families as long as they are needed.

Pigeons will exhaust themselves if they are allowed to raise young the year round. It is far better to separate the hens from the cocks when the molting season starts, around the first of August. Let them rest for several months, and don't start the breeding until February. When you are keeping squabs to increase your flock, be careful not to let them breed too young. Separate males and females when they are fully matured at six months. It's not easy to tell the hen from the cock, but you can learn to do so. The hen waddles when she walks, holding her head and tail high. She is usually a bit smaller than the male, and has a more slender neck and head. The cock struts when he walks, and drags his tail on the ground. He coos in a bossy, aggressive way. If they are allowed to choose their own mates, brothers and sisters seldom pair off, but if you want to be certain to avoid inbreeding, read the leg bands, which will tell you which pigeons are related. If you want to mate a particular pair, you can confine them together until you are sure they have taken a fancy to each other, but during this time, be sure to let them fly a while each day. After they have accepted each other and become a mated couple, let them fly with the other pigeons. They will stay with their chosen mates as long as their quarters are not too crowded.

Never leave an unmated pigeon with pairs, because it will try to steal a mate. If a pigeon dies, take its mate out of the general loft until you find another pigeon willing to accept it as a mate. It's not easy to catch a pigeon in a net. The best way to catch one without a lot of flapping and fuss it to darken the loft, then use a flashlight to find the one you want. Grasp the pigeon in one hand, with your palm under its breast, its head toward your wrist, so that you can hold its legs between your middle and index fingers. Hold it securely, but don't squeeze it, and it will settle down and feel safe.

It wouldn't be practical to keep all the squabs your pigeons raise, but you may want to keep a few of the best ones. The record of how many each pair raises a year will tell you which parents raise the strongest, healthiest young, and these are the ones you will want to keep and continue breeding. Since your pigeons do so much work in raising their own

families, your part is to feed and water them well and to keep
them clean and exercised. Always keep plenty of fresh water
in a drinking dish that has a canopy to keep dirt and debris
from falling into the water. You can buy this kind of equipment in a farm supply store. You can also buy warmers that
keep the water from freezing in cold weather, or you can put
a lightbulb on a stand beneath the water dish. It's interesting
to watch pigeons drink, because they bend their heads low
and suck up the water instead of throwing back their heads
into the air to let it trickle down, as chickens and other
birds do.

When the weather isn't too cold, give pigeons a chance to
take a bath in a big, shallow pan. They love to splash and
preen and generally enjoy themselves. Throw out the dirty
bathwater when they are finished bathing, because you don't
want the pigeons to drink it.

Feed your pigeons twice a day, morning and evening,
from a trough the birds can reach comfortably, but not stand
in. Give them extra rations while they are feeding their
young. Figure on about one hundred pounds of grain every
year for each pair. You can buy pigeon grain ready mixed, or
you can mix your own, using 30 percent uncracked corn, 20
percent each kafir and red wheat, 25 percent Canadian peas,
and 5 percent barley, hulled oats, rice, or some similar grain.
Hemp or millet seed can be added once a week or so. Of
course your pigeons need grit, as do all birds, because they
have no teeth but rather rely on grit in their gizzard to grind
their food. So buy a finely ground pigeon mineral (also called
health grit) that contains salt, and plan on using about five
pounds of this a year for each pair of birds.

Pigeons are the descendants of rock doves, which were domesticated thousands of years ago. A sultan of Baghdad even had a pigeon postal system 3,100 years ago for his personal use. Today there are about 250 breeds of pigeons to choose from, and mixed breeds, often called clinkers, are popular, too. A breed called Carneaux is raised for food, as are white and silver kings. But fancy breeds like the fantails and pouters are raised to compete in shows. Homers, or homing pigeons, are raised to race or carry messages. There are many clubs and associations of pigeon fanciers that can help you choose the best breed for you to raise.

A built-in urge or instinct makes a homing pigeon head for its own loft, just as instinct makes birds find their way back home after migrating long distances. When pigeons are being trained to race, they are taken a short distance, perhaps half a mile from their home, and released. They circle around, but they always fly back to their loft. Gradually they are released farther and farther away from home, which is how they learn to fly longer and longer distances. For its first races, a pigeon may be taken in a basket a hundred miles from home and released to fly back to its loft. Not only can these birds *find* home, but they will fly through storms and even hawk attacks to get there. They can't, however, fly out from their home loft to another destination then back home again, because they wouldn't have any way of knowing where that destination was. They're strictly one-way flyers: toward home. A thousand miles is considered a very long flight for a pigeon, but one United States Army Signal Corps pigeon flew 2,300 miles, which was a record for a wartime carrier pigeon flight.

PIGS

Sometimes people keep a pig as a house pet, but once their little pink piglet has become a huge grown-up pig, they decide that pigs are more contented outdoors. Miniature Vietnamese potbellied pigs were especially popular as house pets for a while because they are so cute and they don't get as large as other breeds. But if you live on a farm or have room to raise a pig in your yard, you'll come to understand why these friendly, intelligent animals like to be outdoors, especially where there is mud. Pigs have few sweat glands. They overheat easily, so they must cool off in water or wallow in mud.

There are many breeds to choose from, such as the black Berkshires, all-white Chester Whites, or black-and-white Herefords. Ask a farmer for advice on choosing and feeding a pig, or read as much as you can about pigs before you bring one home.

By the time baby pigs are three weeks old, you can start helping the sow take care of them. Pick one up to take a good look at its funny blunt nose and beautiful long eyelashes. As you watch the whole litter nosing around the pen, you can see how their barrel-shaped little bodies rock from side to side as they walk. Their short legs may fool you into thinking they can't run fast, but they can, turning and dodging suddenly to avoid being caught. Even if you've chosen a piglet three weeks old, it should stay with its mother for eight weeks. Then it will be ready to wean and to live in its own pen. Pigs like company, so if you can manage, it's a good idea to keep two pigs together.

By eight weeks, a piglet will weigh thirty-five or forty pounds, and its main pleasure will be rooting and eating. Pigs have an amazing sense of smell, which helps them dig out root vegetables and other good things to eat. Your job will be to make sure the pig is clean and comfortable, with plenty of the right food, because it has a lot of growing to do. In only six months, you'll hardly recognize the piglet you chose, because it will weigh about two hundred pounds.

Feeding your pig twice a day will hardly be a chore because it's such fun to see how much the pig enjoys it. If you keep more than one pig, they will grunt and shove one another out of the way to greet you. Use a V-shaped trough that is long enough and of a height they can reach but not climb into. You can probably get a 4-H club bulletin that will show you how to build a trough, or you can buy one at a farm supply store. Some people put the trough close to a low fence around the pigpen, and instead of going inside the pen, they dump the moistened food from the feed pail so that it splashes all over the pigs as they crowd around the trough. The pigs may not mind, but if *you* are sloppy, don't say it's the pigs that are dirty. It's just as easy for you to go into the pen or use a scuttle-shaped pail and aim the food where it's supposed to go. Between feedings, pigs enjoy a friendly rub on the ear, along with an apple or other treat.

DAIRY CALVES

If you are planning to raise a dairy cow, start with the best animal you possibly can, whether you buy her from a local dairy or choose a calf born on your own farm. As soon as the calf is born, you don't need to do anything because her mother, the dam, does the best job. She will lick the calf thoroughly, which not only cleans the calf up but also increases the newborn's circulation and helps her breathing. If the weather is cold, you can help dry the calf by rubbing her with a clean piece of burlap. In any case, wipe the mucus off her nose so she can breathe more easily.

The first few days after a calf is born, the dam's milk is different from regular milk, and it is essential in giving the calf a good start. It's called colostrum, which is high in vitamin A and contains other ingredients that are necessary to start the calf's digestive system working and to protect her from disease. But do not let the calf drink from her mother as soon as she is born. That can complicate milking the mother later, and of course, that's why she's in the dairy — to be milked. Instead, the dairy owner will milk the mother by hand while she is busy and distracted cleaning the calf. After that, the cow is milked just enough to feed the calf, about one quart at a time, twice a day for three days, so the calf gets that all-important colostrum from a bottle. On the third day, the dam goes back to the regular dairy milking routine, and the calf is started on milk replacer, which can be bought at a farm store. Be particular to scour your pails after every feeding and keep them in a clean place. The milk should be warmed. You can use a nipple pail, hung on the side of the calf pen at a height the calf can comfortably reach.

After a week of so of drinking from a nipple, your calf can be taught to drink from a pail. The longer you wait, the more difficult this will be. You start by getting some milk on your fingers and letting the calf suck your fingers. While the calf is contentedly doing this, you lower your hand into the milk pail. Soon you can remove your fingers, because you have tricked the calf into drinking for herself. "Of course they're not that dumb," says one farmer who has raised many calves. "It goes in fits and starts with lots of splashing of milk. But once they have learned, they can't wait to get into the pail and drink, and they usually don't want to give up when the pail is empty. Hang on to the pail while they are drinking, because the little tykes have an instinct to 'bunt,' which seems the natural way to release the milk in the udder."

After ten days or two weeks, it's time to start your calf on solid food. Because a calf still likes to suck on your fingers, you can put some starter grain on your fingers so it gets into the calf's mouth, and soon she will be eating from the feed box. In addition to grain, keep feeding your calf milk replacer until she is two months old.

Build a hayrack in the pen, and each day put in a little of the best leafy legume hay you can get. By the time your calf is a month old, she will have four incisor teeth and will be able to easily manage hay. Steadily increase the amount of hay, giving the calf as much as she demands. Eventually it will be your calf's main food. Always leave fresh, clean drinking water where the calf can reach it anytime.

It is important to keep each calf separate from other calves for two months, because they need this time to get over the urge to suck. When they are together, a calf will suck on another calf, and later on that can cause a disease called mastitis. Sometimes a calf will even suck on another calf's ear, which isn't healthy either. Keep new calves out of the cow barn where, with their immature immune systems, they can pick up pneumonia and other diseases. And be sure they have fresh, clean air. It doesn't matter if it's cold, as long as the calves are out of the wind.

While your calf is still very little and you are feeding her milk, you will become good friends. Don't let this friendship slide as the calf gets bigger. If you know your animal well, you can watch her condition intelligently. You'll know when she is hungry or not feeling well. Put a halter and lead on the calf while she is still small, which will be useful if you ever want to show your calf.

You can make a well-fitting, adjustable rope halter that won't rub the calf's face. First tie the calf to a stake so she will know that the rope won't break or come off. A few short, daily proofs of this is enough. Then teach her to lead. In a show, the lead rope must come out under the jaw on the left side. You walk on the left side of the calf, and slightly ahead. You can begin to train your calf to do this as soon as she has outgrown the darting and balking of the first few sessions.

Brush your calf every day. After she is on pasture, bring her in now and then to look her over and groom her. If you keep the hooves trimmed and filed comfortably, your calf will look better and feel better.

If you have a purebred calf, you will probably want to register her, both for your own satisfaction and to establish her value. You'll need to keep exact records of her birth date — called freshening — and the names of the sire and the dam. Your particular animal must be identified by ear brands, photographs, or color charts. Each breeding association has slightly different regulations. It is worthwhile to get a form from an association, fill it out carefully, and pay the registration. Even if you are not going to register or show your calf, it is wise always to keep complete and accurate records. Your pet may be a valuable animal when she grows up. She may remain on your farm for years, supplying milk and giving you other calves to raise. And she will always be docile and easy to manage, because of your good care.

BEEF STEER

If you are going to raise a baby beef steer (or castrated bull calf) until it is big enough to be sold for beef, you will want to get the best animal you can to work on. When you show him in the ring, he will be up against real competition. Win or lose, you will want to have an animal you can be proud of.

First find out about the various breeds of beef cattle. Farmers in your neighborhood will know the breeds that thrive best in your region of the country. Whichever breed you choose, your calf will be the same as range calves of the that breed. But by confining him and giving him individual care and feeding, you will try to produce a heavier, fatter steer that will sell for a better price than a range calf of the same age. Keep careful watch of your animal and see that his growth is steady. Feed balanced rations that produce the best meat, but keep track of the money you spend on feed. It may not be important for you to make a profit on your steer, but neither do you want to have it cost more than you can make when you sell him.

There are some differences between raising a steer and raising a heifer, or female calf. If you get a newborn bull calf, you'd wean him away from his mother and raise him in the same way as you would a dairy calf. But the most common practice is to buy a seven-month-old steer that has just been weaned. Then it's a matter of feeding, grooming, and training him.

If your bull calf is left with his mother, his main food is milk for four or five weeks, but you can begin to introduce leafy legume hay and grain by putting it in a "creep." A creep is a cool, dry, clean place that the calf can get into but the cows cannot, which you can build in a comfortable, shady part of the pasture. Don't be surprised if the mothers stand outside the creep and bellow until their calves come out. Or you can use a combination of methods, putting the calf with his mother twice a day to suck and the rest of the time keeping him separate, giving him grain, all the hay he can eat, and plenty of water. Always make sure your calf has fresh, clean water and a salt lick he can easily reach.

Your goal is the comfort and contentment of your calf, which will help him become a fine animal. As he grows, he needs sunshine, fresh air, and an open shed to protect him during the hot part of the day. This shed can lead into a well-fenced yard or small pasture, where he can move around and get some exercise. If you have a box stall in a well-ventilated barn, he will be well off there, as long as he is let outdoors for a while each day or is turned out at night. Wherever he lives, his quarters must be kept clean and the manure removed every day. Clean, dry bedding is important because he needs to lie down and rest if he is to grow as much as possible. If flies bother him, he will fret and lose weight, so spray him with a safe insecticide, and hang a piece of burlap where he can walk under it to brush off the flies. Like any other animal, a calf will be lonesome by himself. He will thrive better with company. If you can't keep more than one calf in the pen, make sure his enclosure is near other cattle, so he can at least see them.

Your beef calf must be castrated as soon as he is born. It's a simple operation that will not bother him seriously if is properly done by a veterinarian or an experienced farmer. It should be done in cool weather, before flies are a problem. Never let an uncastrated bull calf run with heifers after he is four months old, because early breeding will retard his development. If you want your calf to be dehorned, have this done soon after the buttons show, when he is about three weeks old.

If your animal is hard to handle, you will have great difficulty with him at a show or even in caring for him at home. A steer is strong and heavy, and you won't be able to manage him unless he is used to you and unafraid of human handling. It's also bad for his development if he's upset. Spend as much time as you can with your calf, and let him get to know you. Put a halter on him when he is little, and teach him to lead as early as possible. He'll be more stubborn if you wait until he is older, bigger, and stronger. If you lead for a while at least three or four times a week and teach him to stop and start, he will be calm and docile. Brush and currycomb him often, too. This not only keeps him clean, but makes him more gentle, too. He will need to look his best at show time, so train him to be so used to handling that he will let you do a good job. Watch his hooves, and trim and rasp them when they need care.

The exact age for showing depends on the rules of the breed association in your community. Make sure that your steer is registered and entered properly, with a record of his exact date of birth if you have it. In a show or at market, steers are usually grouped by age. Calves born between January 1 and April 30 of the current year are called junior calves. Those born from September 1 through December 31 of the previous year are called senior calves. Those born May 1 through August 31 of the previous year are summer yearlings. Show animals are usually yearlings. Calves born after April of the current year are too little to be shown in the fall, when most cattle shows take place. These are the new crop, which you can keep and raise for another year.

SHEEP

If you live on a farm where sheep are raised, you have probably seen a lamb, which needs human help as soon as it is born. You can easily learn to give this help, starting to care for a lamb as a pet when it is small and tottery. Perhaps it will be only a little trembly in the legs, needing you to hold it while it gets the first reviving milk (colostrum) from its mother. Or it might need you to rub its sides to strengthen breathing before you help it to the first milk. Sometimes a winter lamb is chilled. In that case, carry it to a warm room and rub it until it is dry and comfortable. You might even need to hold it for a few minutes in a bath heated to about 100 degrees before you rub it dry. As soon as your lamb seems strong enough, take it back to its mother, and hold it until it starts sucking. If you can't do this, feed it warm milk from a spoon or medicine dropper, using colostrum from the mother.

Though you can raise a lamb entirely by yourself, it is better to keep it with the mother or, if necessary, persuade another ewe to adopt it. The first nuzzling and nursing teaches the mother that this is her baby. If she should reject the lamb or if you are using a different ewe, there are ways to start the suckling. Since sheep first recognize their lambs by smell — later probably by sight as well — rub some of the ewe's milk on her own nose, and also rub it on the lamb. Or use pine tar in the same way.

If, for any reason, adoption does not work, you will find it rewarding to raise the lamb yourself by bottle, although it is a great deal of work. Give colostrum at first, and then use whole cow's milk, heated to body temperature. Buy a lambing nipple, which needs to be strong because your lamb's teeth will come through in a few days. Start out with two or three tablespoons in the bottle at a time. Keep both the bottle and nipple clean and sterile. Feed every two hours, including early in the morning and late at night. Gradually begin to space your feedings further apart, giving a little more each time. Guide yourself by how readily the lamb drinks and how comfortable it seems. Eventually you will need to feed only three times a day, giving a quart of milk each day. In about four weeks, you can start feeding the lamb a little leafy hay or fine grain, using one third cracked corn or barley, one third rolled oats, and one third even amounts of bran and linseed-oil meal. Continue with the milk as well until the lamb is eating plenty of solid food. By this time you will have a real pet, playful and eager for your attention.

If you don't live on a farm or have no experienced person to give you advice about feeding a lamb, you can get help from the county extension service, a 4-H club, or a veterinarian. An expert can also advise you about necessary procedures such as when to dock the tail of a lamb or when to have a male sheep (called a ram) castrated.

You may want to keep your lamb in the yard, where it will follow you around and ask for petting. Even if you put it in a pasture, the lamb will not forget you but will come bounding up to you on spindly legs. It will push its face into your hand, asking for a rub between the ears or maybe a bit of grain or clover. Slowly it will learn to find most of its food for itself, by cropping the pasture grass. But for the first few months, you ought not to let the lamb depend on browsing alone unless your pasture is especially good.

Sheep need to roam and so need strong fences. They will squeeze through ordinary wire and jump over most stone walls. Rams are great fence busters, but they can be contained by one of the new plastic mesh electric fencing materials, which are available in several heights. This kind of fence is ideal for moving from one pasture to another. Sheep prefer high, dry pasture, but they also enjoy a variety of plants. They crop very close to the ground, and if left too long in the same small area, they will destroy the grass by eating too close to the roots. So use as big a field as possible for your lamb, or use a movable fence, and shift it often. Any kind of dry land will do. If you fence your lamb on uncut grass, it will act as an efficient lawn mower. It will also need drinking water and a salt lick. After your lamb is about three months old, it no longer needs special feeding if the pasture is plentiful, and it can join the regular flock.

By late winter or early spring, your pet will be fully grown and its fleece will be thick enough for shearing. You can have it sheared with the rest of the flock at the proper time, and sell the wool. The price you receive will depend on the care you have given, as well as on the quality of wool the animal grows.

GOATS

Of all farm animals, a goat probably makes the most success-ful pet. For one thing, you can keep it for a longer time. Even after a doe, or female, is fully grown and you are milking her, she will remain your pet. She will never lose her inquisitive spirit nor her apparent sense of humor. The old joke about goats eating tin cans was invented because goats nose over everything they see and eat so many different things.

Occasionally a buck, or male, preferably castrated, can be kept for a pet. He can be taught to pull a cart, but he's likely to be rambunctious. If you have a doe — also called a nanny goat — you can supply your whole family with milk and can take over the care of the kids when they are very young. Then you will have not one but several pets, because usually twins are born, often triplets, and even quadruplets now and then. For the first three days, they must have colostrum, so either leave them with the mother to suckle for this short time or milk the doe and give the colostrum from a bottle. Then put the doe out to pasture and bottle-feed your pets entirely. At first, give each kid about two pints a day, in three feedings. The kids are tiny, and their baby hair is soft, so you will enjoy holding them in your lap while they drink from the bottle. Very soon they will learn to drink from a pan.

Steadily increase the quantity you give until each is get-ting three pints a day. By the time the kids are three weeks old, their digestive systems are ready for some solid food. Start them on leafy hay and a small amount of grain of the sort you would give a young calf. Soon they will be browsing for themselves.

The final weaning must be gradual. Plan to have your goats weaned by the time they are five months old, or even younger if your milk supply is short. By this time you'll change the grain to a dairy growing mixture, using about one pound a day for each kid. They should either be grazing on good grass or be given all the fresh green roughage they can eat. They must have clean drinking water, of course. If your grain doesn't contain minerals, add salt and ground bonemeal to the mixture.

For the first few days, your kids should be kept quietly in a clean pen, away from drafts. After that, if the weather is mild, you can let them outside for sun and exercise. During the earliest weeks, they will be at their liveliest, ready for play and lots of attention. Fence them in a small, grassy enclosure, with an open shed for shelter and shade. Build a low platform that they can climb and jump on. You may not even need to build a ramp up to the platform because goats are excellent climbers and jumpers, and you'll often find them standing on top of their shelter. You'll need high wire fences to keep them in. But they are good tightrope walkers, too, so be sure the fence supports are on the outside of the fence, or they will climb out.

Goats are curious and acrobatic. They would like to have your whole yard to play in, but you need to keep them out of mischief. Your family and neighbors would not be pleased to see your goat jump onto the roof of a car, prancing on its shiny surface with sharp hoofs, then leap into a flower bed to taste some juicy buds. As a way of keeping goats out of trouble, you may want to put collars on them and teach them to lead, but you must keep them tethered or in a roomy pen. If you tie your goats, move them often to whatever spot needs mowing, because they do a good job of browsing. Or you can put them in a pasture, where they can graze as cows do. If you supply extra food — hay, silage, grain, and root crops — you can use a rocky section of land that's unsuited to cattle.

By the time a goat is fifteen months old, it is ready to breed. The gestation period — the time from breeding to birth — is about five months. After the kids are born, you can start milking the doe. Ask someone to teach you how to do this. Since the teats are short, you probably won't use your whole hand as you would for a cow but will "strip" with your thumb and forefinger. Wash your hands before you start, and wipe off the teats. It may take some practice to learn to be gentle and thorough, but the goat will soon stand quietly, learning that she is more comfortable after milking. Milk her at least twice a day — and even better, three times — at regular hours. It's not convenient to reach down to milk such a small animal, so build a platform about two feet high for the goat to stand on while you milk her. Either tie her or use a stanchion. If she is uneasy at first, soothe her with a bit of grain. Milk in a clean, odorless place, and keep all the milking utensils scoured. Cool the milk rapidly to prevent the growth of bacteria.

Goat's milk is as nourishing as cow's milk. The content is much the same, but there is far less fat in goat's milk, and the fat globules are smaller and finer, which makes the milk eas-

ier to digest. Some invalids, babies, and people who are allergic to cow's milk or find it hard to digest can often drink goat's
milk. The cream rises to the top slowly and can't be skimmed
off as easily, but you can get it out in a separator. Goat's milk
is almost pure white, with a good flavor. The butter is white,
and not as tasty as cow's butter. But delicious cheese can be
made from goat's milk.

The amount of milk each doe gives varies enormously. If
you weigh the milk of each animal separately and find an
average of nine pounds a day, you will be getting a good yield.
The lactation period — the length of time a goat gives
milk — varies, nine to ten months being what you strive for.
The production depends on the individual animal and on the
care and feeding your give her. It also depends on the breeding of your goat.

People in Europe and other parts of the world have paid
more attention to the breeding of goats than we have in this
country and so have developed many breeds that are high
milk-producers. By crossing some of these imported breeds
with our common American goat, breeders can improve the
quality of their herds. French Alpine and Anglo-Nubian Mal-
tese goats are used in this country, but the two most important foreign breeds are from Switzerland: the white Saanens,
and the brown Toggenburgs.

Before you decide to keep a goat, talk to people who already own one. Find out if your community has any laws
about keeping goats. Make a list of the chores you'll have to
do each day to take care of a goat, and make sure you know
where you will keep this pet, what you will feed it, where you
will store the feed, and where you will milk it.

8.   Ponies and Saddle Horses

A PONY or a horse is more than a pet. So if, as we've discussed, it is important to select the right sort of pet for yourself, it is absolutely essential, if you are going to have a horse, to choose one that is right for you.

By the time you have decided to have a horse of your own, you probably know a fair amount about horses. Maybe you've taken riding lessons, or perhaps you live on a farm or ranch. Keeping a horse or a pony is expensive, and it will require a lot of your time. It's not the kind of animal to buy on a whim. The decision to own a horse is very much a family matter. There will be many things to consider. Is it healthy? Is it the right size, the right breed? Where will you keep it? Are you going to use it for ranch work, pleasure riding, competition, or showing? Whatever horse you choose, if you enjoy riding it and you can manage it, then for you it is the best horse in the world and that's the way you will feel toward it. If you go on the theory that the right horse for you is a good horse, you won't be far wrong. On the other hand,

Secretariat and Man o' War were good horses, but for you, they would have been poor horses.

PONIES

Ponies are small horses, and so are more comfortable for a child to ride. There are several breeds of ponies, just as there are breeds of horses. They are ridden, cared for, and fed in the same way as horses, and, also like horses, some of the best ponies to ride or drive are not purebred but a mixture of breeds.

Technically the top height for a pony is 14.2 hands. A hand, the unit of measure for horses, is equal to four inches, about the width of a man's hand. So 14.2 hands is equivalent to four feet, ten inches. Measurement is taken from the highest part of the horse at the back of its neck, called the withers, in a straight line to the ground. Lots of horses, which overreach the height requirement, are, however, called ponies. We speak of polo ponies, cow ponies, and hackney ponies. The pit ponies once used in mines were generally small, but where high tunnels were dug in mines, some of these ponies were as large as draft horses.

A regular small pony, whether Shetland, a larger Welsh pony, or a native of Chincoteague Island, can be a playmate as well as a mount. If you spend time with your pony when you're not riding, it is likely to follow you around as a dog would. Your pony may scratch its forehead on your back, nibble your shirtsleeve, then suddenly neigh and gallop off. It's no trick for a pony to learn to nuzzle into your pocket for a carrot, and it's easy to teach it to come when you whistle if you offer a reward.

Once you have learned to be comfortable in the saddle, to have a natural balance, and to control the pony with your legs and hands, the pony is going to make you pay attention to what you are doing. If you get sloppy, the pony will realize it right away and play a sudden trick on you. It may pretend to be frightened at a fence post it has seen a million times and shy like a colt. The moment you make the mistake of feeling superior to this kindly pet of yours is the moment the pony may dump you on the ground. Ponies scarcely ever become mean unless they are mistreated. But they can be mischievous. A mount of any size must be continually held to its training by the rider.

If you can control your pony, you will get a better ride than on a larger horse, simply because you fit each other better. Your legs won't stick straight out as they would on a broad-backed horse. Your knees will be in the right spot. Everything will be just right for you, so you can balance comfortably. You and your pony can have a wonderful time practicing until you are an excellent team, with complete understanding of each other. Since you are big enough to control your pony, make sure you do so. It's up to you not to spoil the pony and let it develop any unpopular habits. The pony will enjoy the ride more if it is ridden well and made to go properly, and so will you. While you are not riding, you can play with your pony all you like, and it will be a real pet.

HORSES

After you have been around ponies and horses for a while, you will notice that a really good rider manages to get along nicely with all sorts of horses, even though that person may have favorites. The rider and the horse have respect for each other. An experienced rider will mount a horse that you may have thought was wild because other people have had trouble managing it. That horse will go quietly and well, because the rider knows how to give aids, or directions, so the horse understands what is expected. The same rider will mount a horse that has a reputation as a plug — you may have seen beginners wear their legs out kicking, in an attempt to make such a horse break from a jog to a canter. But with a good rider on its back, that horse will step out smartly at whatever pace is wanted.

HORSE TERMS

The joy of riding a horse that is suited to you is so great that you want to be slow to choose your own. The word *horse* is often used for all ages and sexes, but you will want to be more accurate. A female horse is called a mare. A gelding is a male horse that has been castrated. By far the majority of male riding horses are geldings. This is because stallions — which are also called studs and are males that have not been castrated and so can breed — are usually temperamental. They are more difficult to control than geldings. They will fight each other and be unruly around mares in heat. Racehorses are often stallions, because a large part of their value will be in stud fees after their racing days are over.

A colt is a young male horse, so called until it is four years old, at which time it will be mature and will be spoken of as a gelding or stallion. A filly is a young female horse, so called for the first four years; then she will be called a mare. A foal is a newborn horse of either sex. You will hear of a colt foal, meaning a newborn male, or a filly foal, meaning a newborn female. The word *foal* is used in two other ways. A pregnant mare is said to be in foal, and to give birth is to foal. It is not really all that confusing after you have used the terms a few times.

HORSE BREEDS

The training of a horse and the skill of a rider have a great deal to do with a horse's ability. But the horse's nature is also important. In a general way, breeds of horses have established characteristics, which can be improved on or misused, but not basically changed. Within each breed, inheritance counts heavily. Certain stallions have a particularly strong tendency to pass on characteristics, which is one reason that horse buyers are often interested in bloodlines. Both the stallion and the mare pass on disposition, conformation (build), stamina, and heart. In speaking of the heart of a horse, one means its willingness and courage to do what is asked. A racehorse must have the heart to push itself to the last burst of its speed. A roping horse, trained to a highly specialized skill, must have brains, coordination, and temperament as well as heart.

The Arabian is the oldest known established breed. The type is shown, exactly as it appears today, in an equestrian statuette unearthed in Egypt and dated 2000 B.C. Arabians are speedy, alert, and sensitive, and have great stamina. They are small and short, with one less vertebra than other breeds. Their ears are set on a cleanly shaped head, and there is more width between the eyes than in some other breeds.

Although there are not many purebred Arabian horses in this country or in England, the Arabian bloodline has been powerful in developing our more popular breeds. All Thoroughbreds — which are called hot-blooded, as opposed to cold-blooded horses — are descended from three Arabian stallions: the Darley Arabian, the Godolphin Arabian, and the Byerly Turk. The modern Thoroughbred is the speediest horse ever known, beautifully proportioned, with a long stride and great heart. Sensitive and intelligent, this horse reacts quickly and has a hot temper, characteristics that require an experienced rider. Because of its temperamental reactions, a Thoroughbred can be more difficult to keep, needing great care and good feeding.

Introduction of the hot blood of the Thoroughbred has improved horses of mixed breeds and has helped establish popular breeds. Many of the best cow ponies are part Thoroughbred. The mustang — also known as the Indian pony or Western horse — was never a particular breed but a descendant of Spanish horses brought to this continent during the conquest of Mexico in the early part of the sixteenth century. Before the country was settled, mustangs traveled in wild bands. To survive, they had to be hardy and able to live on range forage in all sorts of weather. Sure-footed and exceptionally agile, they are able to stop on their haunches from a fast run and to turn quickly. These characteristics are necessary in horses used for cattle work or to round up range horses.

Much the same abilities are needed for polo ponies, which are not a breed but a type of small horse suited to specialized training. The quality of both cow ponies and polo ponies improved during the years the army established Thoroughbred stallions throughout the country to be bred to good, sturdy, cold-blooded mares.

Hunters are also not a special breed but a strong, sure-footed type of horse whose powerful haunches make it a good jumper. Usually temperament, fire, and heart are present through Thoroughbred strains, and often a hunter is a purebred Thoroughbred.

A definite and popular breed of American horse, with some Thoroughbred blood, is the quarter horse. This breed was developed in Virginia for quarter-mile racing. The principal sire of the breed was Janus, an English Thoroughbred, with powerful hindquarters, so essential in getting off to a fast start in a short race or in working with stock. Though it does not always have staying power, or the fire and style of the Thoroughbred, it is an excellent utility horse.

Another generally useful breed with some Thoroughbred blood is the American saddle horse. Its light, graceful conformation and precise, stylish gaits have made this breed particularly popular in the show ring. Since it is easy to handle, though spirited, it is also an excellent riding horse. It has been recognized as a distinct breed since 1891, when the American Saddle Horse Breeders Association was founded.

Saddle horses are trained in two ways. Some are trained to do the usual walk, trot, and canter. (The gallop and the canter are the same action, the canter being collected, or held in, and the gallop being extended and faster.) Others are trained to five gaits: the walk, slow gait, trot, rack, and canter. The rack is a rousing gait, seen often in the show ring. Each foot comes down separately in a rapid one-two-three-four beat. It is important — and requires lots of training and skillful riding — to maintain the rack and to keep the horse from breaking into a trot or canter.

The Tennessee walking horse, like other breeds, has a diverse origin, but the definite type was established largely through a single sire. He was a black standardbred trotter of the Hambletonian line named Allan. In turn, his bloodlines included strains of Thoroughbred, American saddle horse, and Morgan. Allan was foaled in Kentucky in 1886 and raised in Tennessee, where he was bred to local mares. The most important characteristic of this breed is that it can be trained readily to a fast, even running walk, which was particularly suitable to conditions in Tennessee, where horses were needed to carry farmers over miles of rolling, open country. Anyone who has ridden many hours at a stretch knows the value of a horse with an even, fast walk. It is a pace that is unnatural to a horse and requires skilled, persistent training, but it is easy on the horse as well as the rider. The Tennessee walking horse was used in harness as well as under saddle, being a generally useful farm animal. Now almost exclusively a saddle horse, it is entered in the ring showing three gaits: the walk, canter, and a running walk.

The Morgan breed was established entirely through a single sire, a small, powerful bay stallion of unknown ancestry. He lived in Vermont from the time he was a colt until he died in 1821, well past the age of twenty-five, when he was already famous. He is named after his owner, Justin Morgan. Though only about fourteen hands, he proved his worth by exceptional strength as a drafthorse as well as speed on the track. His offspring have carried on these characteristics, and present-day Morgans are noted for sturdiness and staying power. In conformation they are broad, short-legged, and powerfully muscled. The head is broad, tapering to a fine muzzle. The eyes are large and intelligent in expression. Originally Morgans were used mainly under harness but now are used more often as saddle horses. There are two modern types, the larger being, in general, more popular in the eastern part of the United States and the smaller in the West.

Though it is interesting to know various breeds of horses and to be able to recognize them, it is not at all necessary for pleasure in riding to own a purebred horse. Many of the best mounts are of mixed blood. Most of the horses for hire at riding stables are grades, which are a mixture of breeds.

Color Terms

Your horse's color will not, of course, affect its temperament or abilities, but you might want to know the various horse colorings and their special names. Solid colors are black, brown, bay (which is a reddish brown), chestnut, dun (which is grayish brown with a black mane and tail), and white. Light chestnut is sometimes called sorrel, and white is often called light gray. Horses of these colorings frequently have white markings. A wide white stripe down the face is called a blaze. White on the leg is called a stocking, and a piebald is a horse with black and white splotches. A skewbald is white and bay, chestnut, or brown. Both of these are also called pintos. A roan has evenly mixed hairs of white and a darker color, so the effect may be either a red roan or a blue roan. A dapple gray is basically gray, with black hairs interspersed in a circular pattern, often with dark head and legs. Palominos are the color of a gold coin, with a silver mane and tail. Appaloosa is not a color but a separate breed with established markings — being white with so many spots of dark hair that the overall effect is dark and showy.

Picking Out a Horse

When you are ready to pick out a horse of your own, you'll find that there are many places to look and many people to help. Horses are sold at auctions by dealers, by breeders, at racetracks, at training centers, and by private owners who put an ad in the newspaper. Because horses are so expensive to keep, some people own a horse with a partner, who shares expenses as well as the use and care of the horse. Wherever you go to look for a horse, take an expert with you, someone you can trust — a member of your family or a friend who knows horses well. And before you make a final decision, ask a veterinarian to give the horse a complete checkup.

HORSE CARE

Once you've chosen your horse, you will, of course, want to give it the best possible care. That depends partly on where you live and how you will use your horse, but the basic needs are the same whether the animal stays in a stall or can be turned out in a field or paddock when not in use.

Your own manner with the horse has much to do with its disposition and behavior. With your first riding lessons, you most likely learned that all horses are trained to expect a person to approach them, to bridle and saddle, and to mount on the left, or near, side. This will become second nature to you, because you will find that handling a horse from the right, or off, side may startle the animal. Naturally you never want to startle a horse, because when frightened, its instinct is to kick out and bolt. If you approach a horse from the rear, as you need to do when it is tied in a stall, always speak quietly to let it know you are there and walk directly to the head so the horse can see you.

No matter how well trained and docile it is, a horse will become jittery if you make sudden, unexpected noises or quick, unexpected motions. Be easy and calm around your horse.

Horses have sharp eyesight, and their eyes are placed so that the slightest motion in the distance or at the side is instantly noticed. A big, familiar object, such as a car passing on the road, will not bother your horse at all, once it is used to it. But a blowing leaf on the side of the road may startle the horse and cause it to shy away. If you stand on a hillside overlooking the country, you may not see a single thing moving, but your horse will prick up its ears and watch keenly a distant moving object that's invisible to you. Once you recognize this alertness, you'll know what to expect from your horse as you ride.

Don't overwork your horse to the point that it becomes overtired, but on the other hand, never let the horse remain in the stall day after day with no exercise. Without regular exercise, a horse will be in soft condition. It will sweat easily, and its wind will not be good. Although a horse's legs are strong, they are made of precise, delicate joints and relatively unprotected bone and ligaments. They can't bear the strain of a sudden jar or knock. Work a soft horse gradually until it is in good condition. Never exercise a horse heavily after it has had a few days of complete rest. If the horse isn't going to be ridden for some time, try to turn it out to pasture in the company of other horses, but avoid letting it overgraze until it is used to grass. As with any animal, a sudden change of diet can be upsetting.

STABLING

With regular exercise, a horse can be kept comfortable and well in a standing stall, but a box stall is better, with a combination of stall and pasture still better. Horses usually sleep on their feet, so constant standing won't be a hardship, as long as there is enough bedding in the stall. But their feet will suffer if they are made to stand on cement or hardwood, or in manure or wet bedding. A well-drained clay floor is practical, but it needs thick bedding. The stable should be light and airy, with good ventilation, and no draft blowing directly on the horse.

The stall should be scraped out and cleaned every day, and soiled bedding replaced with clean bedding thick enough for comfort when the horse lies down. Hay, straw, or wood shavings may be used — whatever you can get most cheaply in your neighborhood. Beware of moldy or dusty hay or straw, because a horse can get sick from eating it. If you use a box stall, be cautious about the kind of latch you use, because horses are ingenious in fumbling with a latch until they find out how to open it. In a standing stall, a horse should be tied securely with a rope long enough to give freedom of head motion but too short to be stepped on. In the winter, your horse may need a blanket, and in the summer, a light, cool stable sheet will help keep off the flies. If you use these at all, do it regularly and never forget to put them on when you stable your horse.

FEEDING

Each stall should have a manger for hay, and the supply of hay should be plentiful, of good quality, and clean. The feed box should be kept clean. Whatever feed you give should be given regularly and not immediately before or after strenuous exercise. A horse's stomach is comparatively small compared to its overall size, and a horse cannot vomit to relieve an upset stomach. So small, frequent feedings of digestible grains are better than one huge feeding a day. The natural feed of horses is grass, which they crop slowly and often, grinding it with a circular motion of the teeth. If your horse can't be on pasture for any part of the day, you can feed newly cut grass as long as you are certain that it hasn't been sprayed with chemicals. The grass must be perfectly fresh, because improperly cured grass will ferment and cause colic or fodder poisoning. Carrots and a few apples are good treats for your horse, especially if you feed them by hand as a gesture of friendship or as a reward for good behavior.

Hay is the main part of a stabled horse's food. It must be fresh, of good quality, and well cured. The three best grains for a horse are oats, rolled for greater digestibility, which build muscle and give vitality; bran, which is not as nutritious but is cooling and laxative; and corn, either hulled or on the cob, which is fattening and heating. Linseed meal is not a food, but a small amount of it several times a week is good for digestion and the coat. Like all animals, horses must have salt, especially in hot weather. The simplest method of providing it is to keep a salt block in each stall or, if the horses are on pasture, to lay a large salt lick where they can reach it anytime.

The amount of grain you should give your horse — and whether you mix three kinds or give only one, or feed it dry or in a mash — depends on many local factors. Follow the advice of local farmers, and watch your own animal. Give your horse the amount that keeps it well filled-out but not fat. The amount and quality of pasture, the age, size, work required, the breed of horse, and other factors besides the cost of grains play a part. A horse in good condition will graze every chance it gets and still be eager for its hay and grain. Specific advice on your horse's best diet in your area may be obtained from your county agent or veterinarian.

WATERING

Horses need a lot of water. The best way to give it is to keep a pail in the stall where the horse can get it anytime. Make sure that the handle of the bucket is fastened to the wall so that the horse cannot catch its head in it and strangle. A pasture should have a watering trough or a stream running through it. If water is always available, a horse will never drink too much at one time. But if you can offer water only at intervals, do so at least three times a day. If a horse is overthirsty and drinks a large of amount of water after eating grain, the grain will swell in its stomach and cause great discomfort. Neither is it good for a horse to bolt down grain, and the safe way is first to give all the water your horse wants, then the grain.

You'll often hear that a horse must not be allowed to drink

when it is hot and tired. It is true that a horse should never be brought in tired and overheated, given all the water it wants, and then be allowed to stand. With or without water, a horse must not be allowed to stand in that condition. After a hard ride, a horse will be very thirsty, and it would be cruel to deny it any water. Just before the ride is over, or anytime during the ride, let the horse drink a reasonable amount so long as you keep it moving after drinking. If you happen to pass a stream on your way home, let the horse take a drink from that.

If the horse is hot and tired and you can't offer water before you reach the stable, when you get in, first loosen the saddle and take off the bridle, and put the horse on a halter. Then offer a small amount of water to make the horse comfortable. Walk the horse for a while, then unsaddle it. Sponge the sweat off its back with warm, salted water. Then rub it down and dry it off. Again walk the horse around until it is thoroughly cooled off. And only then offer a full drink of clean water, and put the horse in a well-bedded stall with hay. Later on give the grain if it is your practice to feed after work as well as in the morning.

If you are going to turn your horse out after a hard ride, you can be less thorough with your rubdown because the horse will probably roll, browse slowly around, and drink the right amount of water on its own time. Actually these precautions should seldom be necessary, because it is such poor practice to bring home a horse in a sweaty, hot condition that careful riders would never do it unless they had been out working and it was unavoidable.

Horsemanship

There are many standard procedures connected with horse-manship that have been handed down over the years. Each of them, from the kind of hat you wear to the pace you ride your horse, has a sound practical reason. The more you are around horses, the more you will understand each detail. The correct way is the sensible, safe way for both horse and rider. If you start off on a ride at a gallop, for example, you're not showing your courage but your ignorance. Like any athlete, a horse's muscles and body should be warmed up before moving at top speed. Otherwise, you might cause a permanent injury.

If you start out on a ride, don't go off a few hundred yards and then back to the stable. That tends to make the horse stable-bound. Do your fast riding in the middle of the ride, and walk the last mile home, bringing in your horse cool and calm. Do this for two reasons: so that the horse need not stand hot and sweaty, and so it won't form the habit of galloping for home. If your horse does that, it may always want to do it, and you'll lose control. It's a very unpleasant feeling to be run away with, but it's usually your fault if it happens to you.

Trail manners are courtesies you observe when you are with other riders, and they are the mark of experienced horsemanship. You never crowd close to the heels of the horse ahead of you, because that might cause it to kick out. You never pass the person in front of you closely at a good clip, because that might start a race that neither of you would be able to handle.

TACK AND GEAR

Among the many traditions of horsemanship is that the tack — which means the equipment you ride with, such as the saddle and bridle, pad and girth, and stirrups and all of that — should be kept in spick-and-span condition. It should be kept dusted, saddle-soaped, oiled, polished, and hanging on racks at a convenient place. This is not mainly because it looks so nice when it is clean, but because uncared-for leather dries out and can break suddenly and unexpectedly. If you don't take care of your gear, you may find yourself with a broken cinch in the middle of a ride, or a rein may snap, leaving you helpless. And if the saddle blanket or pad you use gets dirty and hard, it may rub a sore on the horse's back.

Every horse should have its own equipment: a saddle that fits both you and the horse, and a comfortable bridle with the proper bit. There are many kinds of bits. There is the snaffle, which is hinged in the middle and used with only one rein, called the snaffle rein. A Pelham bit is a solid bar, either curved or straight. This bit has two reins, the snaffle and a curb. A chain runs under the horse's chin. When this lower curb rein is pulled, the bar in the horse's mouth raises and presses against the tongue, so the lower jaw is pinched and the check is more severe than if only the snaffle rein were used. There are even more severe types of bits. Sometimes a nervous horse is given a bit with a roller on the mouthpiece, which can ease its nerves as the horse plays with it, as a person might be distracted by chewing gum. If through mistreatment, a horse has become slightly hard-mouthed, the action of the saliva caused by working a roller softens the corners of the mouth, making the nerves there more sensitive.

It is impossible to say which is the best bit. It depends on the horse's temperament, its training, and the way it will be ridden. The important thing about a bit is how well you use it. A steady pull or too sharp a jerk on a light Pelham bit can be more painful and harmful than proper use of a more severe bit. Your hands must be sensitive, with a light touch, and you must learn to anticipate and give light but decisive aids with the reins. The horse must feel contact with the bit all the time but not be made uncomfortable by it. This contact is not hard to make if you don't get rattled and think of your horse as a machine, with reins as a kind of steering wheel. As you know, a horse is a creature with feelings, a personality, and ideas of its own.

Good hands are essential to good riding, and they are also a part of the pleasure. The contact of hands on reins has often been compared to the feeling of the tiller of a sailboat. They are similar, with one big exception. Poor handling of a tiller may bring trouble and even upset the boat, but a sailboat can be righted. Heavy, insensitive hands on reins can be cruel and ruin a horse's mouth forever. The nerves can be injured so the horse actually does not feel anything less than a hard pull. It is exasperating and tiring to ride a hard-mouthed horse, but it is never the horse's fault.

Your own gear is important, too. If your riding breeches or jeans don't fit well, they will twist and wrinkle, and chafe badly. Most riding stables require young riders to wear a hard hat for protection. These hats look like a regulation velvet

riding hat, but they have saved many people from head inju-
ries. If you wear another kind of hat, make sure it fits snugly
so it won't blow off and scare your horse, or someone else's
horse, and cause an accident.

GROOMING

A horse should be kept comfortably clean. Grooming every
day takes time, but it can be a great pleasure. It's a good time
to talk to your horse and make friends. Take the horse out of
the stall, and tie it securely before you set to work. Learn to
tie a proper knot with your halter rope, one that the horse
cannot undo by pulling, but that you can easily untie. In its
early training, your horse will have been taught great respect
for ropes. It can be a big nuisance if the horse loses that
training and gets into the habit of untying itself. Never tie a
horse by the reins, which can be pulled and broken. If you
have to use reins instead of rope, simply wrap them so they
will pull out before they break.

After tying, the first step in grooming is removing all the
mud and loose dirt with a stiff brush called a dandy brush.
Start at the head and work gently, soothing the horse with
conversation. As you work toward the rear, keep one hand
on the horse's shoulder. Never slap the brush down on a
spot where the horse doesn't expect it. When you come
to the legs and fetlocks, stand facing the horse, and let
your brush travel evenly and comfortably down the legs. In
this way you won't be kicked. Very few horses will kick a
person purposely unless they have been mistreated, but any

horse will kick out if it is surprised. So be careful, but not fearful.

For the next step use a rubber currycomb in a circular motion to bring embedded dirt to the surface. Never use a metal currycomb with teeth sharp enough to scratch the skin. After the basic job is done, take the dust off with a soft brush, then polish the horse's coat with a cloth.

Untangle the mane and tail with a mane comb. There are no nerves at the root of this hair, so you can pull as hard as necessary. Keep the tail trimmed to the length that is suitable to your type of horse. You can decide whether you want the mane to grow or would like it clipped or hogged. If the mane tends to divide, you can easily train it to fall on the right side by wetting it and plastering it down every day. Pick up each hoof, and with a hoof pick remove pebbles and dirt. If there are any nits or fly eggs on the hair of the legs, cut them off so they won't develop into bots, which burrow into a horse's stomach.

SHOEING

Keep your horse correctly shod. Like toenails, hooves grow continually, so that your horse will need to be reshod about every four weeks. Never turn a horse out to pasture for any length of time with its shoes on. The shoeing should be done by an expert, called a farrier. A certain amount of rasping and clipping is always necessary, but beware of a blacksmith or farrier who tries to reshape the hoof to fit the shoe. Each horse presents a slightly different problem, as does the type of ground it will cover. Faults in a horse's stride can often be corrected with proper shoeing.

✿   ✿   ✿

Each horse is different in many ways, temperamentally and in ability. The better rider you are, the more you can ask of your horse. It is a partnership, but you must be the boss. Be precise in giving your aids: by leg, by rein, by position in the saddle, and by voice. If the horse is confused and doesn't know what you mean, it is frequently not the fault of its training, but because you are uncertain how to give directions. Never feel that you have learned all there is to know about riding. It can be a fine art, and it is rewarding and beautiful, because every motion you make has a reason. As your coordination becomes more natural and automatic, you will have a boundless sense of rhythm and well-being as you ride.

9. First Aid and Common Diseases

To prevent illnesses, feed your animals the balanced diet each kind needs, never overcrowd them, and keep their quarters clean. Use reasonable precaution in preventing accidents, remembering, for instance, that a puppy will swallow anything that fits down its throat and some things that won't. Be aware that animals are capable of feeling contented and happy, and also lonely and neglected. Your dog or cat will want your personal attention; your guppy will prefer a friend of its own kind. But few creatures can get along without any companionship. Whenever you associate with your animals, make sure that you are always quiet and calm when near them, and that you treat them according to their needs so that they are never disturbed by fear of you but accept your presence with pleasure — whether this pleasure springs from the fact that you can be expected to fork out a feeding of hay or from real affection.

Naturally, before you get a new animal, you will make as certain as you can that it is healthy. As an added precaution, when you bring it home, keep it away from your other animals until you are sure that it has no contagious ailment. Use common-sense caution, too, in introducing animals to one another. Your established pets are likely to feel jealous and give the newcomer a rough time. All animals have a strong sense of personal property.

It is essential that you have your new animal examined by a veterinarian as soon as you obtain it. He or she will be able to detect any contagious diseases, congenital defects, or other problems that you might not recognize. The vet can also give any vaccines needed and advise you on a proper diet. At the first sign of illness, isolate the animal in case the trouble is contagious, then make sure you have the right diagnosis before you proceed with any treatment. Don't wait until you are in need of help before you decide what professional advice you are going to ask for. Decide ahead of time which veterinarian you will be using, and be ready to call for help the moment you need it. Remember that it is much easier for a veterinarian to diagnose and treat your sick pet if he or she is familiar with it when well.

There is no substitute for good professional advice. Let a veterinarian tell you what to do, and if you are skillful with animals, you can often do the nursing. Be cautious about trying out home remedies, even those you might use on yourself, because they may not suit an animal. As an example, aspirin is often thought of as a safe drug. However, if given to a cat, it may make the cat violently ill. Acetaminophen, a common alternative in people, is even worse; one tablet can be fatal to a cat. The following brief notes on diseases are incomplete. They by no means take the place of professional knowledge and are intended to be used only as a general guide as to what to watch out for and to avoid.

If you should travel by train, plane, or ship with an animal, you should have a strong carrier of a size comfortable for your pet. If you are not accompanying your pet, make sure that someone will meet it as soon as it arrives. You will want to shorten the ordeal for it as much as possible.

Airlines, railroads, and ships have a variety of regulations concerning animals, and these sometimes change from season to season. Each country has its own regulations concerning animal visitors. Some hotels and motels accept pets, and some do not. Plan ahead by finding out how your pet can travel and whether it needs any medical certification. Possibly your veterinarian will recommend a mild sedative.

DOGS

TEMPERATURE

Normal rectal temperature for dogs is 101.5 degrees. This may normally vary one degree higher or lower due to excitement, activity, or environmental temperature.

INTERNAL PARASITES

Dogs, and especially puppies, are subject to worms. These are harmful themselves and also lower the dog's general vitality. They should be eliminated, always under a veterinarian's advice. There are many kinds of worms, the most common being roundworms, tapeworms, whipworms, and hookworms. The correct treatment for each of these is different. It also depends on the age and condition of each dog. If you see worms in the stool, vomit, or bedding of your dog, or if you suspect by your dog's listless behavior that something is wrong, take a specimen of its stool to be professionally analyzed. If worms are present, the veterinarian will prescribe the correct treatment. Usually this will be simple and easily given at home.

Tapeworms do not usually lay eggs in the dog's intestines but pass segments in the stool. These may collect around the anus of the dog, looking something like dried rice grains. If you see this, report it to your veterinarian. It is essential that you do so, because although you have seen them, they will not show up when the stool is analyzed under a microscope. The flea is the intermediate host for the common tapeworm, so it is necessary to control the fleas as well as treat for the tapeworm.

Don't assume that every ailment is caused by worms, but bear in mind that they must be eliminated and that diagnosis is beyond an amateur.

Since worms are particularly prevalent in puppies, find out before you buy yours whether it has been properly diagnosed and treated. If this has not been done, have its stool analyzed at once. It is distressing to start off with an unwell animal. If you have the slightest doubt about a new dog's condition, ask a veterinarian to check it thoroughly before you make your purchase.

Heartworm disease in dogs has become an increasingly

prevalent problem. It is transmitted to the dog by mosquitoes and is present in many parts of the United States. The adult worms lodge in the dog's heart and cause the following symptoms: coughing, lethargy, tiring easily from exercise, and, later, collapsing spells. Heartworm disease can be diagnosed by one of two blood tests. One test detects the larvae of the worm and the other the adults. Your veterinarian may use one or both tests.

You should check with your veterinarian about the prevalence of the disease in your area. He or she may suggest a control program to prevent the disease. This would consist of daily or monthly medication during the mosquito season and two months thereafter. New monthly medications are effective, and prevention of the disease is much easier and safer than treating it.

If your dog has heartworm, it will have to be hospitalized for treatment. The treatment kills the worms in the heart and may make your dog temporarily sick. For this reason it must be done under a veterinarian's constant care. After the treatment for adult heartworms, the larvae, or microfilaria, will be eliminated by another drug.

EXTERNAL PARASITES

Fleas are blood-sucking parasites that damage your dog in two ways. They remove blood from your dog, which may make it anemic. They can also cause skin irritations and loss of hair, especially if your dog is allergic to them.

If you live in an area with fleas, you must constantly protect your dog from them. You can prevent fleas on your dog by the use of insecticide powders, sprays, collars, or solutions that are intended for use on dogs. Follow the directions closely, and avoid contact with the dog's eyes. Your veterinarian can advise you which product he or she feels is the best.

If your dog has fleas, you must also destroy the fleas in his environment. All bedding must be washed thoroughly. Rugs in the house must be vacuumed, and an insecticide spray in the house may be necessary.

Ticks are also blood-sucking parasites. In addition to causing anemia, they can transmit several infectious diseases, including Lyme disease. Unfortunately insecticides do not prevent ticks. During the summer you should inspect your dog daily and remove any ticks. Using tweezers, grasp the tick firmly close to the skin, and pull it off using slow, steady traction. Wash your own hands well after deticking your dog. If your dog has a continuing problem with ticks, take them to your veterinarian to have them classified, and he or she will outline a program for you.

Mange in dogs is caused by microscopic mites. There are two main types: demodetic and sarcoptic. Demodetic mange occurs mostly in young dogs and is first noticed as the loss of hair or a little bald spot. Do not overlook small hairless areas, especially if they are around the eyes or muzzle. Any such areas should be examined immediately.

Sarcoptic mange manifests itself by intense itching, with reddened and scaly skin, especially on the legs and ears. Although it appears serious, it is usually treated with topical or

oral insecticide prescribed by your veterinarian. It is important to note that the mites that cause sarcoptic mange can
also infect people and cause similar clinical signs.

Viruses

Distemper is a highly contagious and serious disease that fortunately is now rare. At best it badly weakens the dog. At
worst it can be fatal or can leave aftereffects that are difficult,
though not always impossible, to cure, such as chorea, which
shows itself in twitching or meningitis, heart trouble, weak
eyes, paralysis, incontinence, or imperfect teeth.

Every dog ought to be inoculated for distemper. Recent
vaccines are nearly 100 percent preventive. You still need to
keep your dog in good general shape and to avoid contagion,
but the vaccines have long been proven effective.

Parvovirus infections in dogs were first diagnosed in the late
1970s. It is believed that the virus that causes these infections
mutated from the one that causes a similar disease, panleukopenia, in cats. It causes severe bloody diarrhea and
vomiting, as well as fever. While both puppies and adults can
be affected, the disease is more severe in the younger animal,
and can be fatal. Because of the serious nature of this disease,
don't try to treat the dog yourself. Infected dogs usually must
be kept in a veterinary hospital for treatment, which includes
intravenous fluids to prevent dehydration and shock, as well
as high doses of antibiotics.

Parvoviral infections can be prevented by vaccination. A

series of injections is initially given to a puppy, followed by boosters at intervals throughout the animal's life. It is common for these vaccinations to be given in conjunction with those for distemper. Consult your veterinarian for a schedule for these shots for a new puppy.

Infectious Canine Hepatitis (which is not related to infectious hepatitis of humans) is a serious and rapidly fatal disease of dogs. Fortunately, however, most veterinarians vaccinate for this disease at the same time that they vaccinate for distemper. If your dog does ever show possible symptoms of this illness — a high fever, depression, vomiting, or bloody diarrhea — it should be seen by a vet immediately.

Rabies is one of the most feared and misunderstood diseases. It may occur in any warm-blooded animal but occurs most commonly in dogs and a variety of other animals, including bats, raccoons, skunks, foxes, cows, and cats, and therefore need not be continuously feared. However, in some areas of the country, particularly the East Coast and Texas, there has been an epidemic of rabies in some species recently. This is one important reason why people should avoid direct contact with wildlife.

Vaccination against rabies provides almost sure protection for your dog. Therefore, for your protection as well as your dog's, you should have your dog vaccinated every one to three years, according to the recommendation in your particular area. You can check with your veterinarian or public health office for recommended vaccination time. Many communities provide rabies vaccination clinics to which you may take your dog to be vaccinated at a low cost.

The disease takes one of two forms: dumb or furious. Both are characterized by a change in personality. If affected by the dumb form, the dog will frequently develop paralysis of the jaw and act strangely. If affected by the furious form, the dog becomes very aggressive and runs around wildly. Any dog showing such symptoms should be examined and possibly quarantined by an official.

It is important to understand that rabies is rare among domestic dogs and that vaccination is effective in preventing the disease and does not harm the dog.

Respiratory Infections

Dogs do not get human colds, but they do get respiratory infections that appear similar to colds. The most common cause of this is the distemper virus. Bacteria and kennel cough virus can also cause respiratory infection. Kennel cough is highly transmissible and often invades boarding kennels. It is characterized by a loud gagging cough. If your dog is coughing and has a runny nose and eyes, it may be a serious infection and your pet should be examined.

Other Illnesses

Seizures can come from various causes and take various forms. The dog may be wild-eyed and semiconscious. It may froth at the mouth and lose control of bowels and bladder. It may run around wildly, knocking into things, or it may stiffen and champ its jaws or fall over and kick its legs.

Attend to the dog immediately. Then call a veterinarian so the cause can be diagnosed and eliminated.

Whatever form the seizure takes, it will be extremely alarming. But if you act at once, there is no real cause for fear, and seizures are usually of short duration. Keep your dog as quiet as you can, and, if possible, in a darkened room. Never make it try to swallow anything, because it might choke. If the dog is running around so wildly that you can't control it, throw a blanket over it in order to keep it from injuring itself and to keep it from biting you. Remember that the dog is not conscious of what it is doing. It will not recognize you, and it may bite. Any human bitten by a dog, even if it's his or her own, should consult a physician.

After a seizure is over, the dog will be weak and exhausted. Soothe and talk to your pet, and let it rest. Do not feed it for several hours. Follow your veterinarian's recommendations for additional care or medication.

Heatstroke occurs in dogs that are enclosed in a warm area and become excited. Symptoms are loud panting, staggering, and collapse. It is particularly severe in short-nosed breeds, such as bulldogs, pugs, and Boston terriers. If your dog appears overheated and its temperature is greater than 105 degrees, put it in a partially filled tub of cold water or hose it down with cool water until its temperature reaches 103 degrees. Cooling it too far may also cause complications. Then immediately call the veterinarian.

SIGNS AND SYMPTOMS

Halitosis (or bad breath) can be caused by bad teeth, foreign matter stuck in the teeth, a stomach disorder, or even diseases such as kidney failure or diabetes. Check the teeth yourself, to remove anything you find stuck between them. If the condition is chronic, have the dog checked by a veterinarian. He or she may find that the teeth need cleaning or may recommend tests for other diseases.

Vomiting. Dogs vomit easily when they are nauseated. If your dog vomits occasionally, especially after eating grass or other abnormal material, don't be alarmed. Simply skip the next meal and limit the amount of water to about half the dog's normal intake for the next six hours. If the vomiting persists, then give Pepto-Bismol every three hours until the vomiting stops. If the vomiting is severe or if it persists over twelve hours, it may be serious and your dog should be examined by a veterinarian.

Diarrhea. Dogs, especially puppies, may have occasional diarrhea, or soft, runny stools. If your dog has diarrhea, stop all food for twelve hours and then feed hamburger, cooked and mixed with boiled rice. Also give Kaopectate at the rate of one tablespoon per twenty pounds of body weight every six hours. Milk may cause diarrhea in puppies and should be discontinued when the stools are soft.

If the diarrhea persists or if it has blood in it, have your dog examined. When you take your dog for the examination, also take a specimen of the dog's bowel movement so that it can be checked for internal parasites.

Constipation. Occasionally your dog may strain excessively to pass bowel movements. If so, it is probably constipated. You may give it one tablespoon of mineral oil to help relieve it. Bones may have caused the trouble, so don't feed them to your dog. Again, if blood is present when the dog strains, have it examined immediately.

If your dog is dragging its bottom on the floor, it probably means that his anal sacs are full and need relieving. Your veterinarian can check and show you how to do it when necessary.

If your dog is straining to go to the bathroom, it may be diarrhea, constipation, or a urinary condition called cystitis. It is often difficult for you to distinguish between these if you see no results of the straining, and veterinary attention may be required.

Eczema (or "hot spots"). During the summer months, your dog may develop intense itching and may bite at itself, particularly around the rear quarters. Reddened moist areas on the skin may develop rapidly, and the hair may mat around them. Clip the hair around the spots, and wash them with mild soap and water. Then get medical attention, because the spots can enlarge rapidly, mainly due to the dog's biting at them. In the meantime, divert the dog's attention so it doesn't bite so much.

ACCIDENTS

Poisoning. Be careful to keep your dog away from rat or insect poison. Also keep your dog from chewing on wood painted many years ago. Old paint may contain lead and may cause poisoning.

In case of poisoning, act at once. Immediately read the antidote on the poison container. It will tell you how to make the animal vomit. This may be done by giving hydrogen peroxide, a salt solution, or syrup of ipecac by mouth. Human poison centers are located all over the United States and can be reached twenty-four hours a day.

Foreign Objects in the Stomach. If you know that a dog has swallowed a nail, a piece of glass, or any object it should not have, give it a large meal of soft food, such as canned dog food, to surround the object. Then watch its stools carefully for the next few days to see if the object passes. If it doesn't, or if the dog is vomiting or has diarrhea, take it to the veterinarian.

Cuts. Almost all cuts need a veterinarian's attention because they become easily infected. If the cut is small, clean the hair and dirt away with mild soap and water. If the cut is severe, bind it firmly but not too tightly with a clean compress or rag, and take the dog to the veterinarian.

If the bleeding is from an artery — as shown by gushes of bright red blood — apply a tourniquet between body and wound as you would for a person. If the bleeding is from a vein — a steady flow of darker blood — apply a compress on the wound. Loosen the tourniquet at intervals if you are not able to reach a veterinarian at once.

Broken Bones. A broken bone or fracture is evident when a dog has severe pain and will not bear weight on the affected leg. Keep the dog quiet and immobile, and seek veterinary help immediately.

GENERAL FIRST AID

Administering Doses. If you give your dog medicine, get it in a receptive mood by talking to it. Hold it still, getting help if it should be necessary. To give liquid medicine, hold the head level with the ground, pull open the corner of the lip to form a pocket, and pour medicine from a spoon or bottle into the pocket. Be quick about it, but don't pour faster than your dog can swallow.

To give pills or capsules, hold the head up and open the mouth. Put the pill at the very back of the tongue, and hold the dog's muzzle closed and pointed upward until it has swallowed several times, thus making sure that the pill has gone down. Don't expect the dog to be honorable about swallowing. It will spit the pill out if it can. Make every effort to a get a capsule or a coated pill down before the coating melts, to spare your dog an unpleasant taste.

If your dog struggles while you are dosing it — or grooming, pulling off ticks, or doing anything else for its benefit — do not try to hold it by cuddling it in your arms. Place the dog on a table. It will feel at a disadvantage there and behave better, and you can control it more easily. Do not scold, but talk soothingly, so the dog will understand that you are trying to help.

Temporary Pain Relief. Aspirin may be given to dogs as to humans, varying the amount according to the age and size of the dog. Consult your veterinarian for the specific dose for your dog. If you can't reach your veterinarian right away, one half of a five-grain aspirin per twenty pounds of body weight every eight hours can usually be given safely for several days. Be aware that aspirin in high doses or for long periods of time can cause stomach irritation or ulcers.

GROOMING AND CARE

Eyes. If you notice a discharge or inflammation around your dog's eyes, clean them by swabbing gently with cotton soaked in a warm saline solution. Like human eyes, they can be injured through internal causes or by dust, scratching, foreign particles, or excessive wind. Don't allow your dog to ride in a car with its head stuck out of the window.

Eye problems may be restricted just to the eye, such as conjunctivitis, or they may represent a more serious illness such as distemper. Occasionally a bluish-white cornea will develop suddenly in reaction to a hepatitis vaccine. This is usually not serious.

Some breeds such as poodles and Bedlingtons have fine hairs on their face, which tend to accumulate on the eye and irritate it, causing weepy eyes. You can help this by gently wiping the hairs away from the eyes with a moist piece of cotton. Do this twice a day and you will train the hairs away from the eye.

Ulcers of the cornea result from foreign particles on the cornea, soap burns, or scratches. If your dog has an ulcer on the cornea, it will squint, its eye will run, and it will show you vigorously that the eye hurts. Look in the eye for a foreign body. If you see anything, remove it gently by washing the eye. Call your veterinarian at once for treatment. Dogs with prominent eyes are prone to this problem, especially Pekinese and Boston bulldogs.

If your dog has a persistent discharge from the eyes, acts painful about one eye, or if one eye appears different from the other, don't fiddle with the eye but take your dog to the veterinarian at once.

Ears. Ear mites or numerous other things may cause ear trouble. If your dog is pawing its ear and shaking its head and you cannot see what is causing it, never probe deeply; get professional help.

As first aid, wipe the inside of the ear, but only as far down as your finger goes easily, with cotton soaked in mineral oil or peroxide. Then dry the ear thoroughly.

While grooming, you will become familiar with the smell of your dog's ears and with the small amount of wax that accumulates there. You should wipe out the ears occasionally with mineral oil on cotton. If there is a foul odor or excessive secretion of wax, have this checked by a veterinarian.

Certain breeds of dogs such as poodles have hair that grows deep into the ear canal. This tends to block the canal and cause the retention of moisture, with subsequent ear infections. You should learn to pluck this hair from the canal every few weeks.

Teeth. Dogs don't usually get cavities, but they can have severe problems with tartar and periodontal disease. They should be checked once a year, especially as to the formation of tartar, and more often if you suspect trouble. The veterinarian can clean off accumulated tartar and, if necessary, remove diseased teeth; this must be done under anesthesia. Dog biscuits and chew toys may help deter tartar formation on your dog's teeth, as will brushing. Your veterinarian can show you how to brush and can give you a "dog-flavored" toothpaste.

Coats and Noses. A full shiny coat and a moist, cool nose are signs that a dog is in good health. If the coat is in poor condition, first make sure that you are giving proper care.

A dog's nose is part of its temperature regulating mechanism, so it will be hot after exercise and excitement and cold when the dog is trying to conserve heat. A hot, dry nose does not necessarily indicate illness. Call for advice only if it persists.

Breeding and Neutering

Breeding. Mature male dogs can breed at any time, but they are not attracted to a female except during her period of heat. The odor at this time is powerful to dogs. If a bitch in heat is allowed outdoors at large, male dogs will congregate from miles around. Often severe fights, even to the death, result.

For this reason, as well as for the sake of the female, all bitches in heat should be confined during the entire period, except for leash walks.

Periods between heats vary, but the average cycle is every six months. Each season lasts from eighteen to twenty-one days. Effective mating can be accomplished normally during the middle of the period, but the bitch is attractive to dogs during the whole period, and so should be confined either at home or in a boarding kennel in order to keep peace in the neighborhood.

The age at which bitches come into heat for the first time varies with the individual and with the breed. It may be any-time after six months.

It is not always possible to tell that a bitch is about to come in heat. But if you keep track of dates and watch your animal, you ought to be able to discover the condition before male dogs can reach her. She will not be receptive to them the first few days but will try to fight them off. You may be able to detect the approach of heat by a coy sentimentality in her affection, or, more specifically, by a swelling of the vulva. Once she is actually in season, there will be a slight, bloody discharge. This can be wiped off gently to protect your rugs.

It is seldom wise to breed a female during her first season, because she may not be fully matured, and the strain of bearing puppies will be too great. On the other hand, a female should not have her first litter too late in life. Two litters a year are possible, but should not be a regular routine year after year because the strain is too much. Once a year is enough. The gestation period — or time it takes to grow within the mother's body — is from fifty-nine to sixty-five days.

Do not raise puppies carelessly. Proper care of the mother and of the puppies and the disposal of puppies are matters for an experienced dog owner. If your dog is purebred, you will want the right stud for her, and you will want to register the puppies if they are eligible. The right stud is not simply a dog of the same breed but one with suitable bloodlines. Consult a reputable breeder. It is better to pay a stud fee, either in cash or a pick-of-the-litter arrangement, than to breed poor puppies. The raising of puppies is fascinating but also time-consuming and expensive. Only real experts can make money at it.

Several breeds of dogs are affected by a hip deformity called hip dysplasia. However, it occurs frequently in larger breeds such as the German shepherd, Saint Bernard, Old English sheepdog, and the Newfoundland. This deformity is inherited — it can be passed on from the mother or the father to the pups. If you have a purebred dog, it is best for you to have it certified to be free of hip dysplasia by a veterinarian. Before you pick a stud, ask that he be certified. It is only fair to your dog not to perpetuate the trait.

Spaying an operation that makes your female dog sterile, or unable to have pups. It is harmless and prevents her from having heat periods. If done before one year old, it also prevents two major surgical diseases of dogs. These are pyometra (infected uterus) and mammary cancer.

If you do not definitely want to raise pups, you ought to have your female spayed. It is wrong to raise pups unless you know you can sell or give all of them away to kind owners. There is too much needless suffering, because pups are raised for which there are no homes.

Neutering, or castration, is an operation that makes your male dog sterile, or unable to father pups. It, too, is a harmless operation and is suggested if you do not intend to use your dog as a stud dog. Neutering usually results in less aggressive or wild behavior and less wandering. It is recommended that this procedure be done when the dog is between six and seven months old.

CATS

TEMPERATURE

Normal rectal temperature for cats is between 102 and 103 degrees.

INTERNAL PARASITES

Cats are susceptible to many types of worms. The symptoms of worm infestation are vomiting, diarrhea, poor condition, and a "pot belly." If you suspect worms, take a sample of your cat's stool to a veterinarian to be analyzed. If worm eggs are present in the stool, the vet will identify them with a microscope and prescribe proper treatment. Never give your cat worm medicine indiscriminately.

Cats are particularly susceptible to tapeworms, mainly because fleas transmit the tapeworms from one cat to another. You may notice small white segments that resemble dried rice grains, under your cat's tail. If so, take the segment to a veterinarian for identification — it might be a tapeworm.

EXTERNAL PARASITES

Fleas. Cats are very susceptible to flea infestations. Fortunately they can be easily prevented and controlled by various flea control products. These should not be used on a kitten less than four months old. Flea powders and sprays may be used on cats to control fleas. However, don't use excessive amounts, especially if your cat licks itself a lot, because it will swallow the poison. If your cat has fleas, wash and clean the cat's bedding and vacuum the rugs, because the fleas and their eggs will be in the environment.

Ticks. Cats are less susceptible to ticks than dogs are. If a tick attaches itself to your cat, pull it off as you would for a dog.

Ear Mites are transmitted from one cat to another. Kittens may get ear mites from their mothers after birth. If so, they will scratch their ears and shake their heads, and a dark brown wax will be evident in the ear canal. Your veterinarian can prescribe topical medication that will kill the mites. Treat all cats in the household, or they will continue to pass the infection from one to another. Remove the brown ear wax with cotton when it comes out of the ear canal.

VIRUSES

Colds. Cats are susceptible to upper respiratory virus infections caused by contagious viruses. If your cat has one of these infections, it will have runny eyes and nose and sneeze often. These diseases are not fatal, but you can make your cat feel better until it recovers. Twice daily, wipe the matter away from the eyes and nose with moist cotton. Often a cat won't eat if it can't smell, so it is important to keep the nose clear. If your cat is eating poorly, try heating baby food meats — often your cat will eat warm food but refuse cold food. If the discharge from the eyes and nose becomes yellow or puslike, call your veterinarian for advice. Remember that these are contagious infections and other cats may become infected.

Many cats that appear recovered remain carriers of the disease and can infect other cats. For that reason catteries and veterinary hospitals have outbreaks of this problem. There are vaccines for the most common respiratory viruses, which most veterinarians routinely administer in conjunction with the distemper vaccine.

Panleukopenia. Other names for this disease are enteritis and feline distemper. This is a serious disease caused by a highly contagious virus. It is most prevalent in urban areas in warmer months. Vaccinations to prevent panleukopenia are almost 100 percent effective. It is essential to have your kitten or cat inoculated yearly to prevent this serious disease.

The first symptoms of the disease are continual vomiting of yellow fluid; diarrhea, which may contain blood; weakness; complete loss of appetite; and dehydration. This is a highly fatal disease, but in many cases the cat may be saved with prompt veterinary attention. There is little that can be done in home treatment by you until the cat begins to improve and eat again. However, at the first sign of the disease, keep your cat in a warm place away from other cats. A tablespoon of salt water by mouth every two hours may help dehydration. Call your veterinarian at once.

The disease may be transmitted to other cats by your clothes or by a cat entering an infected area or household.

Feline Leukemia Virus. This virus was first recognized in cats in the late 1960s. It is transmitted from cat to cat through bite wounds, licking, and urine, and from mother to kitten. Once the cat is infected, it remains so for life. While the virus can cause leukemia, it more commonly results in a variety of serious problems, including anemia, fevers, cancerous tumors, and weight loss. In addition, it makes the infected cat more susceptible to other infections. Your veterinarian can perform a blood test to determine if your cat is infected. If it is, nursing care and medication may be prescribed to treat the secondary problems. Your cat should also be isolated from other cats, because it may spread the virus to them. Unfortunately the effects of the virus usually result in death within a few years of infection. There are vaccines available that can be given to reduce the risk of the cat becoming infected. They are about 90 percent effective, so it is still important to avoid exposure to infected cats. This virus will not infect people or dogs, only cats.

Feline Immunodeficiency Virus. This virus was discovered in the late 1980s. When a cat is infected with this virus, it becomes very susceptible to other infections. Other signs of infection include gingivitis, weight loss, and fever. These secondary infections usually result in premature death of the cat. As with the feline leukemia virus, once infected, a cat remains so for life. This disease is less common than infections with the feline leukemia virus, and it is more difficult to transmit from cat to cat. It is most common in outdoor cats, especially males that have not been neutered. There is a blood test that your veterinarian can use to determine if your cat is infected, but unfortunately there is no effective treatment once the cat is infected. There is currently no vaccine available that will prevent the disease. The best prevention is to keep your cat away from strange cats.

This virus has a similar name to the virus that causes AIDS in people, the human immunodeficiency virus. In fact, the viruses are related. However, the cat virus infects only cats, so you have no need to be concerned about its being transmitted to people.

Feline Infectious Peritonitis. Although this disease is called infectious peritonitis, it actually can take several forms. In one form, the peritoneal, or abdominal, cavity fills with fluid, and the cat usually runs fevers and loses weight. In the other form, the virus infects different organs in the body. The clinical signs will then depend upon which organ is infected. Cats may have eye inflammation, kidney failure, or seizures. Once an infected cat shows clinical signs, there is no effective treatment, and death will result. Unlike the feline leukemia or immunodeficiency viruses, it is possible for cats to fight off an infection with the infectious peritonitis virus early in the course of the disease. The signs the cat shows at this early stage are the same as those for an upper respiratory infection, and there are closely related viruses that cause upper respiratory tract disease. Unfortunately there is no definitive test to determine whether a cat has been infected with the infectious peritonitis virus, because of cross reactions with the similar respiratory viruses. Your veterinarian may make a tentative diagnosis based on clinical signs; a tissue biopsy or autopsy may be needed to determine the exact cause. There is now a vaccine for this disease that will help protect cats that have a high degree of exposure, although it will not protect all cats. As with the other viral diseases, one of the best preventive measures is to avoid contact with strange or sick cats.

OTHER ILLNESSES

Cystitis. If your cat goes to the litter box frequently, and appears to strain, it may be cystitis, an inflammation of the bladder. This is often mistaken for constipation. Check the litter after the cat has been there. If there is a small amount of wetness or small amount of blood, it means cystitis and demands a veterinarian's attention. If your cat is male, he may not be able to urinate at all because of small stones blocking the urine internally. If so, he will sit on the litter box and cry while he tries to urinate. This is a serious situation, and you should call your veterinarian immediately. Male cats get very sick and die from this if not treated immediately.

Dermatitis. Cats can develop skin problems that are very itchy. Often the hair over the back will be thinner than normal and there will be scales and red spots. This is frequently due to an allergy to something in the cat's environment —

fleas are the most common cause. Eliminate the fleas, and bathe the cat in mild soap. If the condition persists, consult your veterinarian.

SIGNS AND SYMPTOMS

Vomiting. Cats may vomit occasionally due to hair balls, indigestion, or abnormal food. Other causes may be internal parasites, gastroenteritis, or uremia. Vomiting infrequently should not be considered abnormal and requires no treatment. You may give one teaspoonful of Pepto-Bismol twice daily to relieve the symptoms. If the vomiting is severe or continues for more than one day, call your veterinarian.

Hair Balls. Long-haired cats and occasionally others may accumulate hair balls in the stomach from excessive licking. If so, the cat will vomit occasionally and possibly be constipated. This may be relieved by mixing a teaspoonful of mineral oil in the food twice a week. Never force mineral oil down a cat's throat, because this can cause a fatal pneumonia. Your veterinarian can also prescribe laxative gels or pastes that accomplish the same result. If your cat continues to show these symptoms, have it examined by a veterinarian. Adult male cats straining in their litter box are often mistakenly assumed to be constipated when actually they are suffering from a urinary obstruction. This situation demands immediate veterinary attention.

Ringworm frequently appears as bare spots, especially about the head of your cat. It is caused by a fungus and is contagious to dogs, cats, and people. It requires treatment under the guidance of a veterinarian.

GENERAL FIRST AID

General first aid for cats is the same as for dogs. However, there are certain drugs to avoid. Never give your cat aspirin, acetaminophen, paregoric, or codeine. Insecticides are frequently poisonous to cats and should be used only with veterinary approval. Hexachlorophene soaps may be toxic to a cat.

BREEDING AND NEUTERING

Breeding. Female cats can breed only during their periods of heat. These periods occur at irregular intervals and sometimes last only a few days, but sometimes much longer. The cat usually makes her condition obvious by extreme restlessness, yowling, and rolling on the floor. After mating, she returns to normal. If she is allowed complete freedom, she may have as many as three litters of kittens a year. She will probably come into heat before she is a year old. If you can manage to keep her confined, it is better for her health not to breed until she is fully matured, at one year, and she should be allowed no more than two litters a year. The gestation period is sixty-three days on an average. If you do not want your female cat to have kittens, you must have her spayed, or she may become neurotic.

There are many unwanted kittens in the world, so if you don't have potential homes for kittens, have your female cat spayed.

Newborn Kittens. The mother will select a secluded dark place to have her kittens. About a week before they are due, you can put down a new cavelike box, comfortably bedded, and large enough for the cat to stretch out at full length. Put this in a spot where you would like to keep the kittens, and hope that she will discover it for herself and use it.

It is easier to tell the sex of the newborn kitten than of one a week old, because the hair is shorter and you can see better. The female has one small slit opening close to the anus, which resembles an upside down exclamation point. The male has one small round opening spaced a little farther from the anus and two testicles between the anus and the penis that appear as small lumps. The male's genitalia resemble a colon.

Care of the Mother Cat. Before the birth, the mother cat should lead her accustomed life, with all the food she asks for. Feed a balanced diet that is labeled so as to meet the nutritional requirements of cats.

Ordinarily she needs no assistance at the birth and prefers to be alone. If there is undue straining, or if there is more than four hours straining without the birth of a kitten, call a veterinarian.

As soon as all the kittens have been born and the mother has settled down, offer her a small amount of food and water. Change the bedding as soon as you can do so without alarming her. This will depend upon how well she knows you and upon her nature. Some mothers want their human families to sit by and provide soothing conversation during the entire birth.

During the nursing period, make sure that the mother has all the food she wants; and if she asks you to, increase her feedings to four a day.

Castration. Neutering is strongly recommended for all male cats, both to prevent unwanted kittens and to make him a more acceptable pet.

An unaltered male is an unhappy animal if he is confined to the house, and he is a tremendous nuisance. His urine has a strong and lingering odor, and he will involuntarily spray the furniture until the whole house is unbearably smelly. If allowed outside, he may prowl a great deal and constantly get into cat fights. And he will add to the already pitiful problem of too many homeless kittens. This can be avoided by having him castrated.

If a male is to be kept indoors, he should be castrated — that is, his testicles should be removed — by a veterinarian. This is not a serious operation if it is properly done. Take your veterinarian's advice as to the proper age for castrating a kitten. This is usually done at six months of age, although some kittens are now being neutered as early as six to eight weeks of age.

Transporting a Cat

Occasionally cats are taught to walk on a leash, but it is very much against their nature, and it is a rare cat and a rare trainer who can accomplish it to the cat's satisfaction. No matter how much your cat loves you, it is not safe to carry it in your arms on an unfamiliar route. If anything should startle it, it will not cling to you for protection. It will struggle suddenly and violently to get away, and dart off and hide. Probably you won't be able to hold it. At best you will be severely scratched while clinging to an angry and terrified animal. Instead of putting your cat and yourself through this ordeal, use a deep, strong carrying case, with ventilation. Your cat may not learn to like to travel this way, but it will be safe and feel safe. It is natural for a cat to huddle out of sight in a box. Make sure the box is strong. If the cat struggles, it will quickly learn that it is useless and settle flatly in the bottom. If you have used a flimsy hatbox lightly tied, the animal may fight its way out and run away.

SMALL CAGED ANIMALS

RABBITS AND GUINEA PIGS

Life Span. The normal life span of a rabbit is eight years. That of a guinea pig is six.

Feeding. Guinea pigs are susceptible to Vitamin C deficiency or scurvy. They will show lameness, weight loss, and a reluctance to move. To prevent this, always feed fresh guinea pig pellets, and supplement them with small amounts of citrus fruits and fresh green vegetables. Do not store pellets for longer than three months, and never substitute rabbit pellets for guinea pig pellets. Rabbit pellets do not contain added Vitamin C.

A guinea pig or rabbit that appears hungry but refuses to eat its pellets may have dental problems. Feed your pet soaked, softened pellets and vegetable baby foods, and consult with your veterinarian.

External Parasites. Rabbits are susceptible to ear mites, which cause brownish crusts around the ear. They may also be infected with fur mites and common dog or cat fleas, causing hair loss and excessive scratching. Consult with your veterinarian for diagnosis and treatment.

Signs and Symptoms. If your guinea pig has abnormal, heavy, rapid breathing, it may have pneumonia. Keep the animal warm, and consult with your veterinarian.

Occasionally guinea pigs will develop lumps under their chin and the underside of the neck. These are abscessed lymph nodes, and you should apply warm compresses to them until your veterinarian can open and treat them.

Diarrhea in rabbits is often caused by a sudden increase in the amount of fresh greens in the diet or a lack of overall fiber in the diet. Always make gradual dietary adjustments and provide your rabbit with timothy hay as a source of dietary fiber.

Respiratory Infections. Rabbits suffer from respiratory infections called snuffles. A rabbit with snuffles will sneeze and have a discharge from its nose and eyes. Keep the rabbit warm, and encourage it to eat with a variety of foods. Call your veterinarian for advice on treatment.

Heatstroke. Hot summer days may be uncomfortable for your rabbit and can lead to heatstroke. Never leave a rabbit in direct sun; always keep it well shaded or bring it indoors during heat spells.

Hair Balls. Rabbits and long-haired guinea pigs may develop hair balls or "wool block" in their stomach during heavy shedding periods. This condition will cause them to lose their appetite and become depressed. Make sure your pet is drinking water and producing fecal pellets, and consult with your veterinarian for advice on treatment. Treatment usually involves force-feeding a petroleum-based laxative and digestive enzymes. Severe cases may require surgery.

Breeding and Neutering. Try to avoid breeding rabbits and guinea pigs inadvertently. Unless you particularly want to raise them, are willing to give the necessary care, and know where you can find homes for the new generation, keep only one sex or have your pets neutered. It is especially important to neuter female rabbits that are not being bred, because they often develop cancer when they get older.

It is hard for a novice to tell the sexes apart, but anyone with a little experience should be able to do so. By six weeks, the sex of a rabbit can be determined by gently pressing the sexual opening, which is in front of the anus. In the doe, the slit is long and narrow. In the buck it is round, and if you press with a scooping motion of your fingers, the penis will pop out. Male guinea pigs are noticeably larger than the females of the same litter.

The gestation period of rabbits is twenty-eight to thirty-two days. That of guinea pigs is fifty-nine to seventy-two days.

WHITE MICE

Odor. Complete cleanliness — and refraining from keeping too many mice — prevents a disagreeable mousy odor. A cage-floor covering of wood shavings absorbs odors more thoroughly than paper. Change the shavings and thoroughly wash the cage frequently. Cleanliness is for the mice's health as well as your own comfort.

Cannibalism. Sufficient space and exercise, comfortable bedding, and plenty of the right food are the best precautions against cannibalism. Do not keep too many mice together. Overcrowding can lead to aggressive behavior.

Parasites. If your mice scratch themselves often, suspect parasites. Most commonly these are mites, although they may be lice or fleas. Consult your veterinarian for advice on treatment.

Disease. As soon as a mouse looks sick, separate it from the others and take it to a veterinarian. Take along some of the droppings for the veterinarian to examine as well.

Keep the mouse warm and quiet in transit, and do not handle it too much. Give the cage a thorough cleaning and new bedding, in case the trouble is infectious.

HAMSTERS

Avoid indiscriminate breeding by learning to tell the males from the females. This is easy to do by the time hamsters are two weeks old. The female's nipples show by that time. The shape of her body under her tail is rounded, and the sexual opening is round. The male's body is more pointed under the tail, and the testicle opening is a slit.

Misshapen teeth sometimes make eating difficult. A veterinarian can file the teeth to the proper shape.

You may suspect external parasites if your hamster scratches and has a rough coat. Your veterinarian can identify the parasites and suggest an effective treatment.

Hamsters are exceptionally hardy and free from disease. The most common problem is diarrhea or "wet tail." This is a serious, life-threatening condition. If one should appear sick, separate it from the others, keep it warm, and take it to a veterinarian. Clean and disinfect the cage.

GERBILS

In general gerbils are healthy, and if you allow them space for exercise and give them the right food, they are not likely to get sick.

If the nose and eyes are running, perhaps the gerbil has a cold. Separate it from the others and take it to a veterinarian.

Sometimes gerbils wound one another in fighting if you have not been watchful enough to separate those that seem to dislike one another. Clean the wound with an antiseptic, and consult with your veterinarian.

Occasionally gerbils have seizures much like human seizures. These pass quickly and do no permanent harm. The cause is not known — possibly rough handling, strange surroundings, or sudden noise.

CAGED BIRDS

CARE AND FEEDING

An unbalanced diet, cramped or dirty quarters, and drafts are the most common causes of sicknesses in caged birds. Give your bird a balanced diet recommended by your veterinarian. A seed mixture alone does not contain all the nutrients your bird needs. If the bird neglects one kind, limit the supply of its favorite until you have taught it to take it all. Do not neglect the suggested extras, because they are needed to keep your bird in top condition. Keep the cage in a protected location free from drafts and out of reach from other pets. Clean the cage and provide fresh food and water daily. Make sure the cage is large enough and contains enough toys to keep your pet entertained when you are away.

EXTERNAL PARASITES

Mites and Lice. Symptoms of scaly leg or face mites are a crusty skin in the area of the legs, beak, and eyelids. Other lice and mites may attack feathers and cause much itching and picking by your bird. These mites may be seen on the skin, feathers, or the cage itself. Your veterinarian can treat this condition with medication. All birds in the same cage must be treated whether or not they all have symptoms. The cage must also be thoroughly disinfected.

RESPIRATORY INFECTIONS AND SINUSITIS

Symptoms of a respiratory infection are general malaise, a discharge from the nares (nostrils), heavy breathing, and sneezing. The bird will often stop eating and will appear weak and fluffed up. At the first sign of this, place a forty-watt lightbulb ten inches from the cage for heat. Keep the cage covered to restrict drafts, and encourage your bird to eat by offering foods it is particularly fond of. Call your veterinarian for examination and treatment immediately. When transporting the bird, make every effort to keep it warm and covered to avoid drafts.

SIGNS AND SYMPTOMS

Loss of Voice. If your bird loses its voice, it may indicate thyroid disease, respiratory infection, or general depression. If the voice is absent more than two days, have your veterinarian examine your bird.

Molting normally occurs twice a year. However, many caged birds molt more often. The feathers are lost gradually, so there is not a large bare part of the bird's body. While molt-ing, the bird may be listless and sing or talk less than usual. If the molt seems very long, or some of the feathers don't re-turn, consult your veterinarian.

Broken Feathers. If a young feather breaks and bleeds, the entire feather and shaft should be removed to prevent bleed-ing. It will not be replaced until the next molt.

Diarrhea may be caused by a sudden change in environment (such as drafts), change in food with too much fruit, or severe fright. If your bird has diarrhea, feed it only dry foods such as seeds or pellets, fresh water, and vitamins. Monitor the bird's condition closely. The diarrhea should stop in twenty-four hours. If not, call your veterinarian immediately. Birds with diarrhea rapidly lose weight and become seriously dehy-drated.

GRIT

Gravel or grit is no longer recommended for pet psittacines (parakeets, cockatiels, parrots, etc.) on a regular basis. Overuse of grit can lead to serious intestinal blockages in some birds. Consult with your veterinarian for advice on this matter. Charcoal is also not recommended, and if used can lead to serious vitamin deficiencies. However, the use of oyster shell as a grit substitute is an excellent source of calcium and is highly recommended for most birds.

AQUARIUM AND VIVARIUM PETS

FISH

There is not a great deal that can be done for a sick or injured fish, so take all the preventive precautions you can. Keep the aquarium in good condition. Make sure the water is always clean, at the correct pH, and at a steady temperature suitable to your species of fish. Do not overcrowd it, and give it the proper amount of light. Give the varieties of food your particular fish need. Do not put assorted sizes and species of fish together until you have checked with a pet shop to be sure you are attempting a safe combination. They might fight. If you use tap water, let the chlorine evaporate before the water goes into the aquarium. This can be done by drawing the water twenty-four hours ahead of time and letting it stand. To speed evaporation, heat or stir the water.

Many diseases of fish are highly infectious. Guard against the spread of any disease by quarantining a new fish, segregating an ailing fish, cleaning the entire aquarium from which you have taken a sick fish, and sterilizing the net you have used to move your fish.

The safest and most generally effective treatment is to put the fish in a shallow container filled with warm salt water for one hour at a time: the proportions being two and a half tablespoons of household salt to a gallon of water. Be sure not to use iodized salt. Rock salt, sea salt, or kosher salt are best.

The most common disease of goldfish is a white fungus that attacks all parts of the fish but usually the fins. It looks like a white, transparent film. Use the saltwater treatment.

The most common disease of tropical fish is ichthyophthirius, known as Ich or pepper-and-salt disease. It shows up in white spots. Use the saltwater treatment, and increase the heat of the tank. There is also an Ich remedy on the market, which should be available at your pet shop.

TURTLES

An incorrect diet and inappropriate environment are the most common causes of sickness in turtles. Many diseases can be prevented by providing an optimal environment and diet. This can be achieved by thoroughly researching the specific needs of your species of pet turtle *before* you acquire it.

Common dietary disorders often involve calcium, vitamin D, or vitamin A deficiencies. A calcium or vitamin D deficiency may result in a soft or deformed shell. A vitamin A deficiency can cause swelling of the eyelids or a discharge from the eyes or may lead to a respiratory infection. Treatment for these disorders involves correction of the diet and may include vitamin injections.

The most common infectious disease of turtles and tortoises is pneumonia. This often results from an unclean, poorly ventilated environment, maintained at an inadequate environmental temperature. Signs of pneumonia include lethargy, loss of appetite, discharge or bubbles from the nose, and open-mouth breathing. Water turtles may swim at an angle or may prefer to stay out of the water altogether. A sick turtle will benefit from having the environmental temperature raised to 90 degrees. Your veterinarian should be consulted as soon as possible. Pneumonia can be a life-threatening condition.

LIZARDS

Lizards also suffer commonly from diseases brought on by errors in husbandry. Providing an adequately sized clean cage, with proper lighting and heat, as well as a well-balanced diet is essential to their good health. A little research into the requirements for your specific species of lizard will be needed to ensure the optimal set up.

Dietary deficiencies of calcium, vitamin D, and protein in young, growing lizards often result in stunted growth and multiple broken bones. Very severe calcium deficiencies can lead to seizures and death. Your veterinarian should be consulted if any signs of weakness, lameness, muscle twitching, or seizures occur in your pet.

SNAKES

Snakes must be kept in a secure, clean, dry cage with an adequately sized water bowl for bathing. An appropriate environmental temperature is essential and usually falls between 80 and 90 degrees. Snakes should be fed on a regular basis, and a record should be kept of successful feedings, defecations and urinations, and skin molts or sheds. Many diseases will cause disruptions in feeding, defecation, and shedding.

Newly acquired snakes should be kept separate from other animals and brought to the veterinarian promptly to check for parasites. A fecal sample should be brought in along with the snake if one is available. Snakes often suffer from skin mites and intestinal parasites that are infectious to other snakes and debilitating to the infected animals.

Skin disease or blister disease, mouth rot, and pneumonia are common infectious diseases in snakes. They often result from being kept at an inadequate environmental temperature or in a dirty or damp cage. Signs of pneumonia include foaming at the mouth or nose, lethargy, loss of appetite, and open-mouth breathing. Consult your veterinarian immediately if you suspect a problem. These infections can be serious and will require antibiotic injections. Some animals will have to be hospitalized for treatment.

Snakes may also suffer from skin burns if allowed to sit directly on heating elements, hot rocks, heating pads, radiators, or lightbulbs. These burns can be serious and can lead to life-threatening infections. Keep all electrical heating devices out of reach of your snake and make sure heating pads are well insulated. If you suspect your snake has suffered a burn, take it to your veterinarian as soon as possible for treatment.

Large snakes should be fed dead rodents or rabbits if at all possible. Feeding live animals can lead to many problems. One of the most common problems occurs if the snake does not eat the rat in a timely manner, and the rat bites the snake. Severe rat bites can result in deep wounds, scarring, and serious infections. Your veterinarian should be consulted as soon as possible. Never leave a live food animal in the cage with your snake for longer than an hour.

FARM ANIMALS

First aid for farm animals is an important part of the general management of any farm. If you live on a farm, your farm pets will be watched and cared for in the same manner as the other farm animals, according to the latest tested methods of raising healthy, profitable stock. In order to fit into that plan the special attention you give your pets, learn all you can concerning the diseases and other troubles to which your kinds of animal may be subject, and be ready to carry out both the measures used for preventing illness on your farm and the practical nursing recommended by your veterinarian if sickness occurs. The most important way of keeping healthy animals is to provide daily care and clean housing, feed a proper diet, and give recommended vaccines to your animals.

If you do not live on a farm, but are raising perhaps chickens, or goats, or any farm animal on your own, you need to know more than this book has the space to give you. Turn to the bulletins of the Department of Agriculture, your state Extension Service, or other recognized agency for full information and essential knowledge of how to proceed in the prevention and care of specific diseases.

Your veterinarian can advise you on vaccines needed.

PONIES AND HORSES

INTERNAL PARASITES

Horses are often heavily infected with worms, which can cause colic, poor condition, and lack of energy. The worms can be removed by medicine. However, the horse can pick up worm infestation again by grazing where manure collects. In order to reduce the amount of worms, keep the manure cleaned up and allow your horse as large a grazing area as possible. Have your veterinarian set up a deworming schedule and recommend appropriate medications.

INFECTIOUS DISEASES

Vaccinations. Your veterinarian will probably recommend that your horse be vaccinated for sleeping sickness (equine encephalomyelitis) and tetanus. He or she may also recommend other vaccinations, such as rabies, depending on where you live.

Respiratory Infections. Symptoms of respiratory infection are a discharge from the nose and eyes, coughing, and loss of appetite. Place the horse in a box stall without cold drafts. Call a veterinarian for treatment. Many respiratory infections can be prevented by proper vaccinations. They also can be highly contagious, so isolate your horse from others.

Other Illnesses

Colic is acute abdominal pain, which can have several causes. Quantities of gas may form and cause spasms of the intestines or cramps and extreme discomfort. In more serious cases, the intestines can twist and cut off blood flow to other parts of the intestine.

Among the causes are too much water immediately after grain, overeating or bolting food, too much grass in the spring, or a sudden change of food. Internal parasites, called strongyles, are often the underlying cause. All horses and ponies should be dewormed routinely every few months. Your veterinarian can help set up a schedule and advise you on deworming medications.

If affected by colic, the horse may bite or kick at its sides. It may keep trying different positions, getting up and lying down frequently, or rolling. The stomach may swell. The horse may break into a sweat.

Blanket the horse, and lead it around. Keep it moving steadily. If relief is not immediate, call a veterinarian.

Azoturia (Black water) usually occurs if a horse is exercised heavily after a few days rest while being fed much grain. The horse will become weak and sore while exercising and eventually lie down. It will be hot and sweating, and its leg muscles will bulge and be hard. It may pass reddish-brown urine. Call your veterinarian immediately.

SIGNS AND SYMPTOMS

Lameness. If your horse is lame, it may be a serious problem or rather minor. First examine the hoof. Compare the lame leg with the opposite one for swellings. Feel up and down the leg for painful areas. Notice if the horse is lame at all times or only at certain gaits.

If the lameness is not easily identified, call your veterinarian for diagnosis and treatment. Do not use your horse in the meantime.

Laminitis (Founder). Acute laminitis is manifested by severe lameness or reluctance to stand, warm feet, and frequently by sweating. Call your veterinarian immediately for treatment. Chronic laminitis is evidenced by a misshapen hoof. Consult a veterinarian or farrier for advice on trimming and shoeing.

GENERAL FIRST AID

Wounds. Small wounds should be cleaned daily with soap and water and an antiseptic or antibiotic ointment applied. Wounds larger than one inch require veterinary attention. The skin of a horse heals slowly and may form an excessive scar if not properly treated. Horses are very susceptible to tetanus and require an antitetanus injection when a wound occurs.

GROOMING AND CARE

Teeth. Your horse's molar teeth may wear unevenly and cause a sore mouth. If so, your horse may eat poorly and dribble its food when eating. Your veterinarian may float, or file, the uneven edges. Swelling along the cheek is often caused by an infected tooth, which may need to be pulled.

Eyes. If the eyes are reddened and watery, it may be due to dust irritation or other trauma. Wash the eye with warm salt water, and apply boric acid ointment twice daily. If the discharge is yellow or does not clear up in two days, it is probably an infection and requires treatment by your veterinarian.

Harness and Saddle Sores are caused by friction from the tack. If they occur, clean the sore with soap and water and apply antiseptic or antibiotic ointment. Do not use the horse until they are healed. In the meantime, clean the leather well and make sure the tack fits properly.

For Further Reading

Alderton, David. *You and Your Pet Bird*. New York: Knopf, 1992.

Hickman, Mae, and Maxine Guy. *Care of the Wild Feathered and Furred*. New York: Michael Kesend, 1993.

Price, Steven D., editorial director. *The Whole Horse Catalog*. New York: Simon and Schuster, 1993.

Rosenfeld, Arthur. *Exotic Pets*. New York: Knopf, 1992.

Sweeney, Roger. *Garter Snakes: Their Natural History and Care in Captivity*. London: Blandford, 1992.

Vine, Louis L., D.V.M. *Common Sense Book of Complete Cat Care*. New York: Morrow, 1978.

Index